# THE FAR JOURNEY

*Other books by Loula Grace Erdman*

THE YEARS OF THE LOCUST

LONELY PASSAGE

THE EDGE OF TIME

THE WIND BLOWS FREE

THREE AT THE WEDDING

# THE
# FAR
# JOURNEY

## Loula Grace Erdman

*Dodd, Mead & Company*          NEW YORK

*For my mother*

WHO KNOWS WHAT IT MEANS TO JOURNEY FROM
MISSOURI TO TEXAS

# PART 1

# CHAPTER 1

———◆———

CATHERINE MONTGOMERY STOOD IN THE MIDDLE OF THE SITTING ROOM FLOOR WITH HER MOTHER AND HER AUNT MAE MONTGOMery kneeling at her feet, adjusting a flounce on the changeable silk taffeta dress they were making for her.

"Turn slowly," Jessie Montgomery said. "No—that's too far. Back a little."

The girl followed her mother's directions with scarcely more will than a puppet. But even as she did so, she was thinking that the situation gave her an advantage she was not often privileged to enjoy.

The windows of the room were abundant and so arranged that she had only to lift her eyes to see the outward dimensions of her world. The Old Montgomery House, as everyone called it, sat on a high knoll overlooking the little town of Grafton, Missouri. When it had first been built, in the early forties, Montgomery land had stretched out in all directions. Now, forty years later, the town edged up almost to the front gate and on the other three sides small farms lay. In Catherine's own lifetime she had been witness to the gradual shrinking of the place; she had been aware of the slow sure tide of people advancing, had seen the little farms eating away at the edges of

Montgomery land until now it was only a shadow of what it had been when she was born, eighteen years ago.

But in the house itself there had been no change. Jessie had seen to that, withstanding even so much as the rearrangement of a single piece of bric-a-brac, as if by so doing she would be able to deny the fact that her own personal world had fallen to pieces. Della and Hiram's cabin, back of the house, had been there as many years as Catherine could remember. Aunt Mae frequently remarked that the room she occupied had been hers since she was a girl; Jessie sometimes mentioned that her own room was the one she had come to as a bride, twenty-five years ago. Catherine herself had known no other room than the one she now had, with its white ruffled curtains and spread to match.

"Turn a little—to the right," Aunt Mae told the girl. "Not too much—there, that's good."

Catherine shifted her position just enough so that she could see the porch and, leading off it, the door to the room which was called, aptly enough, the "Little Room." Always it was kept neat and clean with fresh linens on the bed and towels on the rack and water in the flowered pitcher on the washstand. Regardless of how many guests were in the house no one was ever assigned to this room, for here it was that Uncle Willie Keith came home from his wanderings, slipping in so quietly that often the first notice anyone had of his arrival was when Della came from her cabin to prepare breakfast for the family. If the door was closed, it meant he was there.

Catherine had learned early that she was never to go into the room to play. Once she had done so, finding it an ideal place to set up doll housekeeping. When her mother found her there, she was greatly upset.

"You mustn't go in there—that's Uncle Willie's room," she said.

"But I don't see why—Uncle Willie loves me. He'd *like* for me to play in his room, even if he wasn't there."

"We have to keep it nice for him," her mother explained. "See—you have left a chair out in the middle of the floor. Push it back against the wall."

Catherine had put the chair back in its place against the wall, pouting a little as she did so. Uncle Willie wouldn't care if a chair *was* out of place; he was always teasing her mother about having things so neat and prim.

"What if he came in during the night—he might stumble over that chair and hurt himself."

That made sense. More often than not he did slip in at night. She could remember how delighted she was to come downstairs in the morning and see the door to his room closed, knowing that it meant he was home. It was open now, as it had been for several months.

She craned her neck, ever so little, until she could look toward the east, beyond the farthest hill, bright now with the loveliness of June. Far to the east lay Virginia, still home to Jessie's heart although she had spent much of her life here in Missouri.

"Stand still, Catherine," her mother admonished her. "We have to get this flounce draped exactly right, and we can't do it as long as you keep wiggling."

"I wasn't wiggling," Catherine defended herself stoutly.

"Well—you're looking out the window, and that throws the dress out of line. Try looking at the floor for a while."

Catherine looked down obediently, her eyes not on the floor but on her mother and her aunt. It occurred to her that seldom, if ever, did she have these two humbled before her— these women who formed the boundaries of her inner world. She had been standing still for a long time now, but she forgot her weariness in contemplation of the novelty of the situation.

Her mother's hair, soft and brown and abundant even though she was past forty, was parted in the middle and drawn into a soft coil at the back of her neck. A few tendrils escaped the pins and clung to the skin—firm and soft and creamy white. The Keith skin, Jessie Keith Montgomery called it. But about the woman herself there was little of softness. Her body had the tautness of a coiled spring. Her hands were trembling as she threaded in the pins; they often trembled, as if there was a force in her frail body too great either to be contained or to be released. Catherine, studying her mother now, wondered as she often did how the woman's size, so delicate as to suggest frailness, could house a will so strong.

"There—I think it'll do now," Aunt Mae Montgomery said, getting stiffly to her feet and standing, tall and gaunt and gray. The woman had a way of dwarfing any room in which she stood, as a familiar rock dwarfs the landscape around it. Such Catherine had found her all her life—a strong and sure force, a person who neither trembled nor moved quickly enough to frighten a child.

"Now you look at yourself, Catherine," Aunt Mae said to her, "and see what you think."

Catherine turned to face herself in the long mirror at the end of the room—herself, the very core of her world.

Above the multicolored tones of the dress she saw her face, an irregularly shaped triangle rather pleasantly arranged with a low broad forehead and a look of height to the cheek bones. Her eyes—brown, and deep-set—held a hint of brooding, of great sensitivity. Her nose, finely shaped and large enough to denote character as Aunt Mae sometimes told her, had a tendency to tilt upward, giving her face an air of piquancy. Her mouth she had always thought too large, although, as a matter of fact, it was part of her charm. Wide and generous, with a full underlip, it indicated warmth and a capacity for deep feeling. And, overlying it all a certain hesitant dignity peculiar to the young person who has been brought up almost entirely among older people.

"It's lovely," Catherine said. She lifted her arms, began to unhook the dress. But before she had so much as touched the first fastening, her mother stopped her.

"I'm not sure the waist isn't too tight," Jessie said, turning her head to one side to survey the dress more carefully.

Now that the two women were on their feet, Catherine was a child once more. She did not think the waist was too tight. She liked the way it outlined the delicate shape of her body, emphasizing ever so slightly the small bosom, showing off to an advantage the rounded lines of hips and thighs, before it swept down to the fashionable flounce Aunt Mae and her mother had spent the morning adjusting. She thought she would feel very stylish when she wore this dress in Virginia.

"It doesn't seem too tight," she ventured.

Even in uncertainty she had a lovely speaking voice—low-pitched, yet clear, slurring some of the syllables slightly after the manner of her Virginia-born mother. But the tone and timbre were Aunt Mae's, a fact of which the girl was aware without ever knowing for sure whether this was accidental or deliberate.

"I want it to be exactly right," Jessie said. "Goodness knows, you aren't going to have many things to take to Virginia, at best."

Her high, thinly sweet voice filled the room. It held a quality that, after so long a time, made listeners want to get away. Anywhere, for any reason. About it was a curious monotony, like water dripping on a rock in some dim distance. After a while the rock would wear out, but the water would continue to drip.

"Oh, the waist is all right," Aunt Mae said. "It looks exactly like the picture."

She pointed to the illustration from *Godey's Lady Book* pinned to the lace curtain so they might check it as they worked.

"Yes," Jessie agreed, looking at the picture once more. "I believe you're right, Mae. Now just sit down, Catherine, and see if it hikes up. Goodness—I'm glad I thought of that. What if it had pulled up just as you were sitting down in Cousin Pattie Lou's parlor!"

Catherine sat down, glad for the chance to rest even though it was not her mother's reason for having her do so. This was the final test—that Cousin Pattie Lou should find the girl's clothes right, holding the correct degree of style, cut and color.

"Yes, it's all right," Jessie said, taking another chair. The success of the fitting had put her in excellent humor.

"You are going to enjoy visiting Cousin Pattie Lou," she continued. "Such a lovely place—or at least it was before the war."

She said the word darkly, as if the whole thing had been contrived deliberately by the North in order to confound and humiliate the South. An unwarranted interference by meddling neighbors. It went beyond that. For Jessie Keith Montgomery, the War Between the States had been a tragedy transcending even the fact that her husband, whom she adored, lost his life fighting in a border scrimmage against the Kansas Redlegs. Herself a transplanted Virginian, she had brought to Missouri all the customs and beliefs which, for her, made life rich and meaningful. For a few years she and her husband were privileged to enjoy this ideal existence and then the war had come. For her, General Lee's surrender was not so much a military defeat as an end to a way of life. She had no notion of following his example in her own domain.

As a defense against this new world which emerged she

built up a barrier of aristocratic snobbery, with its taboos and traditions, retreating behind it and holding fast to all her remembered gentility. Behind this barrier she had taken her family as well as herself.

"And think how much fun it is going to be for you to see your Cousin Keith again," Jessie reminded Catherine now.

Her words held a child's naïve transparency, accompanied by a child's bland self-assurance that no one saw through her. From the moment that young Keith Hopkins had arrived in Missouri for a visit with his relatives the fall before, Jessie had worked toward a single goal, one which she considered as good as accomplished. Two months from now—in August—she and Catherine were going back to Virginia for a visit. Not for one minute did she doubt the ultimate success of the trip.

Actually, while Catherine was pleased at the prospect of going to Virginia, which she had not seen since she was old enough to remember much about it, she did not share either her mother's reason for wanting to go or her confidence in the outcome. She had not found her Cousin Keith as altogether wonderful as her mother had—or professed to have done.

He had arrived casually and almost without warning, after the manner of the time and the custom of the Keith family. Jessie accepted him with complete and unreserved joy. Besides being a kinsman—distant, but still of the blood—he was an ambassador from Virginia. She welcomed him to her house and to a way of life not greatly different from the one he had left.

It was a state of affairs which he recognized and of which approved.

"I declare, Cousin Jessie," he said, "this is just like home."

And indeed he was comfortably like the people he visited.

He was small for a man, with delicate bone structure. "The Keith build," Jessie called it, implying there was some special

merit to it. He carried his head a little to one side in the manner of an artist appraising a painting. In fact, he had wanted
to paint, but had to forego the pleasure because "The Mater
wants me to manage the place."

"I should think you'd be delighted to do it," Jessie told
him. "Such a beautiful place . . ."

"Rather a nuisance," he told her languidly.

He had been content to sit with Jessie for hours, tracing
their mutual kinship.

"Now let's see," Jessie mused. "Wasn't it Cousin Malcom
who married that Boston woman?"

"Why Cousin Jessie," he drawled, "the very *idear* of your
forgetting that!"

He spoke in such exact imitation of the Boston cousin-in-
law that Jessie laughed until the tears came into her eyes, and
even Aunt Mae, who did not seem to find the young man as
funny as did Jessie, could not refrain from smiling.

Keith Hopkins had a gift for mimicry, one which Jessie
found thoroughly enjoyable but which, for some reason Catherine could not quite explain, made her squirm uncomfortably
each time he indulged in it. Perhaps she felt that, once Keith
got back to Virginia, he would be equally adept at mimicking
the Missouri kin, herself among them.

Jessie however had no reservations about him. She accepted
him wholly, blossoming out during his visit. This was natural,
for he was always telling her how lovely her hair was (which
was true) and what nice skin she had (which was also true).
He remembered to bring her shawl and pick up her gloves and
always listened attentively to whatever she had to say. In fact,
he seemed to enjoy being with her as much as, or more than,
he did being with Catherine. When he first arrived, the girl
had thought it was going to be great fun to have someone her
own age in the house. Actually, having Keith was not much

different from being with her mother and Aunt Mae. Jessie
took her to task for this lack of enthusiasm about her cousin.

"You aren't very nice to him, Catherine," she said. "Sometimes when he's talking you'll pick up a book and start reading
—just as if he wasn't around."

"I didn't know those people you all were talking about,"
Catherine defended herself.

"They're your own cousins," Jessie cried, scandalized that
Catherine should think such a thing, much less say it.

"Now see here, Jessie," Uncle Willie put in. He had come
home for one of his "visits" while young Keith was there and
seemed no more impressed with the boy than Catherine was.
"Now, you let her alone. You can't expect her to be interested
in a bunch of people she's never seen."

"But she could at least be polite to Keith," Jessie argued.
"Her own cousin—and a fine young man, besides."

"He's her fourth cousin," Uncle Willie pointed out. "And
if you ask me, he's a little on the sissy side. I don't blame her
for not being interested in him. You ought to let her see some
real young people now and then."

Jessie sniffed. What young people were there for Catherine
to know? Certainly not the children of the emigrant farmers
to whom she had been forced to sell portions of her place down
the years; certainly not any young people from Grafton, which
had also been carved out of Montgomery land. For the most
part, the town now was made up almost entirely of families
who, before the war had come and changed everything, were
little more than trash. Once they would have been shy and
hesitant even so much as to speak to her unless she spoke first;
now they walked boldly to her front door and asked about buying a bit of land, naming their own price.

It was no wonder, therefore, that Jessie Montgomery em-
braced with great joy the opportunity to take Catherine back

to Virginia for a visit. She made no attempt to cover the fact that she was confident this trip would settle Catherine's future once and for all. Thinking this, she had spared no pains and no time and effort in getting clothes suitable to the visit. It would take every minute, with her and Mae working as fast as they could, to have things ready by the last of August, the time set for leaving.

She sat back now, regarding the dress with narrowed, speculative eyes.

"I still wonder," she said, "if it would have been better to have ordered the silk from Kansas City."

"Nonsense, Jessie," Aunt Mae told her. "Mr. Delaney carries just as good materials as anybody in Kansas City. And cheaper besides."

"Humph!" Jessie snorted, dismissing the subject, as she always strove to dismiss the man himself—with as little discussion as possible.

For Mr. Frank Delaney, who ran the Grafton General Store, she had a grudging respect but no real liking.

To begin with, he was from Illinois, a state which, according to her judgment, had produced few men to admire. Even the late martyred President. Least of all, him.

Mr. Delaney had first gone to the aid of "Poor Bleeding Kansas" which Jessie felt deserved to bleed, and worse, as payment for harboring that unspeakable old man, John Brown, the one who went about setting slave against master. True, Frank Delaney had eventually seen the error of his ways, and leaving Kansas to work out its own salvation had moved across the line into Missouri to establish a store in Grafton. But so far as Jessie was concerned the stigma of his original intent continued to cling to him.

There were other lesser—and greater—counts against him. She suspected him of being trash, because he went about in his

shirt sleeves (with black sleeve holders on them) and was blunt
and direct in his manner.

He would stand watching her with poorly concealed impatience as she stood trying to make up her mind about some
item—brown sugar or shoelaces or a length of silk—his attitude
saying plainer than words could have done,

"Well, do you want this?"

"I'll take it," she would say, feeling that she had made
her decision with more haste than wisdom.

Usually she tried to send Della or even Catherine for
groceries or other items that might be needed, but even so there
were times when she had to go herself. Mae was no good at
all—she merely took whatever was shown her.

And never did she walk into the store without remembering that it stood on land which had once belonged to the Montgomerys. Frank Delaney had come to buy it, and a plot on
which to build his house as well, and she had sold to him—
hating to part with the land but hating more the fact that,
even though he was of a different stripe from those others who
came asking, he still showed her no more deference than they
did, nor did he seem more impressed with her. In fact, that
was one of her chief though unconfessed reasons for disliking
him. She always had the uneasy feeling that he knew more
than she did—read more widely, thought more deeply. And
although she would try whenever his name was mentioned to
dismiss him with an airy, "Well, what can you expect of a
Yankee!" she was, in his presence, apt to be careful of what
she said or did. It was not so much from a desire to win his
approval as from the certainty that, should she step out of line,
he would be capable of putting her in her place with a few
quick, incisive phrases.

Now when Mae said that Mr. Delaney's materials were
cheaper than those in Kansas City and just as good, Jessie knew

she was quoting Mr. Delaney—and that the statement was correct. The knowledge took away a little of the pleasure in the new dress.

"Stand up, Catherine," her mother said. "And let me have one last look before you take it off. Turn around, very slowly . . ."

Catherine, turning as her mother directed, saw out of the corner of her eye that two men were walking up to the house. It was only the briefest glance she had but even so she thought one of them looked like Mr. Delaney himself. This she dismissed at once as impossible, for the man did not make calls on the Montgomerys. In fact he did not make calls at all. A bachelor in his sixties, he divided his time between his store and his rather cheerless house.

Catherine did not share her mother's dislike for the man. As a matter of fact, she found his bluff heartiness somewhat engaging. He was always most polite and helpful when she had to go to the store on an errand for her mother. She liked to linger and talk with him after the purchases were wrapped. When she was a little girl, he had always given her candy; now he invited her, with a large generosity, to go back and "poke around among the laces and velvets and things—stay as long as you like."

It was in that way she had run across the taffeta for the dress she was now fitting. Seeing it, she had felt a peculiar tingling sensation as if here was something she must have—something on which all her future hung. She had come home to tell her mother about it and Jessie, after seeing it, had agreed, though not without some hesitation and grumbling and with considerable prodding from Aunt Mae.

"You can take it off now," Jessie said when the girl had made the complete turn. "Be careful of the pins."

But Catherine had not had time to begin removing the dress when Della came to the door.

"Miss Jessie," she began, and then seeing Catherine standing there in the new dress, she stopped and with the freedom of the privileged servant cried, "Why, Miss Catherine—honey —you look lovely. You look good enough to eat."

Catherine smiled at her. There was a peculiar quality to the girl's smile. It seemed to come from somewhere deep inside her, to gather force as it traveled to her face and, once it found itself there, to lend a special radiance to her whole being. It was something that differed with her moods—when she smiled at older people it was gravely pleased; now, as she smiled at Della, she seemed very young and happy. People who saw her smile would think, "Strange—I hadn't realized before that she is beautiful."

"Like it, Della?" she asked.

"I sure do, honey." And then she turned to Jessie. "Miss Jessie, Mr. Frank Delaney's here asking to see you. He's got his nephew with him."

"Mr. Delaney—" Jessie spoke with quick impatience. "And his nephew—goodness, Della, he doesn't even *have* a nephew."

"Well, he's got a young man with him and he says it's his nephew and he wants to see you," Della told her, with the air of one who is taking no sides in the matter.

"That was Mr. Delaney . . ." Catherine was thinking, even as she understood her mother's impatience.

"My goodness—what a mess he's caught us in." Jessie complained. She looked around the room, littered with bits of material and patterns, and at Catherine, wearing the dress with all the fitting pins showing plainly. She halfway considered sending word back that she could not see anyone at the moment. But knowing Mr. Delaney as she did, she suspected that he'd just sit down outside the door and announce he'd wait until she could see him.

"Oh, let him come in—" she said resignedly.

Catherine was still standing when the two men walked into the room.

"Good morning, Mrs. Montgomery," Mr. Delaney said, in his bluff way. "This is my nephew, Edward Delaney."

"How do you do." Jessie spoke, politely, but cool enough to convey the impression that the call was certainly unusual.

"How do you do," the young man said. He turned and looked directly at Catherine.

The girl's first impression was that he was quite tall, although at second glance she realized that he was not much over middle height. Perhaps it was just the way he carried himself, with his shoulders erect and his head high, which gave him the look of height. He had dark brown hair. His eyes were deeply blue, probably a heritage, along with his name, from some distant Irish ancestor. From this one, too, he might have got his restless eagerness. It moved ahead of him so that the room seemed suddenly charged with vitality and purpose, shifting the concern about the dress fitting back into its proper place—pleasant work for women to occupy themselves with while men went out to larger endeavors.

It was a quality emphasized by his eyebrows, dark and strongly marked, with one of them—the left one—lifted slightly, giving his face a constant look of inquiry even in repose.

The two young people stood looking at each other with heads lifted, eyes widened, lips parted slightly. An arrested look, as if both of them were caught in the unexpectedness of the moment, held by the novelty of it as much as by their interest in each other.

"My nephew just got in from Illinois, and he needs some young people to be with instead of an old codger like me. And

I thought to myself—well, there's not a nicer girl in this town than Miss Catherine, so I took the liberty of bringing him over," Mr. Delaney continued.

"I'm sure you're delighted to have him," Jessie said, ignoring completely Mr. Delaney's explanations as to the reason for the visit.

"Miss Mae, my nephew," Mr. Delaney continued.

"How do you do," Edward Delaney said again. He spoke politely enough, but there was no denying he lacked the polish Keith Hopkins would have displayed in a similar situation. Jessie hoped Catherine was aware of this, then had the curious feeling that she was and counted it all to the good.

Catherine, who had been standing when the men entered the room, now found herself taking an involuntary step toward the young man. She knew her mother would reprimand her for this later, but even so she did not draw back. Edward came toward her at the same moment and so they met in the center of the floor.

"Miss Catherine, my nephew Edward," Mr. Delaney said. He looked quite pleased with himself and the way things were going.

"How do you do," the two young people said, almost in the same breath. Catherine extended her hand, and the young man took it.

His hands, long fingered and strong, closed over the girl's in a confident, positive way, making of the gesture something more than a mere social courtesy. And suddenly Catherine found herself thinking—that's the way he is. He goes forward to meet things and when he gets there he doesn't hesitate. She stood still, not wanting to withdraw her hand from that warm, strong clasp. Jessie, watching narrowly, found herself wishing that the young man were squat, ugly and ill-mannered.

"Won't you sit down?" she suggested crisply.

At the sound of her mother's voice, Catherine withdrew her hand, flushing a little. Edward Delaney took a chair Jessie indicated, but as soon as he was seated he looked at Catherine again.

The girl was conscious of her mother trying to signal her to go upstairs and take off the taffeta dress. After all, the flounce was held on only by pins—securely anchored, it was true, but still pins. She deliberately avoided her mother's eyes. In some strange way the dress seemed to contribute to the excitement of the moment—shimmering as it did in waves of color, now predominately blue, now violet, now green, now rose. It added to the sense of vitality which the presence of the young man had brought. The girl's eyes glowed darkly; she moved her hands restlessly in spite of all she had been taught about keeping them folded neatly in her lap. And instead of sitting up straight and firm, she leaned forward a little as if she were preparing to get up and go away somewhere, very fast.

A silence had fallen over the room. Jessie, as hostess, was forced to give up her attempt to make Catherine change her dress. She turned to her guests.

"How do you like Missouri?" she asked, speaking directly to Edward.

"Oh," he told her, "very well . . ."

He spoke in crisp, rather clear-cut tones, certainly unlike the slightly slurred speech pattern of Missourians. Hearing him, Jessie lifted her eyebrows slightly. That was the way all Yankees talked—so abruptly they sounded almost rude. Mr. Delaney, in spite of all the years he had been in Missouri, had never quite lost these brusque undertones.

"Will you be staying long?" she asked.

"I don't really know. I'm on my way West, but I ran out of money so I decided to stop off with Uncle Frank until I could earn enough to go on."

Jessie could not bring herself to answer that immediately. In her code, one did not mention money—either its presence or its lack. One might even do as she had done—sell his land acre by reluctant acre, signing each deed with tight-lipped dignity, but still he did not say it was because he needed the money. When she finally spoke it was to bring the conversation around to his family, surely a safe enough subject.

"Your people are all from Illinois?" she asked.

The young man brought his glance reluctantly away from Catherine long enough to look at Jessie while he answered her. In spite of herself the woman was impressed by the way he looked at her—a straight, level glance, clear and direct.

"I believe my mother's grandmother was from Virginia," he told her. "Outside of that, they probably have all been from Illinois."

"Oh, Virginia—" Jessie was immediately impressed. "We have many relatives there. What was her maiden name?"

"I don't believe I ever heard my mother say," Edward told her casually. "She died when I was quite young."

Jessie recoiled as from a blow. To her nothing was more unthinkable than that one should fail to know the maiden name of his grandmothers—far, far back into the history of the family. Those who forgot did so for some very good reason.

The young man stirred restlessly in his chair. "This is a nice place you have here," he said. He looked at Catherine when he spoke, his meaning as clear as if he had said the words which were really in his mind. "If you have no objections, I'd like to go out and look around a bit."

He got to his feet quickly in a co-ordination of wish and fulfillment which gave his actions a look of fluid grace. Catherine rose, too.

"I'll show you around," she said.

She was conscious of her mother's eyes on her, signaling

her that she should not go walking in the taffeta dress. She
knew that was only an excuse. Her mother did not want her
to go walking at all with the strange young man, so different
from any other boy she had ever known. So vastly different
from Cousin Keith who would not have thought of crossing his
Cousin Jessie by walking out when she so clearly did not want
him to do so. Certainly, even had he wished to be alone with
Catherine, he would never have shown it so plainly and forth-
rightly.

And strangely enough, with Keith she would have been
guided entirely by her mother's wishes. Now she merely led
the way out the side door.

"This is the croquet ground," she explained. "Would you
like to play?"

"Why, yes, I would," he said, apparently forgetting entirely his wish to explore the place.


In the days that followed, Edward Delaney came almost
every day to the Montgomery place. The fact that Jessie re-
ceived him coolly did not seem to discourage him in the least.
He was invariably polite to her, but beyond the first greetings
he paid her little attention. He had not come to see Jessie.

Usually he came in late afternoon when his uncle could
best spare him. Jessie tried to find tasks to keep Catherine busy
at these times, hoping to discourage the visits. Often she arranged for a fitting of one of the dresses for the Virginia trip,
preparations for which she was now pushing forward with re-
newed haste and energy. But when she sent down the message
by Della—that Catherine was busy at the moment—the young
man simply sent word back that he would wait until she could
see him. Actually, Jessie found it was worse than useless to try
fitting a dress after he appeared—Catherine was suddenly un-
interested in anything save going to meet him.

"Oh, take off the dress—I'll manage without you," Jessie would finally say. "There'll be no peace until you go down there where that Yankee is waiting, anyway."

Catherine could scarcely get dressed fast enough. She was not greatly concerned with her mother's disapproval; in fact she was hardly aware of it. The presence of Edward in the sitting room was a magnet which drew her there almost without her being aware of her going.

Generally they started out avowedly to play croquet. But more often they found a bench once they were outside and sat down to talk.

"This is a large place you have here," he said once, looking across the rolling acres of the farm. It didn't matter what he talked about; for Catherine the subject immediately took on dignity and worth.

"It used to be much larger," she told him, a delicate excitement flowing through her veins. "Before the War it was larger and prettier. The War was hard on all of us around here."

"The War was hard on everyone," he said gravely. "You Southerners have a way of thinking it was hard only for you. My father was in prison camp—Andersonville. He never was well after that. He wanted to be a lawyer, but he had to work outside so he took up carpentering. He never liked being a carpenter."

"I'm sorry," Catherine said impulsively feeling that in some way she was at fault.

He smiled at her and the lines deepened in his face, those two curved lines which ran from just below his cheek bones to his chin, forming parenthesis marks enclosing his mouth. She thought they gave a special significance to whatever he said, set it apart from the utterances of other people, just as she thought now that they lent a certain quality to his smile, giving it both strength and understanding. She felt very warm and happy, having him smile at her.

"I wanted to be a lawyer, too," he told her. "But there wasn't any money. Anyway—I got to thinking a man's chance lies in the West these days. So I set out to go."

Light died in her face and she got quickly to her feet.

"Let's play croquet," she said, her voice breathless and quick, like a runner fleeing some great danger.

He did not go however, whether from lack of money or for another reason Catherine would not let herself dwell upon. The weeks slipped by—it was July now. Edward was still working for his uncle, and coming often to the Montgomery place. On those rare days when he did not drop by Catherine found the time was one of complete bleakness for her. Always with him there was a sense of excitement and, oddly enough, also a feeling of content. Even when there were others in the room she found herself listening for his voice, hearing it above all others, although certainly he did not talk loud.

It was a feeling he seemed to share, for when she spoke he always turned in her direction to listen, regardless of who might be attempting to engage him in conversation at the moment; and no matter how far they might be seated from each other at the beginning of the call, they soon found themselves close together. Almost at the same moment they would have the impulse to stand up and say, "Let's go outside and play croquet."

Edward was an excellent player; there was a neat precision about the way he sized up the situation and then with deliberate care raised his mallet and brought it down against the ball at exactly the right spot, sending it spinning across the grass to the destination he had determined for it. Catherine played only moderately well.

"It's because you don't take any pains aiming," Edward told her. "You've got to decide where you want that ball to go and then send it there."

He took the mallet from her, tried to show her how to aim, how to give the smart snap to the ball.

"Hit it," he told her. "My Lord—you act as if you were afraid it would blow up in your face if you did anything more than tap it gently."

They laughed together and Catherine had the fleeting thought that, with the exception of Uncle Willie, she had never had people to laugh with. It was delightful. She laughed again, just for the pure joy of it.

"You know," Edward said, surveying her thoughtfully, "you ought to laugh more. When you do you have a dimple in your left cheek."

By the end of July Edward was able to come for only the briefest of visits, and those at no set time. He might show up in the middle of the morning or late afternoon. Usually he could stay for only a few moments. Apparently Mr. Delaney, having discovered the convenience of a helper, was making full use of him.

The main purpose of each of Catherine's days was to keep watch and then, before her mother sensed what was going on, hurry outside to meet him. She had no intention of wasting any of their precious time together sharing him with her mother and Aunt Mae. When she saw him coming she would walk out of the door, move to meet him.

"Hello."

"Oh, hello . . ."

Together, as if by common consent, they would make their way to the bench by the croquet ground. It sat under a great maple tree, well hidden from the house and the watching eyes of Jessie. Here they would sit down and talk.

"You know," he said one day, "you aren't a thing like I thought you would be."

"What do you mean?"

"I mean—well, when Uncle Frank told me about you, I thought you sounded sort of—sort of prim and stuck-up. I don't like people like that. Do you?"

"No," she said, not quite sure what he meant, knowing only that if he disapproved she would be willing to follow his judgment.

"I almost said no when he wanted to come calling on you."

Almost said no! What if he had refused to come! What if he had pushed on West before she saw him! Her eyes grew wide and dark at the thought.

He picked up a blade of grass, put it between his fingers. She watched his hands—strong and purposeful, long-fingered and supple. He adjusted the grass blade with meticulous care, then raised it to his lips and blew on it. A piercing whistle split the air. Catherine jumped and they both laughed.

"Scared you, didn't I?"

"Here—let me see if I can do it. Uncle Willie used to try to teach me but I never could learn."

He had scarcely reached for another bit of grass when Jessie's voice came from the porch.

"Catherine—" she called.

"Golly," he said ruefully, "Now I've gone and done it!"

"Catherine—" Jessie called again, urgently. "Come here right away. I want to try this dress on you."

They stood up.

"See you tomorrow," he told her.

He walked away rapidly, swinging his arms, whistling as he went. Catherine made her way toward the house.

Ordinarily Jessie would have been aware of what was going on. But now her preoccupation with preparation for the trip kept her from noticing how often Edward dropped by. Or if she noticed, she evidently did not attach too much significance to the visits.

Catherine had mentioned the forthcoming trip to Edward, but only in the vaguest terms. As if it were something not yet definite; or, if really a fact, one to be carried out at some distant date.

It was just twilight of an early August evening when Catherine looked out the window to see Edward coming up the path. She was surprised—he had been there briefly earlier in the day when he was out delivering some groceries for his uncle. She got up and started toward the door.

"What's the matter?" Jessie asked. "Surely that Yankee isn't back again."

Catherine did not answer. She went out of the house quickly, walked to meet him.

Even before he spoke to her she knew something was wrong. Scarcely were they seated on the bench when he began.

"Is it true—that you're going back to Virginia to marry your cousin?"

Catherine flushed quickly. Even her mother, for all the fact that her intentions were so crystal clear, had never put the thing into words. Now when Edward flung the accusation at her she winced a little, both from shock and embarrassment.

"What an idea," she stammered. "Who said that?"

"Uncle Frank—he says that's what people are telling. Is that why you're going back?" he asked again.

"We're just going on a visit," Catherine said uncertainly. "You've known that for weeks."

"No I haven't. You always talked about it as if the time was most indefinite—that maybe you wouldn't go at all. And now today I find out you're leaving in a few weeks—and why."

Catherine wished he wouldn't be so blunt. He could see she didn't want to discuss the matter. He had set his jaws so that they made a square firm line; all the lines of his face were set and hard. Then she saw a little knot of muscles flexing in his throat and suddenly she knew the reason for his brusqueness. *He doesn't want me to go,* she thought. *That's why he's acting this way.* She dropped her eyes quickly to cover her gladness.

"You don't belong back in Virginia," he told her, his voice stiff and constrained. "You may think so, but you don't. East is not for people like you."

"How do you know?" she asked, almost in a whisper. "You've never been there."

"I don't need to go there to know what it's like. You'll just see people who believe the same things, who never grow and never want to. You have to push West if you want to keep growing. Go East and you'll die—inside yourself. I tell you, it's not for you."

"I know," she said softly.

She wanted to cry out to him that she had never really wanted to go, that the idea had been her mother's. But this would have been disloyal in her so she remained silent.

"Catherine," Edward began and then stopped. A flush rose in his face. "Catherine—" he went on urgently and reached toward her.

Above the thundering in her ears one thought came clear to the girl. She should resist. Girls of her time, her way of life, resisted automatically—not so much from maidenly reserve, although that was part of it, as from the knowledge handed down from mother to daughter that this was a part of the technique of getting a husband. More than that—it was insurance against the future. If a girl proved hard to win the husband would never remind her afterward that she had been eager enough to get him and, therefore, had no grounds for complaint no matter what happened. The woman who acted on this knowledge was forever after in a position to make a better bargain.

Catherine knew this as well as any other girl. But still she did not resist. Instead, she went into Edward's arms willingly and without hesitation. She did not even draw back when he kissed her, although it was strange to find a man's lips on her own.

She was not prepared for the feeling that came from being kissed by him. She had a great desire to try to tell him how she felt except she knew she could not put the moment into words even had she tried. He was sharing the experience—perhaps he knew without being told.

She drew back from him a little, lifted her hand and ran it across the triangle of his left eyebrow, down the parenthesis marks on his cheeks; touching him gave her a feeling of strength, of being steadied by some sure force.

Edward took her hands. He bent to kiss her again. Then he spoke.

"Catherine," he said. "Don't go to Virginia to marry anybody else. Stay here and marry me."

Again her course was indicated, clearly and with no deviation. She should hesitate and tell him she would think about it. But what she really said was, "Yes, Edward—of course I will."

She said it, knowing that all her life, without realizing it, she had been waiting for this moment.

# CHAPTER 2

NOTHING CATHERINE MONTGOMERY COULD HAVE DONE WOULD HAVE SHOCKED HER MOTHER AS MUCH AS DID THE GIRL'S ANnouncement that she had promised to marry Edward Delaney. It cut directly across every cherished tradition, every hope and belief of Jessie's life.

True, she had good reason to be prepared, for the young man had haunted the place ever since that unfortunate day when his uncle—God forgive him, for Jessie could not find it in her heart to do so—had first brought him to the house. She had been blinded to the true state of affairs, she defended herself, by the belief that no daughter of hers could ever be attracted by a Yankee whose uncle ran a village store—a boy whose background was so different from hers that the two of them might as well have been from separate planets.

"You scarcely know him," she protested. No girl, reared as Catherine had been, could consent to marry a man she had met a scant two months ago.

"I know him well enough, Mother," Catherine said softly. Her cheeks were flushed, her eyes bright. About her there was a glow, a brightness that came from within, like light shining through alabaster.

"And just when you were getting ready for that lovely trip to Virginia."

That was the core of the thing—the final defeat, the ultimate bitterness. It was not a trip alone that Catherine rejected; it was a long dream, her entire future.

"I'm sorry, Mother," Catherine said gently. She was genuinely sorry for the hurt she was causing her mother, understanding quite clearly the nature of it, aching that there was no way of avoiding it. But even as she spoke she was seeing the image of Cousin Keith Hopkins, sitting in the parlor with a group of middle-aged women, paying them pretty compliments. And she was hearing Edward's voice saying, "You don't belong in Virginia."

She wanted to add, "I never really wanted to go, Mother." But she restrained herself.

Jessie tried another tack.

"You don't know a thing about his people," she said. "What did his father do?"

"He was a carpenter."

"Oh—" Jessie's monosyllable relegated the work to the background, something the least said about the better. "Do you want to ask him to the wedding? I believe he said his mother is dead."

"His father's dead, too," Catherine said. "He died before Edward came to Missouri. As long as he lived, Edward felt he had to stay with him."

"Does he have any other close relatives?"

"No—just Mr. Delaney. That's why he came to him."

"Catherine," Jessie said, "it's a risk you're taking—marrying a man who is almost a stranger to you, whose people are strangers. You think you're in love with him—but you haven't been around him long enough to be sure."

"I'm sure," the girl told her with quiet conviction.

She wished she could explain to her mother how she felt about loving Edward. As if, at long last, she had become a real person instead of a shadow—from somewhere out of a world of men there had come this one who was the other half of her. She was as sure as that, and as confident. Something about her attitude impressed Jessie. Reluctantly she had to admit, but only to herself, that this was no mere infatuation on the girl's part.

"All right," she finally said, coldly and with nothing of happiness in her words, "if you are bound to go ahead, I reckon there is no stopping you. But don't say I didn't warn you. He's got two counts against him from the start. He's Yankee and he's part Irish. Almost I could wish the Yankee would come out ahead. For if that happens, at least he'll make a living for you. If the Irish wins, you'll have to make out on dreams."

"Edward will take care of me," Catherine said. "I'm not afraid."

She had never been less afraid in her life. And feeling as she did, she could understand in a measure her mother's objections to the marriage, so that, even while she went ahead in the face of her mother's disapproval, she still wanted to make things as easy for her as possible.

Jessie might have accepted the fact of the approaching wedding, but that did not mean she gave up her objections. She continued to voice them, losing no chance to bring them into the conversation.

"You're both too young," she insisted. "You won't be nineteen until after—until September."

Not if she could help it would she mention the wedding date—August 28. To do so might imply the approval which she certainly did not feel.

"How old is *he?*" she continued. Nor could she bring herself to call Edward by name. The few times she had tried, the word stuck in her throat.

"Twenty-two, Mother," Catherine said, thinking that it

sounded very adult and exactly right. A man's age—impressive, correct.

"You and Richard weren't a great deal older when you were married, Jessie," Aunt Mae pointed out.

"That was different . . ."

She did not reveal the nature of the difference, nor did Aunt Mae or Catherine ask her to.

"He doesn't even have a job . . ." Jessie went on.

"Oh, Mother, but he does. I told you his uncle asked him to help in the store. Mr. Delaney isn't feeling too well—he said it would be a real blessing if Edward would help him." She said this proudly, as if it were a great tribute to Edward's worth.

"Oh, that—" Jessie dismissed the job curtly as something not to be remembered at all, especially with any pride. Clerking in a store—a small country store—was not a work to which one could attach any distinction. How could she write the news back to Virginia—news already bitter enough—and have to add, "At the moment, he is helping out in his uncle's store." She considered suppressing the fact of Catherine's marriage altogether. Keith girls simply did not marry clerks.

Then a way out occurred to her, one that might salvage some lost dignity, be a kind of compensation for this difficult thing she was facing.

"I have a much better idea," she said. For the first time since Catherine had broken the news to her she was alert and purposeful, reasonably composed. "I would like very much for Edward to help me manage the place. Hiram is getting old and I need someone."

That would sound much better. "My son-in-law is taking over the management of the place. Really it is too much for me." She was thinking how she could write that and be believed. Catherine's marriage might take on an air of melancholy dignity, something done almost as a duty.

"I'll speak to Della right away," Jessie said, getting to her feet, "and have her make the upstairs guest room ready for you."

Actually the suggestion did not seem at all out of order to Catherine. The farm, though smaller than it had once been, was still large enough to require more help than Hiram was able to give. And certainly there was room enough in this house. Nor was this a custom unsanctioned in the family. She would not be the first bride who had come here to live since the house had been built. Even so, she stopped her mother's headlong rush out of the room.

"I'll mention it to Edward," she said.

"Oh—" Jessie stopped uncertainly. It had not occurred to her that she would be unable to settle the matter at once and without further discussion. "There's no reason why he should refuse," she said stiffly.

"I'll ask him," Catherine promised.

She felt few, if any, doubts about Edward's approval of a suggestion so right as this. Although she had not admitted it, even to herself, she was not too pleased with the idea of his helping in Mr. Delaney's store, even while she was grateful to the old gentleman for the offer. She told herself Edward was capable of better things. Now when her mother offered such a sensible alternative, she was delighted.

That evening when Edward came calling, she told him.

They sat together in the parlor—the first time they had done this. Always before they had talked outside or in the sitting room where they first met.

The parlor was correctly formal with its rosewood piano, damask covered furniture and dark portraits of departed Keiths and Montgomerys. Catherine felt it was hard to bring their love inside to the chill of the parlor. Not only that, but they were both conscious of Aunt Mae and Jessie sitting across the hall in the warm, familiar sitting room—with doors discreetly open between them. The knowledge put a restraint on both young people. It was no wonder that Catherine broke the news as a child might have done—a child, conscious of her elders keeping watch over her.

Edward sat, stiffly erect, on a rose damask chair while Catherine, sitting with equal stiffness on a love seat, was torn between the hope and the fear that he would move over beside her and take her in his arms. Hope, because as they sat now there was a stilted formality between them, so that they could not talk with any ease or naturalness; fear, because the long silence that would follow would betray the situation to the women across the hall as clearly as if they had been watching. The awkward moments continued; she began to wonder if he was tired of her already. Maybe he was sorry he had interrupted his westward journey to marry her.

And since he made no move toward her, made no indication of wishing to do so, she felt it necessary to keep conversation going.

"Edward," she said, almost as formally as she might have asked him to show her a length of ribbon at the store, "Mother would like very much to have you help her run the farm."

"I can't," he told her. "I wouldn't have time—I'll be too busy helping Uncle Frank."

"I mean—live here—and not work in the store . . . "

Suddenly Edward stood up. His face was flushed, his eyes more darkly blue than she had ever remembered seeing them. She watched him, fascinated, thinking he did not need to say anything in order to let her know he would have none of her mother's suggestion. But he said it anyway, and with such firmness that the words most certainly carried to the women in the sitting room.

"No, I'm going to work in the store. And we aren't going to live with your mother."

For a moment Catherine felt like a child rebuked for some misdeed she was scarcely conscious of having committed. Partly it was the reaction from the pleasant confidence she had experienced in thinking she was going to offer him an excellent solution, both as to his job and the matter of a roof over their heads. Now it would seem Edward would have none of them.

She looked at him with uncertainty, blurted out self-consciously, "But I don't see why—" Her lip trembled a little as she spoke and Edward, aware of her hurt, moved toward her. He put his arm around her gently as he would have done to a child—which, at the moment she was.

"Because," he said, "it's my business to get the job—and the home. I'm the head of the family. See?"

And suddenly she thought—a home of our own. Then we won't have to worry about somebody knowing I'm in his arms, about somebody thinking it's time he went home. He won't have to leave at all.

Her eyes grew wide at the thought, and deep. A delicate flush crept up her neck, flooded her whole face. She dropped her eyes suddenly, and Edward's arms tightened around her.

"I'll find a home for us," he said almost in a whisper, as if her thought had communicated itself to him, too. "Just don't worry, darling."

"I won't," she said. She slipped her arms around his neck, tilted her face up to be kissed. She forgot all about Aunt Mae and her mother.

The matter of a place to live was solved in a manner which, while not entirely to their liking, was still one they could both accept.

Mr. Frank Delaney said they could move into his house.

Now that he had Edward to take over the store, he wanted to go back to Illinois to see his family and old friends, something he had not done in all the years since he had left. He might stay six months. At any rate, the young couple would be welcome to his house in his absence.

Edward brought the news to Catherine.

"His house?" Catherine spoke hesitantly. She had been inside Mr. Delaney's house once when she accompanied Aunt Mae on an errand. She could remember little about it, except that it was small, with the dull utilitarian furniture a bachelor would select. There were no curtains at the windows, no pictures on the walls.

"Now Catherine," Edward said, speaking a little stiffly. "I know it isn't what you've been used to." He brushed his hair back with a gesture somewhere between apology and embarrassment.

"Oh, darling, I don't mind—I don't mind at all." There was a rich, impulsive warmth in her voice. Hearing her, Edward grinned at her shyly, like a small boy who has been forgiven and is grateful. She ran toward him, stood on tiptoe to put her arms around his neck, to drop her head on his shoulder.

He rubbed his chin across her hair, rumpling it into a fine state of disarray.

"Fact is, looks like I can't give you anything at all," he went on.

"Don't you say that," she cried. "You're—you're giving me —" she hesitated a moment searching for words. "You're giving me just *everything*," she finished triumphantly. "Just everything I *want!*"

Aunt Mae stood solidly behind the young people in their decision to live in Mr. Delaney's house. Not so, Jessie.

"Live in that house," she protested, "You might as well move into the barn. Or Della's cabin."

"Young people ought to be to themselves," Mae remarked quietly. "Remember how you felt when you had to move in here."

"There was nothing else we could do," Jessie said. "Your Pa was sick, and somebody had to help you look after him, and the place."

"That's what I mean," Mae told her. "You and Richard did it because you had to, not because you wanted to."

"There wasn't any other way," Jessie repeated stubbornly. "We had to come. And—and afterward, I stayed on to make a home for him and you . . . "

"You made a home for all of us, Jessie," Mae said softly. "And we've appreciated it. But let Catherine and Edward have a home of their own."

Strange, Catherine was thinking, it's never seemed quite real to me before—Mama and Papa coming to this house as bride and groom, loving each other as Edward and I do, full of hope as we are.

She had been so young when her father died—barely two—that she had no actual memory of him. Most of what she knew she had got from Aunt Mae and Della.

"He was a brave fine man," Aunt Mae had told her. "And handsome, too. You look more like him than you do your mother."

"Yes," Della had said—Della who had been first slave and then servant and always the devoted friend, "yes, he was a fine man. Full of fun. And how he and your ma did love each other. The two families were a little bit of kin, and your ma and your Uncle Willie and your pa—well them and the families used to run back and forth between here and Virginia all the time, a-visiting."

"Don't try to talk about him to your mother unless she brings up the subject," Aunt Mae had warned Catherine as soon as she was old enough to understand, "She's never gotten over his death."

So Catherine satisfied herself with what she got from Della and Aunt Mae, and with looking at the pictures of him that were all over the house—a young man with a smiling mouth in the picture on her mother's dressing table, a solemn little boy looking anxiously out on the world in Aunt Mae's room, a half-grown lad regarding her gravely in her own room. But strangely enough, none of them ever made him come as clear as did the conversation between her mother and Aunt Mae now. And, also, she had a better understanding of why her mother should feel as she did about the approaching marriage.

She put out her hand, touched her mother's arm timidly.

"We'll be so close, Mama," she pointed out. "I'll come over here every day."

"I don't doubt it," Jessie agreed grimly. "You'll be glad to get away from that Delaney house every chance you have."

Aunt Mae looked thoughtful.

"You know, Jessie," she said, "you may be right. That house does need something done to it. I'm going to speak to Mr. Delaney about it."

Aunt Mae did go to Mr. Delaney to discuss the advisability of "freshening things up a bit" before the young couple moved in.

"Go right ahead," he said. He liked Mae Montgomery. She was a quiet, soothing sort of woman. People thought she was weak and spineless, putting up with her sister-in-law the way she did. She wasn't weak—she was a strong, good woman. "Go ahead," he repeated. "Pick out what you need here at the store. But don't you stick in a lot of junk that'll just get in my way once I come back."

Mae promised to stay within the bounds of reason and made certain selections she deemed necessary. Then she and Della cleaned and scrubbed and polished. They hung curtains. Catherine wanted to help, but in this matter Jessie was adamant.

"You stay away from that place until after you're married," she ruled. "People are talking enough as it is."

Sometimes Catherine thought that, without Aunt Mae, there might not even have been a wedding. On her fell all the planning, the preparations, Jessie's one stipulation being that it be kept simple. There would be no house full of guests, no cousins coming back from Virginia or even any Missouri kin, who, though hardly as dear as those from Virginia, still expected to be represented at weddings and funerals. Only Mr. Delaney and the immediate family would be present, three people in all, exclusive of the minister and the young couple. And of course Della and Hiram hovering solicitously in the background in such a way that they could be "watching" without actually attending—a situation understood and carefully observed by everyone concerned. In after years, Della could say to Catherine's children,

"Honey, I watched your Ma when she got married."

Not, "I was at the wedding."

For Della, the whole thing held all the delight that Christmas would hold for a child. She lost herself in Catherine's happiness; she was caught up in preparations for the wedding, simple though it might be. She baked a wedding cake without which, to her, the whole affair would scarcely attain legal status. With Hiram's help she cleaned the house until it shone, even though there would be no kin to poke around looking for dust and disorder. She baked a ham and dressed chickens, although why she scarcely knew. That was part of the ancient ritual of marriage as she had practiced it for other brides in other, happier days. She was up early and late, treading the path between cabin and kitchen a dozen times a day.

And then one morning when she came up on the porch, she saw it had happened—the door to the little room was closed. Mr. Willie had come home during the night. She sighed, as much for the fact that she must be the one to tell Miss Jessie as for anything else. She busied herself with preparations for breakfast until finally her mistress came into the kitchen.

"Good morning, Della."

"Good morning, Miss Jessie." And then, with gentle compassion, "Mr. Willie's home, Miss Jessie."

Jessie lifted her head quickly. All the lines in her face were etched more sharply; her nose was drawn in until it looked like only a thin wedge on her face. For a moment she did not speak and then it was to ask a question, uncertain and even helpless.

"How—is he?"

"I don't know—I jest thought I'd wait and we'd look together."

"Yes—that was good . . ."

Long since, Jessie Montgomery had accustomed herself to her brother's unexpected arrivals and his no less unexpected departures, although she had never reconciled herself to the manner of them. She accepted them because he was her baby brother and she had helped to bring him up. He had come back from the war; her husband and Mae's fiancé had not. Down the years she had come to realize that there can be other casualties in war besides physical death. Men may also die inside themselves, as Willie had done when he came back to find the girl he was to marry had burned to death when the Kansas Redlegs had set fire to her father's house. Mae had never recovered from the death of the man she loved. Jessie often thought it was a good thing that she herself was the kind who could stand up to life. She wondered where they would all be now if she, too, had given up.

But there was no time for such thoughts now. She and Della had work to do. Together they went to the door of the Little Room, opened it. One look at the man on the bed—his head hanging over the edge, still wearing his clothes, even to his shoes—told them all they needed to know.

"He's pretty sick, Miss Jessie," Della ventured, expressing the thought for both of them.

"Yes—go get some hot water." She turned to the wash-stand and began gathering up towels and soap. "First I'll see that he has a bath. Put on some broth to heat. See that the coffee is extra-hot and strong . . . "

So many times they had met this problem together, she hardly needed to give directions. Nor did Della need to say, although she said it, "Yes, Miss Jessie."

In some ways, the arrival of Uncle Willie, only three days before the date of the wedding, was fortunate. It kept Jessie so busy looking after him that she had little time to bemoan the approaching event. Catherine and Aunt Mae went ahead, unhampered by Jessie's objections, to plan things pretty much the way they wanted them. Mostly Jessie made no objections, once the plans were announced. This, however, did not hold with Catherine's decision concerning her wedding dress.

The girl wanted to wear the changeable taffeta, the one she had been fitting the first day she and Edward had met.

It pleased her to think how greatly different the destiny of the dress would be from that which was orginally planned. She was to wear it "Sundays and for best" back in Virginia. The bustle and the carefully draped flounce—those were meant to catch the eye of Keith Hopkins, who was a great one for notic-ing women's clothes. The color, rose shot through with blue and green and violet, made her eyes look darker, her skin more faultlessly creamy. "The Keith skin," Jessie called it, thinking happily that it would not escape the notice and the approval of the Virginia kin.

Now Keith would not see the dress. But Edward would, and he would know why she wore it and love her for it.

Jessie, when informed of the decision, was shocked.

"Why, Catherine—you can't do that. *He's already seen you in it!*"

No reason could be more final than that. A groom did not see his bride in her wedding dress before she came to him at the altar. Jessie might give way in other matters concerning the wedding, but this she refused to sanction.

"You can't do it, Catherine," she repeated firmly.

"Now, Jessie," Mae said. "If she wants to, there's no real reason she shouldn't. It isn't as if this were a fashionable wedding with a lot of guests. Let her wear it . . . "

"What's Mae taking such a stand about?" a voice asked at the door.

The women turned, and there stood Uncle Willie.

"Oh, Willie—" Jessie said. "How do you feel?"

"Fine—never felt better."

He spoke with a gay debonairness, with the light mockery the vagabond reserves for the earth-bound plodder. But the deep lines running from nose to mouth belied his carefree manner, as did an indefinable sadness mirrored in his eyes. In fact, his whole face was one of contradictions—contradictions which were repeated in the worn shoes, so carefully polished, and the clean but threadbare clothes he wore.

Jessie might have succeeded in building a wall around herself but she could never induce her brother to join her in the retreat. Even when he came back for his so-called visits he did not seem a part of the place, delighting instead in telling stories of the world she had rejected, peopling it with such charm that one would forget, in listening to him, that he had not fared too well himself at its hands.

"You ought to settle down to something," Jessie used to urge him.

"Too many fascinating things to do," he assured her. "Prospecting, freighting, railroading, each a separate adventure."

"Adventure," she had sniffed with high disdain. "Why don't you stay here and help me run this place? That's adventure enough for anyone."

"Now Jessie," he had protested, "you don't seriously expect me to do that, do you?"

She did not answer, perhaps sensing that his very protest covered a secret yearning for the life he professed to disdain.

It was this understanding that made her always gentle with him. She turned to him now to ask, "Have you had your breakfast?"

"Yes, Della fed me. Ah, there's poetry in her food!" He pushed back his brown hair, only slightly graying, with one hand as he spoke; as he did so, he snapped the fingers of the other lightly.

"Now tell me what's upset Mae," he said. "She's usually as calm as a spring morning."

"She wants Mother to let me wear my taffeta dress at my wedding," Catherine explained.

"Your wedding . . . " Uncle Willie said. "Yes—Della was telling me about it. And why, Jessie," Uncle Willie said, turning to his sister, "shouldn't the child wear her pretty new dress at her wedding if she wants to?"

"Because the groom has already seen it on her," Jessie snapped. Already she knew how the discussion would turn out, but even so, that did nothing to allay her anger.

"All the more reason, it would seem to me," Uncle Willie

said. "That way he will be sure to recognize his bride—no matter how excited he is."

Catherine got up and moved rapidly toward her uncle. Always the tie between them had been strong and sure. He it was who made willow whistles for her in spring and snow men in winter. He it was who took her fishing. He it was who taught her to laugh.

"I'm so glad you got home for the wedding," she told him, kissing him lightly on the cheek.

A strange look came over the man's face, fleeting as a shadow across the sun. Welcome he had in this house, and shelter, and nursing. But save from Catherine not always joy at his return.

"I'm glad to be back kitten," he said, kissing the girl. "And it seems to me that a little happiness in this occasion is badly needed. The way you look, Jessie, one would think we're going to be celebrating a wake instead of a wedding."

"He's a Yankee and she hardly knows him," Jessie wailed, letting the burden of her discontent spill out.

"Well, he's her choice," Uncle Willie pointed out. "If he's the one she wants, she ought to have him."

"She doesn't know what she wants," Jessie said bitingly. "She's had so few chances to be with young men."

"Just her Cousin Keith," Willie retorted, grinning so impishly that in spite of herself Catherine smiled with him. "I admit that wasn't much help."

"Stop talking about Keith Hopkins," Jessie cried, all the bitterness of her lost hopes welling up in her voice. "He is a gentleman. At least she can say she knew one in her life."

"She'll probably know a lot of others, her husband included, before her life is finished," the man said. "They are to be found in more places than you suspect, Jessie. You've done the girl a great wrong, keeping her off to herself the way you have."

Catherine, listening to the two, was thinking that she had grown up knowing little contact with other children. True, she had gone to school in Grafton, but she had ridden her own pony instead of walking as the others did. When the weather was bad, Hiram drove her to school in the carriage and called for her at the end of the day. She would have liked walking with the other children, feeling a part of them. But when she asked to do so, Jessie was so firm in her refusal that the child gave up. At school she got along all right, making a small place for herself. But once she mounted her pony or got into the carriage she was alien and apart.

It was a separateness which increased as she grew older. Jessie seldom allowed her to go to the homes of children in the community and by and by the invitations ceased to come. For the most part, all the company that ever came to the Montgomery house was cousins and friends from Warrensburg or Jefferson City or Independence or, occasionally, from Virginia.

Uncle Willie was right in saying that her mother had kept her from knowing people beyond their own kin and friends.

"Well anyway," Uncle Willie went on now, "it's a good thing I'm here. I can give the bride away. It would have been most unfortunate for a Keith bride to be given away by someone other than a Keith."

As a matter of fact, no preparations had been made for this detail. As far as Jessie was concerned, the young couple could simply walk up to the minister unattended; to do otherwise would have implied a family approval which she was not prepared to bestow. And anyway—until Uncle Willie arrived, there was no man to perform the office. She would almost have been willing to ask Hiram to give Catherine away rather than to allow Mr. Delaney, the only choice, to do so. Knowing this, Catherine and Aunt Mae had planned for Catherine to come into the room alone.

"Her name is Montgomery," Jessie pointed out coolly.

"You are quibbling, Jessie," Uncle Willie chided her. "It is my place to give her away and I am going to do it. And—I'd like to meet the young man, if you please."

Hiram was accordingly dispatched for Edward, who came at once. Uncle Willie indicated that they were to be left alone. In half an hour or so, the two men came out of the room together, with Uncle Willie's hand on Edward's shoulder.

"I enjoyed talking with you," Uncle Willie said.

"Thank you, sir," Edward responded.

They shook hands. Then Edward looked around restlessly. Jessie knew that the next minute he'd be asking for Catherine, here on the day before the wedding when propriety demanded that the bride remain in seclusion. But of course one couldn't expect a Delaney to know about such things.

"Good morning, Edward," Jessie said formally.

Edward hesitated a moment. Then he said, "Good morning, Mrs. Montgomery," and made his way to the front door. Uncle Willie walked with him, his hand still on the boy's shoulder.

"I'll see you tomorrow," Uncle Willie said.

"Yes, sir," Edward said, smiling at him.

The two men shook hands again; Edward walked out the door, closed it behind him. They could hear him going off the porch, out of the yard, whistling as he went.

"That's a fine young man," Uncle Willie remarked thoughtfully. "You need never fear, Jessie. He'll be good to Catherine."

Jessie sniffed. But inwardly she felt relief. Some man in

the bride's family ought to have a talk with the prospective husband. Thank heavens Willie had got home in time for it.

The wedding took place the following evening.

It could scarcely have been more simple. Jessie walked into the parlor a few minutes before the hour to find Mr. Delaney, Edward and the minister already there. She spoke to them civilly enough, but with no real warmth. Her mind was too occupied with thoughts of the contrast between this and the kind of ceremony which was Catherine's right. That would have meant flocks of relatives, many of them from as far away as Virginia, filling the large, high-ceilinged rooms and spilling over to the porches and up the stairway. Girl cousins would be giggling in Catherine's room now, putting the last-minute touches on the wedding dress. The house would be filled with flowers, and all the precious china and cut glass and silver would be out, ready for the reception to follow.

Instead, there were no guests except Mr. Delaney, whom she scarcely counted as such, and Hiram and Della, watching from the double doors that connected the parlor with the dining room.

Presently Aunt Mae came in quietly and took her place at the rosewood piano. She struck the notes of the wedding march and almost immediately Catherine entered on Uncle Willie's arm, exhibiting what Jessie felt was an almost indecent haste, betraying the fact that she had been waiting just outside the door for the music to start. Edward moved over in front of the mantel to wait for her. Della and Aunt Mae had banked some late August flowers in front of it, had brought in the fern from the sitting room to form an altar of sorts. But to Jessie the whole thing looked shabby and pitiful.

"She might as well be marrying in the office of the justice of the peace," she thought bitterly.

For Catherine herself, however, there was no lack. She entered the room on Uncle Willie's arm, wearing the taffeta dress. Edward, seeing her, took a swift step toward her, his face intent and serious. Then he smiled, and suddenly she felt that they were the only two people in the room.

She took her place beside him; Uncle Willie stepped back to stand behind her mother's chair. The minister cleared his throat, began to speak the ancient, beautiful words of the ceremony.

He's talking to us, she thought—to Edward and to me. . . .

The age-old strength and dignity as well as the promise of what he was saying came through to her so that she could see the pattern of their life together—eternal, strong, everlasting as time itself. And she knew the quick wish that she might make her mother see this, as she herself did.

"Do you take this man . . ." she heard the minister saying.

She turned to Edward.

"Yes." she said, thinking as she did so that her mother would probably feel she had spoken too quickly, too eagerly.

"I pronounce you man and wife," he said.

The simple reception followed the ceremony.

"You were sure pretty, honey," Della whispered, handing Catherine the silver knife with which to cut the wedding cake. The colored woman had tied the customary white streamers to it, just as she had done before for other Montgomery brides. She had decorated the cake as she would have done had the wedding been the sort Jessie herself might have planned. These touches somehow helped to atone in a measure for the stiff smile on Jessie's face.

Uncle Willie's cheerfulness helped, too, as did Mr. Delaney's brisk heartiness.

"Well," he said, "I'd better be getting along. Almost time

for my train. I'm the one that's taking the wedding trip," Mr. Delaney finished, laughing at his own joke—a laughter in which the others, with the exception of Jessie, joined.

Hiram slipped over to Edward now, whispered a word in his ear. Edward looked at Catherine—she nodded slightly. Then she turned to her mother.

"Hiram's ready to drive us over, Mother," she said softly.

"Oh . . ."

This was Jessie's idea—that Hiram drive the young couple to their new home in her carriage. In some obscure way she seemed to feel that the stigma of going to Frank Delaney's house to set up housekeeping would in this way be partly alleviated. Now that the moment had come she thought she could not bear it, even under these conditions of her own making.

Catherine looked at her mother's face and then, uncertainly, at Edward. He stepped forward, put out his hand.

"Good-by, Mrs. Montgomery," he said gently. He looked as if he wanted to say more—to reassure her against all the doubts and fears he knew she was holding at the moment. Something of the goodness of his wish must have come through to her, for she relaxed a little, took his hand.

"Good-by," she said, speaking with more naturalness than she herself would have thought possible.

"Good-by, Mother," Catherine said. She went into her mother's arms like a child. They clung together for a brief moment and then Catherine kissed her. "Good-by," she said again. And then she turned to Edward.

"All right, I'm ready."

She kissed Aunt Mae and Uncle Willie. Together she and Edward walked out of the house and got into the carriage.

Hiram stopped with a flourish in front of Mr. Frank Delaney's house. Edward got out, reached his hand to help Catherine.

"Good night, Miss Catherine," the colored man said.

"Good night, Hiram."

"Good night, Mr. Edward."

"Good night—and thanks for driving us over."

"Oh, that's all right, Mr. Edward. If ever I kin be of any help . . ."

He drove off.

Together they walked toward the house, dark against the sky. Edward unlocked the door. Then he turned to her, lifting her up, the folds of her taffeta dress cascading down across his arms, the little wedding shoes swinging free of the ground. A step, and they were across the threshold.

She was aware of the smells of the house—new varnish and furniture polish and the good clean odor of cleansing powder and soap. There was, too, the pungency of the marigolds Aunt Mae had placed in a vase on the hall table, and the unmistakable smell of the new curtains she had made.

But the house itself was in darkness—it was as if Catherine was taking the whole thing on faith, having no knowledge at all of what lay ahead of her, depending entirely on Edward to guide her.

He put her down; she could feel the firmness of the floor beneath her feet.

"I'll light the lamp," he said, his voice constrained and self-conscious.

He took a match from his pocket in a gesture she sensed rather than saw. Standing apart from him, she had a feeling of strangeness, a sensation so sharp that it was close to fear. She reached out quickly to him, seeking reassurance with his touch. His arms went around her and the match dropped, unlighted and unheeded, to the floor.

# CHAPTER 3

WHATEVER DOUBTS CATHERINE MIGHT HAVE HAD AT FIRST ABOUT MR. DELANEY'S HOUSE WERE QUICKLY DISPELLED, ONCE SHE AND Edward were settled there. It became a dream cottage, completely right, entirely wonderful. It was, however, a sentiment not shared by Jessie.

"It doesn't even have a pantry," she pointed out. "Where are you going to keep the food?"

"In the kitchen safe," Catherine told her.

"In a safe—in the kitchen—" Jessie managed to imply that food thus stored would scarcely escape contamination.

"My goodness, Mother, that's all right. I don't have so far to walk for it then."

Jessie also resented the fact that Catherine and Edward ate breakfast—and sometimes even supper—in the kitchen.

"I can't see how you can bring yourself to do this, Catherine," Jessie protested. "You never ate a meal in the kitchen in all your life."

Secretly Catherine thought that perhaps she appreciated the experience more for this very reason. She found it delightful to eat breakfast in the kitchen, especially since Edward enjoyed it.

"That's the way to eat these cool mornings," he said. "Not

51

three feet from the stove and the hot coffee. Want to pour me another cup?"

She jumped up quickly, anxious to serve him, moving so swiftly that he put out a hand in protest.

"Here—not so fast. You'll spill it all over me."

"There's just no pleasing you," she said. "I've a good mind to slosh a little of it right down your neck, just to teach you a lesson."

"You do, and I'll beat you," he told her calmly.

She began to pour the coffee into his cup, and as she did he tilted his face, pursing his lips a little. She bent to kiss him lightly. The next thing they knew, cup and saucer were filled with coffee, and a stream of it trickled out on the cloth.

"It's all your fault," she told him. "You mop it up."

Which he did.

She couldn't tell her mother this, however; she couldn't explain why she hoped they'd always eat breakfast in the kitchen—all their lives together.

"It's—well, sort of cozy," she said simply.

"Cozy!" Jessie sniffed. "It's about as cozy as a barn. I tell you what I'm going to do. I'll send over some things from home that will help out a little—pictures, dishes, rugs and so on."

Catherine was not unwilling to let her do this, thinking that even a dream cottage could stand a few extra comforts. When she mentioned the matter to Edward, however, he told her she'd better leave things as they were—after all, Uncle Frank might not like any additions. Besides, they were here only temporarily. Accordingly, Catherine passed the word on to her mother, softening the refusal with Edward's remark about their temporary status.

So practically all the young couple brought to their new home was their own personal belongings. For Edward this included some books, old and much-used.

"My father's law books," he told Catherine.

"Oh, you've kept them!"

"Yes and I like to read them when I have a little time," he told her diffidently.

"How wonderful," she cried. She was thinking how much this would impress her mother.

"Now, Catherine," he said, apparently sensing her thoughts, "don't you go telling anybody. If people around here knew I was reading law, they'd think I was neglecting the store. Besides, there's no need to talk about it. Just because I read, it doesn't mean I'll ever get to be a lawyer."

She was glad Edward had enjoined her to secrecy, once she found out the complete picture.

"Bing Sutton is helping me," he told her.

"Bing Sutton—" the words burst from her in both distaste and unbelief. Bing Sutton was the town drunkard, the town idler. In summer he spent his days sitting on a bench in front of Mr. Delaney's store, moving inside to a spot near the big stove at autumn's first chill. True, he had a sharp wit; there was even a rumor, never verified, that back in his home town in Ohio he had once been a person of some consequence. Now he was the town bum.

"Listen here, Catherine," Edward said quickly, "he's a smart man, and he knows law. I'm lucky to have him take an interest in me."

"But Edward—people will talk . . ."

"People don't need to know. Even so, what if they do talk. He was a lawyer once; fact is, he was a district attorney. He is helping me no end."

She ceased to protest, and Edward continued to read the law books and to be guided in his reading by Bing Sutton. But she could not overcome her distaste for the association, nor could she even pretend to hide her fear that her mother would find out. Every time she saw Bing Sutton—sitting on his bench and making no attempt at earning an honest living—she drew back a little.

Outside this, she and Edward had no reason for disagreement at all. They settled down in the little house, finding the experience completely delightful. Catherine discovered she had an unexpected gift for cooking—surprising in view of the fact she had done so little of it. Della was not much for letting anyone, even Jessie, assist in the preparation of meals.

Della insisted on coming once a week to give the house a thorough cleaning. She also gathered up the soiled clothes and took them home with her. In two or three days she would be back, carrying a basket filled with clean laundry. Then she and Catherine would sit down in the kitchen for a good chat, an experience almost as pleasant for Catherine as it was for the colored woman. It was all comfortably like the days when Catherine had still been at home and had dropped in on Della for a little visit in the kitchen.

Certainly, there were inevitable adjustments, but these in themselves were only a part of the delight. Living with women, Catherine had grown up with some unavoidable primness about her. Edward found it highly amusing that she should fold her clothes neatly and put them over a chair at night with her shoes underneath it, toes pointing straight out.

"They look like an old maid at a missionary meeting," he told her. "So stiff and straight."

She giggled and asked him how many old maids he had ever seen at missionary meetings. But she did not change her way of leaving the shoes.

He also thought it was another mark of overniceness that she refused to wear underwear or stockings a second time without first washing them.

"You'll wear them out, washing them so much," he protested.

"All right," she said, "tomorrow I'll start going around looking like a dirty pig."

But she continued to put on fresh underwear and hose each day.

Even his way of talking was new and strange. Sometimes he would cut through some of her feminine subterfuges with a curt, "Now, why don't you say what you mean, Catherine, and stop beating around the bush?" He approached life with a man's head-on, direct simplicity—a characteristic which Catherine found disconcerting at first, but quickly began to appreciate.

At first, too, Catherine was taken aback by Edward's frankly admitting that they had almost no money. Brought up on her mother's delicate refusal to discuss such matters at all, Catherine felt a faint distaste for her husband's ready admission that they couldn't afford something.

"I'm trying to save money enough to go West," he usually said, explaining the necessity for some economy.

"I'm sorry I married you and kept you from going," Catherine told him once very early in their marriage when he mentioned the matter. She drew down the corners of her mouth, trying to look contrite.

"The devil you are," he said, grinning slowly. "If you'll just name one time you've been sorry . . ."

"All right," she said, "I'm glad." And then she looked at him again, not with simulated contriteness, but with something of doubt. "Aren't you?"

"You guess."

"I won't—I won't—you tell me!" She was more than half indignant.

"Come here and I'll tell you."

"I won't—you come here."

Their glances locked. She stood firm, her face flushed, her eyes wide and mutinous. Neither spoke. Finally Edward held out his arms to her; she hesitated a moment, and then she ran to him. He put his arms around her, and she buried her face in his shoulder.

"When it's time to go West, we'll go together," he told her, holding her very tight. "Together, like we're going to do everything else."

"Together—" she repeated the word slowly. "Oh, Edward, isn't that the loveliest word in the world!"

Really they had no problem at all. Edward was doing well in managing the store—people liked and trusted him. The only thing which gave Catherine cause for concern was the relations between Edward and her mother.

They still did not like each other; sometimes Catherine thought they did not even try. Edward was always polite enough to her but it was a politeness born of duty instead of any real wish to exhibit liking, a fact he was not always successful in hiding. He called her "Mrs. Montgomery," although he always said "Aunt Mae," a distinction which Jessie never mentioned but could not fail to notice. She, too, was polite to a point of overdoing it. For instance, she was careful to send Hiram each Saturday to extend an invitation to Sunday dinner with her.

"I don't see why we have to go," Edward invariably grumbled. "It's the only day I have at home."

"But we can't disappoint her," Catherine said. "It's such a little thing to do. Besides, Della is a much better cook than I am."

"You suit me," he told her.

"Oh, you—" she said fondly, feeling mature and very much married.

Trouble started the first Sunday. Edward liked to smoke

as soon as the meal was finished. Already after only a week of marriage, Catherine had discovered that this smoke was almost a ritual for him. He did not want her to start gathering up the dishes or, as a matter of fact, to move about at all until he was finished. For her part, she was more than willing to sit quietly talking with him until he was finished.

It was not until the first Sunday dinner at Jessie's was almost ended that Catherine remembered she had not told him how her mother felt about smoking.

"Mind if I smoke?" he asked with perfunctory politeness. He took out his tobacco and his cigarette papers, serene in the assumption that he would receive the customary permission, given as automatically as he had asked. Instead, Jessie set her mouth in lines of disapproval and did not reply.

"It gives her a headache," Aunt Mae explained hastily, when the silence had become a little embarrassing.

Edward stood up. "Will you excuse me?" he asked, and walked out of the house. The women got up, too, and went into the sitting room. From the window they could see Edward in the back yard, chatting with Hiram who was also smoking.

Jessie said nothing, but her look implied she could not have been more horrified had he chosen to go into town for a game of "craps" with the Negroes, a sport indulged in by the less stable of the town's young men.

Presently Edward came back into the house, looking very cheerful and, Catherine thought, smelling delightfully of tobacco. He was met by Jessie's cool silence, so naturally he froze over, too. All in all, that first dinner did not turn out too well.

The ones that followed were no better.

"What the devil does she want me to do all afternoon?" Edward fumed, once they were home. "Sit around and embroider?"

"Not on Sunday, darling," Catherine giggled. Then real-

izing that he was in no mood for levity, she went on soberly,
"You don't suppose you could wait until we got home to
smoke?" The moment she suggested this, she knew it was no
solution.

"I will not," Edward said emphatically.

"Well, go right ahead," she went on hastily. "That's the
way Uncle Willie does. Only, try not to act so grim about it."

Of course it was too much to expect Edward to handle
the situation with Uncle Willie's light touch.

"Stop raising such a fuss, Jessie," the man would tell her
lightly. "I'd think you'd be glad to have me smoke—makes you
know you have a man around this woman-ridden house."

Edward could never be that casually offhand with his
mother-in-law. The best he could do would be to continue as-
serting himself with what Catherine thought privately sometimes bordered on defiance.

Jessie's first visit to the young couple came off little better.
She arrived unexpectedly, opening the kitchen door without
knocking, which was quite as things should be. Edward, preparing to shave, was standing before the mirror, wearing neither
shirt nor undershirt. Jessie started and then drew back with the
red-faced confusion of a prim spinster rather than the normal,
casual acceptance a matron should have displayed.

"Oh, excuse me," she said, starting to back out the door.

After that she always came to the front door, knocked discreetly and waited for someone to answer the knock. And when
she entered she never failed to look around her quickly so that,
in case her son-in-law was indulging in any masculine coarseness,
she could immediately avert her gaze.

Catherine dreaded these encounters between her mother
and her husband and wished that she could find some way to
prevent them, or at least to keep them to a minimum. When
they were together, she must remain constantly on the alert,

ready to smooth over any argument that might develop between them. Not that Edward argued—he was very careful.
But she could see the strain that he was under, trying to maintain that self-restraint. For her part, she not infrequently came
home with a headache; always, she was tense and nervous, a
feeling that did not leave her immediately.

They went as usual one Sunday in November to Jessie's
for dinner. This one seemed to be going better—Della's excellent meal had put everyone in good humor. Now they were
lingering over dessert, one of her incomparable Jeff Davis pies.

"A couple of fellows were in the store yesterday," Edward
said, trying consciously to make polite conversation. "They
were telling me about some good land that could be bought
cheap."

"Where?" Jessie asked, courteous on her part.

"Kansas," he told her.

"Kansas—" the very word was anathema to Jessie.

"That's right—out in western Kansas. Lots of people are
going to be heading out there before long. That part of the
country is due for a boom."

"The country's always been full of people headed West,"
Jessie told him tartly. "Covered wagons filled with trash who
couldn't make a go of things at home. I can't see how they
would make any place boom, once they got there."

"You came West when you came to Missouri," Edward
reminded her.

"That was different," she said, her voice rising sharply.
Missouri was not West; there was something distasteful to her
in the very suggestion that it might be. Missouri was old and
settled and proper, a piece of the South, transplanted. West
was young and new and crude. Besides, she had never set foot
in a covered wagon. She came by train, bringing slaves and
cherished heirlooms and traditions with her.

"I don't see how it was different," he continued stubbornly.

Just at that moment Della came in with fresh coffee.

"Della," Catherine said, speaking hastily—too hastily, "I wish you'd show me how to make Jeff Davis pie. Edward won't eat mine at all."

She caught Edward's hasty look in her direction, hoped he wouldn't announce that Jeff Davis pie was one dish she had yet to set before him.

"No trick at all, honey," Della assured her. "Jest you come over here in the morning and I'll teach you right quick. Want another piece, Mr. Edward?"

"I sure would, Della. Catherine's right—it's a lot better than hers."

He winked at his wife, the merest flutter of an eyelash. Catherine relaxed—he wouldn't bring up *that* subject again today.

But Jessie reverted to it the next morning when Catherine went over for her instructions in pie making.

"I hope Edward isn't thinking about dragging you out West," she said. "If he says anything more about it, you put your foot down."

"You jest handles the crust light," Della interrupted with polite firmness. "Light, like you handles men. So as it don't catch on it's being handled."

Catherine took the pie home.

"It's better than Della's," Edward told her. "And lots better than the other ones you made for me."

He grinned at her engagingly. "Did she talk any more about how silly it is to go to Kansas?" he asked.

Catherine hesitated. How could she tell him what Kansas meant to Jessie—that it was an affront to every memory she had. Because of it, they had all lost some portion of their happiness—Jessie herself, Uncle Willie, Aunt Mae. To her mother, years could make no difference, no good could ever come out of the place.

"Edward," Catherine said soberly, "it might be just as well if you didn't talk to her about it—I mean, well, it just makes things unpleasant . . ." Her voice trailed off. Looking at him, she knew she had put the matter very poorly. She hadn't meant for him to give up the idea—she just wished he wouldn't talk about it before her mother.

"All right, Catherine," he said quietly, and there was a formality in his voice which hurt more than if he had spoken in anger. "I won't say anything about it to her. But that doesn't mean I've given up the idea."

"Oh, darling—you mustn't give it up!" she cried. "I don't want you to."

Nor did she. Once he had told her that she would not fit back in Virginia. Now she could see that perhaps he did not belong here in Missouri. She did not quite understand this dream of his about going West—sometimes she thought it wasn't very clear even to him. But still it was there—only half articulate, but real and strong anyway. A belief that somewhere beyond where the sun dipped into evening lay promise and hope and adventure.

"Don't think of giving it up," she said urgently.

"I don't mean to," he told her, and this time he spoke warmly. "Just as soon as ever we can get a little money together we'll go."

It looked as if his chance might come sooner than he expected.

Mr. Delaney came home from Illinois. Yes, he had had a good time—seeing relatives and old friends.

"Funny thing," he chuckled, "they all thought, just because I am an old bachelor, that I must have scads of money hidden away. I left before they found out—thought they might stop cooking up those good company meals for me."

Edward and Catherine immediately offered to find another place to live but he vetoed this idea.

"You stay right here," he said. "I like having you. Don't even mind those danged curtains like I thought I would."

So the young couple stayed on, all the more willingly because the other alternative would be moving in with Jessie, something Catherine knew would not work at all. Either that or hurting her feelings beyond any healing if they set out to find another place.

Mr. Delaney was thoughtful and considerate—he made it very easy for the young couple to be in his house. But even so Catherine found the arrangement somewhat short of perfect: it did interfere with the delightful alone-ness she and Edward had experienced before his return.

One evening Edward came home to report that he had a real chance at some land in Kansas.

"It's a good thing," he said, discussing the idea with his uncle at the supper table.

"That so?"

"Yes—it's rich land. I could prove up a section or so, easy as not. The railroad is not too far off and there's water on the place."

"How do you know?"

"I talked with John Sharp—he's just been out there to look for himself. He's going back, and wants me to go along."

"Sharp's a reliable man. If he says a thing it's so."

"That's what I think."

"What's holding you, then?"

"Well, sir, there's the matter of money. We'd have to have some to get started—can't go off with empty pockets."

"Oh, that— Look here, Ed, I don't have anybody but you that I want to help out very much. If you want to go to Kansas, strike out. I'll stake you."

Catherine sat there listening to them, thinking it was her future they were deciding without so much as feeling it necessary to include her in the conversation. Of course, she had told Edward she wanted him to go, if that was what he wanted. But he might at least ask her again, if for nothing else but manners' sake. He must have sensed her thoughts.

"What do you think of homesteading in Kansas?" he asked, turning to her.

"It looks as if that's what I'm about to do," she said. For a moment she shrank from the sound of her own voice. It sounded almost exactly like her mother's. She caught his quick puzzled look.

"I think it will be fine, Edward," she added quickly. "If you want to go, that is. . . ."

They began to make their plans. Jessie at first refused to believe they really meant to go. When it began to dawn upon her that they were serious, she took to her bed with a sick headache which lasted for almost a week. Catherine, torn between the needs of the trip they were to make and the necessity of trying to help Della and Aunt Mae look after her mother, began to feel anything but well herself. She mentioned this to Della, who regarded her shrewdly.

"You're going to feel a lot worse before you feel better," she said. "Unless I mistake me, you are."

"You mean—?"

"Yes'm, that's what I mean. But you go see a doctor."

Even before she went, she knew Della was right. She was pregnant.

She told Edward and he put his hand on her shoulder, gripping it so hard that she felt something almost like pain. Then he put his arms around her.

"Of course we can't go now," he said. "We'll have to wait."

"I don't see why," she told him. "I'll bet women have babies out there the same as they do here."

"Oh, you . . ." he said. But Catherine knew she'd never forget the way he looked at her—like a man who had been given back a dream he had thought was lost.

If they believed the matter could be settled that simply, they had reckoned without Jessie. When she found that they were actually planning to go, even with Catherine expecting a baby, she was horrified. She arose from her bed, looking very white and peaked but fired with determination nonetheless.

"It's unthinkable," she told them, drawing her mouth down into a thin determined line. "There probably aren't any doctors there. Besides, the trip is enough to make you lose the baby before it's even time for it to be born. You've no right to insist on her going, Edward. It's very selfish of you."

"I'm not insisting that she go, Mrs. Montgomery," Edward said, his anger visibly rising. "She thinks the trip won't hurt her any. We'll go by train, except for a very short distance from the station out to the claim."

Jessie looked at him in shocked unbelief. She was not accustomed to having her statements questioned, certainly not by someone who knew as little about the subject under discussion as Edward knew of this one.

Catherine, watching, saw the rift widen between her mother and her husband, wanted to do something to prevent

it and yet felt powerless. Worse than that—she felt that her
mother, in ways too obvious to be overlooked, and Edward,
without being aware of doing so, were both waiting for her to
take a stand. Had she been alone with either one of them, that
might have been possible. But now she could only say weakly,
"Oh, it shouldn't hurt me any, Mother."

"Catherine," Jessie went on. "I can tell you it isn't wise
for you to attempt this trip. Three years before I had you, I
lost a baby. It was two months on the way when I insisted on
going back to Virginia for a visit."

"I didn't know, Mother," Catherine said softly. Edward
stirred uneasily.

"It was no use to tell you. It would have caused only sadness, and there's enough of that in the world anyway." She
turned to Edward. "Now," she continued, "you see it is not
just a foolish notion which makes me try to prevent you from
going. Surely you would not risk Catherine's life, just by being
selfish enough to insist on the trip at this time."

Edward flushed a bright, angry crimson. Then he grew pale.

"I have no intentions of taking Catherine if there are—
are possibilities such as you imply," he said stiffly, and with
even more than the usual formality with which he addressed
Jessie. "Surely you know that."

"You're thinking I'm exaggerating the whole thing," Jessie
said. "Ask Mae. Mae, didn't I lose my baby and nearly die
myself while I was in Virginia?"

Aunt Mae, brought so suddenly into the center of attention, blinked as if a bright light had been focused on her. She
squirmed a little, unwilling to give testimony which would
hurt Catherine's case, and certainly not wanting to fall short
of telling the truth.

"Didn't I, Mae?" Jessie prodded her sharply.

"Yes, Jessie," Aunt Mae admitted softly, "you were real sick in Virginia."

Finally they gave up going West. There seemed to be nothing else to do. Catherine urged Edward to go on without her, stake out his claim. Then, as soon as it was safe for her to travel, she and the baby would come to him. This he would not do.

"Do you think I'd go off and leave you at a time like this?" he said. "I told you we'd wait and go together, and that's what we'll do."

"But the claim may be gone by then."

"There'll be other claims."

She knew she should have been relieved to see him taking the matter so sensibly, but strangely enough his attitude gave her a sense of guilt she could not quite shake off. His wish to go had not lessened; he had simply postponed it because of her condition. She was doing what she had thought she would never do—making him lose his chance to go West.

But this alone was not the heart of her guilt. That lay in the fact that she knew she had not really wanted to go. It was not only that the trip might be the risk Jessie had pointed out. For her own sake Catherine wanted to be near her mother during her pregnancy and confinement. This was an unknown world into which she was advancing—one filled with little real knowledge but rather with dark hints, half-truths and old wives' tales of symptoms and dangers and agonies which she, in her inexperience, could not even fathom. Of these things her mother and Della—and perhaps even Aunt Mae to a lesser degree—would have full and complete understanding. Catherine was unwilling to leave this help and comfort to go into new and unknown land, away from doctors or even friends, with only Edward, whose knowledge would be even less than her own.

It was an undertaking from which she shrank, even as she was ashamed of her feelings and hoped devoutly that Edward did not suspect them.

She tried to salve her conscience by telling herself, and Edward, that as soon as the baby was big enough to travel they would go. . . .

As a matter of fact, Catherine got along fine. She had never felt better or happier or more sure of herself.

"You're jest meant to have babies, that's why," Della said. "You can always tell the women that are—they gits prettier every day while they carries their babies."

"I feel so well, that's why."

"I thought women spent most of their time lying on a sofa before their babies were born," Edward told her. "You seem to have as much energy as you ever did."

"I guess I do," she said. And then, "It's too bad we didn't go to Kansas, the way I feel."

She watched him carefully as she made the statement, half expecting him to burst into quick reassurance that they had done exactly right, that they would have been foolish to have taken the slightest risk. But all he said was,

"Oh, well—we didn't know it would be like this."

Did she only imagine there was regret in his voice? Was he thinking, as she had already done, that perhaps she should have gone to a doctor and checked about the possible dangers involved instead of taking her mother's word as absolute authority. Or did he suspect the truth—that she had not wanted to go, had been relieved to find he was willing to postpone the trip.

For the first time something had come between them which

they were either unable, or unwilling, to talk over freely. This
knowledge served to heighten her sense of guilt.

Whatever she might have known of fear or doubt left her
on that September morning when little Edward Montgomery
Delaney made his wailing, protesting way into the world. Holding him in her arms, she forgot all about lost claims and other
irrelevant matters. And watching Edward's face as he looked
at his son, she could see no feeling other than complete happiness and content.

The baby was a week old. Catherine was sitting in a chair
in the little sitting room, waiting for Edward to come home.
He came at last, moved across the room rapidly and kissed her.
She reached up, put her arms around his neck.

"Hello, darling," she said.

"Got a little something for you," he told her, dropping a
small box into her lap.

"Why Edward, how sweet," she said, turning the box over
in her hands. "My goodness—you sent to Kansas City for it!"

"Sure, that's why it's late. Aren't you going to open it?"

She undid the wrappings, drew out the gift. It was an oval
locket hanging from a flat chain. On the front was delicate and
intricate carving, so fine it looked like etching.

"Why it's beautiful," she cried, holding it up against her.

"Turn it over," he told her, with a boyish mixture of shyness and pride.

She looked at the other side, saw there his and her initials
entwined and below them the date of their marriage. And underneath that, another date. That of the baby's birth.

"There's a place inside for pictures," he said. And then,
grinning at her, "You'll notice there's plenty of space beneath
Ned's birthdate . . ."

She looked at the smooth surface beneath the baby's

name; she looked at him, her eyes widening. He put his arms around her and she clung to him, her heart beating strong and quick. For the moment she was neither wife nor mother but a bride, looking down the long corridor of the years, contemplating a rich happiness toward which she had taken only her first tentative step.

# CHAPTER 4

---

THEIR PLAN TO GO TO KANSAS AS SOON AS NED WAS BIG ENOUGH TO TRAVEL DID NOT MATERIALIZE. BY THAT TIME, THE CHANCE AT the claim was gone.

"You're a mighty little bundle to trade a claim for," Catherine told her son.

The baby responded with some delightful jabbering, waving his hands aimlessly around.

"That's right—tell your mother you're worth it," Edward told the child. "Look, Catherine—he's grinning at me. Why you little son-of-a-gun."

"It's better anyway to wait until he's older," Catherine said. Again, she was relieved. Kansas sounded far away and wild. Maybe there wouldn't be doctors. If Ned got sick, she wouldn't know the first thing to do about it. Now she could call her mother or Della or Aunt Mae for the least emergency. She was finding a great comfort in her mother these days. Fortunately Ned was never sick, but it was fun to talk him over with Jessie, assuring herself that his progress in all things was absolutely right and normal.

Catherine's life fell into a delightful pattern of the commonplace now. Scarcely a day passed that she did not go to her mother's—or that either Jessie, Aunt Mae or Della did not come to her house. The women would sit together, sewing or mending or merely chattering. Mostly they talked of how Ned was growing, of his smartness, of his beauty. Endlessly they could enlarge on this subject. For the time being at least, Jessie's disapproval of her daughter's marriage gave way to her delight in her grandson.

There were other, more subtle components of Catherine's happiness. For one thing, Jessie had gone directly to Mr. Delaney, asking if he minded if she sent over some of Catherine's things for the house "to make it cozier for Catherine and the baby." By this time he was so delighted with Catherine and Ned that he would have consented to almost anything proposed in the name of their comfort. And so a quantity of rugs and pictures, of dishes and bric-a-brac, of rocking chairs and linens, found their way to the Delaney house. Actually the additions were all to the good, a fact which Mr. Frank Delaney was first to admit.

The house took on a warm and friendly charm. Catherine wondered why she had ever felt any reluctance about living there. She began to look around it appraisingly, with an eye to possible additions. The lines of the house were really good. There was no reason a room could not be added at the back, a big porch on the front. She could see other minor alterations that might be helpful. Her mother's earlier suggestion about a pantry now seemed a most excellent one.

She bided her time however, mentioning her thoughts to no one.

Gradually the conviction began to grow in her that Grafton was the best place for them. For one thing, Mr. Delaney had turned most of the running of the store over to Edward. The job was certainly not an easy one, for the old gentleman's way of doing business was extremely casual.

"My Lord, Catherine," Edward said, "I think half the people in the county owe bills."

"Can't you collect from them?"

"I've tried. Some of them pay. But you can't make a widow with a bunch of kids settle a bill her husband ran five years ago."

"No—I guess not."

"Uncle Frank had no business letting it run in the first place. Now, there's nothing to do but forget about it."

"Why don't you talk things over with him; he knows these people better than you do. Maybe some of them are just pretending they aren't able to pay."

"I don't like to bother him. Seems to me he hasn't been feeling too well these last months."

Edward was right. There was no difficulty one could really lay a finger on—a growing weakness, a lack of interest in business, a wish to sit at home in a chair playing with Ned.

He frankly adored the child, a love which was freely returned. Ned would hang around the man by the hours, chattering like a magpie.

"He's a smart one," Mr. Delaney said, regarding him fondly.

He looked at Catherine thoughtfully. "Always did like young 'uns," he said. "Wanted to do things to help 'em. You are just real nice, Catherine, to stay here and let me enjoy this little fellow."

"Why Uncle Frank," she said, the name slipping off her tongue easily, considering this was the first time she had called him anything but "Mr. Delaney," "It is *you* who have been kind. You've given us a home, and I appreciate it—we all do."

"Humph," he said, "I'm the one that's got all the benefits. Come here, Ned, and I'll tell you about a little pony I used to have."

And again the dream flitted through Catherine's mind—that she and Edward would buy this house from his uncle and change it to suit their needs. Edward was making a place for himself in the town—people liked and respected him. Catherine noticed evidences of this with great content, but not without a sense of guilt. She knew that her gladness went beyond the natural pleasure of a wife whose husband is making good and realized that it was based instead on the hope that once he made a place for himself here he would not want to leave. She even found herself regretting that he was too busy to read law with Bing Sutton any more. This might be just one more tie to bind him more closely to the safeness and security of this little Missouri town.

Each time she saw evidences of restlessness on his part, each time he seemed lost in thought, she knew a quick stab of fear. Could he be planning once more to go West?

When she discovered just after Ned's third birthday that she was pregnant again, her first thought was, Now—there'll be no talk of leaving for a while. She put the idea hastily from her, telling herself that if Edward wanted to go, she wouldn't hesitate. But there was no use of getting the thought into his mind. Maybe he had forgotten all about it—maybe her mother was right in saying that people who were making good entertained no notions of moving somewhere else. But still, if he wanted to go later on—after the baby was old enough to travel —she wouldn't protest.

It never occurred to her that, in carrying this baby, she would not repeat the experience she had had with Ned. In this assumption she was wrong. Almost from the first she felt wretchedly ill, scarcely able to drag around. Much of the time she was forced to stay in bed, an arrangement necessitating that her mother or Della or Aunt Mae come to look after her and take care of Ned.

"You must be very careful," the doctor warned her. "Otherwise you will lose this baby before it comes to full term."

She took the greatest care but that was not enough. The baby was no more than two months on the way when she lost it.

After it was over, she lay in bed, spent and weak, while they tried to comfort her.

"It was just one of those things, Mrs. Delaney," the doctor said. "You did all you could, and so did I. It was nobody's fault."

"You're all right, honey," Edward told her. "That's all that matters . . ."

That was not all that mattered. There was the empty space on the locket where the happy date was to be engraved. There was the emptiness in her heart. Ned would not have the little sister or brother. For a moment she considered putting the date on the locket anyway, then knew she could not do this for a life that had had no real entity except for her. She leaned against Edward and began to cry.

"Anything hurt you, honey?" he asked anxiously.

"No," she said thickly. "It's just that—we can't put the date on the locket now."

"There'll be other dates to put there," he told her, holding her tight. "Don't cry, honey . . ."

Catherine's strength came back slowly. Even after she was up and around the house the doctor insisted that she lie down for a long rest every afternoon. Mr. Delaney volunteered to take Ned over at these times.

"No need for your mother to have to give up all her time," he said.

He displayed a great adeptness in caring for the child. Catherine, watching him, felt embarrassed to remember that she had once felt reluctant to move into his house, had later been a little sorry that he chose to live with them.

As a matter of fact, her enforced rest periods gave her much time to think. She had stayed here, where things were supposed to be safe and easy, and still she had lost her baby. Had she gone to Kansas, she could have blamed the trip. Now she had nothing to blame. She supposed one could never be safeguarded against trouble. It was too much to ask of life that it give you immunity from sorrow and heartache. It was foolish to think one could avoid these things in any way—either by staying in one place or by changing locations.

Edward was kindness itself. But even so she realized that their relationship had lost something. Of course the bright expectancy, the delicious adventure of exploring each other's personalities that had been present at the outset of their marriage was gone. These she did not really miss, finding they had been more than compensated for by the mature happiness which had replaced them. But even that seemed threatened now in some vague way she could not quite analyze. She tried to tell herself that as soon as she felt stronger she and Edward would renew their old closeness. A sick wife was almost no wife at all.

Finally she made herself face the fact that this might not be the real difficulty. Maybe Edward was wanting to go West again, was unwilling to mention it to her because of her ill health. She wondered if she ought to bring the matter up. This idea she immediately rejected. "But," she promised herself, "the next time he mentions wanting to go, I'll not discourage him."

Having made this resolution, she immediately felt better. She got up, combed her hair and put on her prettiest housedress. Strength came to her, and purpose. She'd cook a real

meal for a change—maybe even bake a pie. A Jeff Davis pie!
Something about the idea brought back their first bright plans
to go to Kansas.

She had the last dish on the table when Edward came
home for supper.

"Somebody sure does look pretty," he said, kissing her.
He sniffed appreciatively.

"And something smells mighty good."

"I made a Jeff Davis pie," she told him.

"Good as the ones you made when we were first married?"
he asked. They laughed together, the sound linking them in
love and remembrance.

"Tell you what," Uncle Frank said. "Seems more like living with you up and running things. The others mean well, but
they don't have your touch."

Tonight she felt in love with the world. She leaned over,
dropped a kiss on the top of his head. She squeezed Ned close
to her.

"I'm ashamed of the way I've been neglecting my boys,"
she said. "Ned—you're as dirty as a pig. Uncle Frank, you don't
look well—sort of peaked. What's wrong?"

"I haven't been feeling too good today," he admitted.
"Sort of dizzy-like . . ."

She was up early the next morning. No more lying abed
for others to wait on her. She cooked breakfast, feeling strong
and full of energy. She sent Edward to call Uncle Frank, thinking how pleased he would be to see she felt like getting the
meal herself. By and by Edward came back alone, with a
strange look on his face.

"What's wrong?" she asked.

"It's Uncle Frank—I can't rouse him. I'm going to call
the doctor."

"Is he—" she could not bring herself to say the word.

"I'm afraid so . . ."

Catherine ran to the room where the old man lay in his bed, his face still and composed. The doctor did not need to tell them what they already knew.

Uncle Frank was dead.

Catherine felt a very real grief at the old man's passing. In looking back, she liked to remember that last evening—how pleased he had been to have her like herself once more. She even recalled with pleasure the quick impulsive kiss she had planted on his head. It was the first time she had done this, and he had looked at her with grateful pleasure. She remembered how he had enjoyed Ned, and it comforted her to believe that they had really, as he had told her once, made him happy.

If they were to judge by his brief will, they had indeed been successful. Its provisions were simple. After the outstanding debts were paid all his property—the store and the house—were to go to "my beloved nephew, Edward Delaney, and his wife, Catherine, their son Edward and any other children they may have. They are to keep these properties or sell them and have the proceeds, just as they wish." He left instructions that he was to be buried back in his old home in Illinois.

Catherine was deeply touched, as was Edward. He took the body to Illinois for burial, saw that it was put into the family plot there. Immediately upon his return he began straightening out the business.

"No use trying to sell it until I get things all ironed out," he told Catherine.

"Oh—you're going to sell it." She tried to keep the disappointment out of her voice and knew she succeeded but poorly.

"Of course—I thought you knew that."

"And the house too?" she asked.

"Why, yes." He looked at her keenly, and she noticed again, as she had used to notice in those first days she knew him, how square his jaw was, how steadfast and sure the look in his eyes. "I'm selling and then we'll head West."

"Oh, West . . ." she repeated, trying to put conviction into her voice.

"See here, Catherine, you've known all along that was what we would do, the first chance we had. Now it's here. You don't want to turn it down do you?"

"No—of course not," she assured him quickly. Too quickly, she feared. "Of course we'll go."

Certainly the time seemed ideal for the venture. Except now, instead of Kansas, talk had turned to Texas.

"It's the place," people were saying. "Land—why man, the biggest part of it is level as that floor. And so rich you can't believe it. Soil that's never had a plow in it—you buy it from the state for two dollars an acre, with thirty years to pay. All you got to do is to stay on it six months and make some improvements. Then you file your claim and start paying."

"Of course," another one said, "you got to stay right on the job that first six months. If you don't someone will come in and jump you."

"I tell you," the first man said, "the ones who turn down a chance to go to Texas are just plain fools. But anyway, it's a good plan to go out and check for yourself. The Panhandle's the best place to go. Still, there's some poor land there—breaks and so on. Best to go have a look before you decide to settle."

Edward, listening to them, knew that here at last was the place for him.

He set about the business of getting the store ready to sell. The job was not an easy one.

For one thing, there were a great many debts out against the store. Technically some of these notes might have been outlawed, but this he refused to do, a decision in which Catherine was in hearty accord. The fact that they were to benefit by any money that remained made them more careful to see that all debts were paid. It was, in a way, a tribute they could pay to Mr. Delaney's memory.

Finally a buyer was found, one who wanted both the house and the store.

"It's a good thing we have this house, Catherine," Edward told her soberly. "Actually, the money we get from it is going to be about all we'll have."

Which was right. When the last of the debts was paid, there was just a little under a thousand dollars left.

"But it's enough," Edward said. "With that, we can go out there and make our down payment. We'll have thirty years to pay the rest of it."

Thirty years! It was a life sentence he was passing.

"We ought to be settled before winter," he went on. "It's August now—we'll have to move fast. I think we'll go by train to Dodge City and take the stage from there to Mobeetie. We'll buy the supplies we need at Dodge and have them freighted down."

"Won't that be more expensive?" Catherine asked.

"A little. But every day we wait, the good claims are being snapped up." And then he grinned at her. "I guess your mother is real relieved that we're going to Texas instead of Kansas," he said.

"She doesn't like the idea of our going at all," Catherine told him soberly. "You know that as well as I do."

Which certainly he did. Jessie had missed no opportunity since the first hint of the plan had come her way to give her views on the subject.

"Oh, well," he said and shrugged his shoulders, "it just can't be helped. Better start packing things, Catherine. It's not going to be long now."

She set about packing, with Della and Aunt Mae's help. (Jessie refused to give aid to so ridiculous an enterprise.) As she worked, she tried not to feel that each article sent back to her mother's, or put away into a box to take with her, was a separate stab at her heart. She made an effort to conceal her feelings from Edward, who was excited and happy over the prospective move. Sometimes she thought she was succeeding —at other times, she was not so sure.

Everything was nearly ready for them to leave when the letter came. It was addressed to Edward and bore an Illinois postmark.

"Now who could this be from?" he mused as he opened it.

He read it, a puzzled frown between his eyes, the left eyebrow mounting as he skimmed down the closely written lines.

"Anything wrong?" Catherine asked.

"I—don't know." And then, "Yes—yes there is. Listen to this."

The letter was written by a trustee of an orphans' home back in Illinois.

"I see by the paper," it said, "that my good friend, Frank Delaney, has died and been buried in our old home town. I now take pen in hand to tell you his wish concerning a part of his estate. He wanted our orphans' home to have it. I am sending you a letter from him to me which will show you what he wanted."

The letter was enclosed.

It had been written years ago, long before Edward had come to Grafton. It said, and there was no mistaking Mr. Delaney's writing, that he would like very much to have a hand in helping out with the home for these orphans. "Best way for a lonely old bachelor to feel he has been of some use in the world." The letter went on to say that he would leave instructions to the effect that, at his death, the sum of five hundred dollars was to be paid to the home.

"Five hundred dollars—" Catherine repeated the words in shocked unbelief. "Why Edward, we wouldn't have anything left."

"We'd have something," he corrected her. "Not as much as we would send them, but something."

"Let me see that letter," Catherine demanded. "Maybe it's a fake. Some smart lawyer got hold of them and made them think they had a case."

Edward handed the letters to her but even before she took them she knew there was no mistake. The very naïve simplicity which had prompted the man to send Uncle Frank's letter on was proof enough that the trustee was open and above board. Had he merely quoted the contents, it might not have been so believable. But here was Uncle Frank's handwriting, like a voice from the grave coming back to make his wishes known.

Catherine was confident that in his last years Mr. Delaney had forgotten ever having written the letter. "Way for a lonely bachelor to feel he has been of some use in the world," the letter read. He had entertained no doubts about his usefulness when he had given Edward and her—and later, Ned—a home. He had been confident and sure of his place, happy in the knowledge that things were as they were. He had wanted Edward and his family to have the property.

"What are you going to do about it?" she asked.

"There's only one thing to do—send the check. You can't cheat orphan children."

"You can't cheat your own child either," Catherine burst out.

It was monstrous, this thing Edward planned to do. She believed in being honest and meeting one's obligations and all that, but there was a limit beyond which it was both unnecessary and unwise to go. Edward's proposed action went past that limit.

"It's not a question of cheating our child," he said coldly. "Here is the letter written in Uncle Frank's own hand and signed with his own name. We have no choice."

He looked at her keenly.

"You agree, don't you?"

"I'm not sure I do, Edward," she told him honestly. "Isn't there something about a later will making an earlier one invalid? Surely as much as you've studied law, you'd—well—be able to work that out . . ."

Her voice trailed off, seeing the look on his face.

"I could know all the law there is to know," he said, "and I'd still see this as a moral obligation, not a legal one. The sort of thing no decent man would want to evade, even if he thought he could."

It was the first time he had ever spoken to her like this— a detached coolness, tinged with disapproval. She was hurt that he should reprimand her impersonally as if she were a stranger, but most of all she was resentful because, in some obscure way, he made her feel selfish and small-souled and guilty when she had meant only to be practical and foresighted.

"Oh, I suppose you are right," she said stiffly. "Go on and send the check."

"It's what we have to do, Catherine," he said quietly. "If we kept it, every time we looked at Ned we'd think we took something from children who had no one to look after them."

Catherine was reluctant to have her mother learn about Edward's generosity, feeling that it would only give Jessie something else to criticize in her son-in-law. But find out she did and, just as Catherine had feared, Jessie did not fail to imply that the whole thing was added justification for her own earlier evaluation of Edward's impractical approach to life. However she took it far better than her daughter had anticipated.

"At least," she said, "that means you can't afford to go to Texas now."

"But we are going," Catherine assured her.

"Going—but you haven't any money left."

"Edward says there's enough, if we manage right."

Jessie took the matter directly to Edward.

"Catherine says you still plan to go to Texas, even when you've scarcely any money left."

"Yes . . ." he ignored the latter part of her speech.

"Texas is a big state. Just where do you plan to go?"

"To Mobeetie—In the Panhandle. I understand there's a lot of good land around there, open to homesteaders."

Jessie reached for the atlas lying on the table at her elbow. She thumbed through it until she found the page she was looking for.

"I guess you know that region is labeled a desert. And that Mobeetie isn't even marked there."

"That's an old atlas," he told her. "Mobeetie's there now all right. It grew up around Fort Elliot."

"Oh, a fort. Thank God for that—at least you'll have a place to go to when the Indians threaten to scalp you."

"There aren't any Indians. They've all been placed on reservations."

"Humph!" Jessie sniffed unbelievingly, and then she continued, "That claim of yours—there'll be no house on it. Where will Catherine and Ned stay while one is being built?"

"I thought they could stay in town, in Mobeetie."

He was patient with her, realizing that was the least he

could do. Looking at him, Catherine thought the strain was beginning to tell on him a little—the lines were etched deeper in his face. Sometimes when he was trying to explain something to Jessie his hands moved restlessly, betraying his own efforts at self-control.

"But," Jessie pointed out, "you won't have money enough for that now. I can't help telling you, Edward—I think you acted very unwisely in sending this money off to those orphans. I know you wanted to be fair, but does it ever occur to you that you owe your own child a duty as well?"

"Yes," Edward told her quietly, "I've thought about that a lot. But I still think I—" he stopped, corrected himself, "I still think we had to do what we did."

He looked at Catherine, seeking support for his statement. She dropped her eyes and her face colored slightly. Then she spoke, but even as she did so, she knew it was with haste and emphasis which only served to betray her own feelings in the matter. "Oh, yes, Edward—that's right."

Jessie's inquisitions continued.

"You don't know for sure you can get the land, once you're there, do you?"

"Everyone says it's there, just for the taking."

"There's good land here, just for the taking. This farm. You can run it for me, Edward. You can live here in this house."

"It's generous of you, Mrs. Montgomery. But I want to go West."

"West—" Jessie said bitterly, "West—" On her lips the word took on the taste of defeat, the last refuge of failures.

"Well," she said at last, coldly and with the implication she was wasting her words, "if you insist on going, the least you can do is to let Catherine and Ned stay here until you've actually got that claim you want and built some sort of shelter for them."

"If I did that, I'd have to come back for Catherine and Ned later, and that would take too long. We're anxious to get there and be settled before winter starts."

The last thread of Jessie's patience snapped.

"You mean *you* are anxious to get there," she said, her voice rising shrilly. "Catherine doesn't want to go at all. Surely you are not blind enough to fail to realize that!"

Edward turned to face Catherine quickly, a startled look on his face. She shrank back from his intent gaze, feeling it rake the very center of her heart. Now was the time—now she should stand up firmly and say whose side she was on. Now she should, once and for all, refute not only her mother's words but her own lingering doubt and hesitancy. Edward was watching her, expecting her to do this. Her mother was also watching, no less avidly, sure she had spoken correctly for both her daughter and herself.

There was a stillness in the room. Like doom, it hung over them all, reaching not only back into their past but far into the future as well. Catherine was aware of it; she was aware, also, of a constriction and a stillness in her own heart. She wanted to speak but she could find neither the will nor the words. She felt Edward's eyes on her, trying to force from her the admission that her mother had been wrong. Finally she cleared her throat, hurled words into the vacuum.

"Oh, Mother," she protested, "what a thing to say!"

Not denial; just protest that her mother had spoken. The blood rushed to her face. "Of course I want to go," she finished lamely. She did not dare to look at Edward.

They went home, scarcely speaking on the way. Together they put Ned to bed, exchanging the few necessary words politely, like strangers accidentally engaged in a common task. When they finished they went into the sitting room. Then the storm broke.

"You don't want to go."

"I never said that . . ."

"How else would your mother know?"

"I didn't tell her."

"But she knew. She's right—you don't want to go. You've never wanted to go."

He would not speak to her in that way unless his words had been grounded in hurt—a smarting shame that Jessie should be the first to know a thing so close to their own lives.

"You were glad when you got pregnant. You knew it would make us stay here. Both times, you were glad . . ."

And now she was shamed and hurt—making their babies seem the result of something other than their love. He could not mean what he implied. She looked at him, saw the square unyielding set of his jaw, the lines around his mouth. They were hard now; steel-taut, accentuating the hardness of his face.

"Edward—I'm going with you," she reminded him. "Why do you talk like this. Why are you so angry?"

"But you don't want to. You aren't willing to risk it for yourself and Ned. You know things will be even harder, now that we don't have very much money. That's why you didn't want to turn the money over to those orphans."

"Edward," she protested hotly, "you know better than that!" Anger had taken over; she was shaking with the force of it. "You've no right to say such things to me," she cried.

For a moment he did not answer. Finally he spoke. "I'm sorry, Catherine," he said. "It's just this devilish temper of mine."

Her anger cooled. She looked at him timidly, ready to go into his arms now that the half-apology had come. But he made no move toward her. And then she knew this quarrel was different. From the very start, it had been different . . .

By the next morning he seemed quite in command of himself once more.

"I've been thinking, Catherine," he told her. "Your mother may be right. It might be sensible for me to go out and file on the claim, build a house and then come back for you and Ned."

He made the proposition sound right and sensible. Only he did not look directly at her as he spoke.

"I believe I'll try doing it without using the money we have. Freight wagons run from Dodge City to Mobeetie. I'll get a job with them, working my way out. Might even be able to make enough for a down payment on the claim."

This, too, sounded like a good idea. But when he mentioned the money his voice was stiff and constrained.

"Oh, Edward," she cried, "what would Ned and I do while you are gone!"

Even as she spoke she knew what his answer would be. Knew, because it was in her own mind too.

"You could stay with your mother," he said, still not looking at her.

Long ago he had promised, "When we go West, we'll go together." He had said it, and they had both believed him. She was reaching for those words now, wanting to batter them against the wall that was between them. But before she could speak he went on.

"It's the only sensible thing to do," he assured her.

He's going without me, Catherine thought. I can't bear it. A part of me will die with his going. I can't let him go alone. If only he would look at me. If he would even fly into a temper. Anger she could meet better than cool, impersonal logic.

"I—" she began her protest.

"It shouldn't take too long," he interrupted briskly. "This time next year we will all be in Texas."

He has settled the matter, she thought wildly. He has settled it in his own mind without even giving me a chance.

# PART 2

# CHAPTER 5

APRIL SPILLED LAVISHLY ACROSS MISSOURI, WITHHOLDING NOTHING —NEITHER FLOWERS NOR GREEN THINGS NOR SONG OF BIRDS. Della, walking up the flower-flanked path from her cabin to the kitchen, felt this loveliness. She drew a deep breath of it into her lungs; she filled her eyes with the sight of it.

Something of her bright mood left her when she stepped up on the porch and saw the closed door to the Little Room. Mr. Willie sure had been sick this time. Maybe it was because he had stayed away so long—since before Miss Catherine and Ned had moved in. Poor Miss Jessie had had her hands full these last two days and nights since he got here. Della hoped she would sleep late this morning; she sure needed it.

She tied on her apron, set about preparations for breakfast. Soon she heard a step at the door and turned to face Catherine.

"Oh, good morning, Miss Catherine," she said, a rich and loving tenderness rippling through her voice. "How do you feel?"

"I feel fine, Della."

"You sure look it," Della said.

She regarded Catherine carefully. There was something about the girl this morning that made her look different—a

93

delicate glow of happiness, overlying each separate feature, lending it brightness. Della had not been pleased with Miss Catherine's looks of late; she had seemed older, graver, almost plain.

"Somebody's mighty happy this morning," Della said as she put a slice of ham into the skillet.

Catherine smiled, and now suddenly she was radiant.

"Yes—I heard from Mr. Edward."

"Now that's good—no wonder you look like maybe you swallowed some of this bright sunshine. He well?"

"He's fine, he's wonderful." Her voice spilled over with joy as bright as the morning's. "Things are going well. He's coming for Ned and me, Della."

"Coming for you—" Della knew the reason for the joy now. She pushed the skillet to a hot place on the stove. Then she brought her hands together quickly in a gesture of pure happiness such as a child might use.

"Oh, honey," she exulted, "that's grand. It's—" she hesitated, searching for words adequate to the occasion. "It's just real grand," she repeated. "You told Miss Jessie yet?"

Some of the brightness left Catherine's face. Once more she was hesitant.

"No," she said, "I had the letter late yesterday. I was afraid she wouldn't sleep if I told her then. I'm going to this morning."

"You done right, Miss Catherine," Della told her. "You done exactly right. She ain't been sleeping too good anyway, what with Mr. Willie sick and all—" her voice trailed off.

"Yes, I know. That's why I waited. She's just worn out."

"Yes'm, things have been pretty upset. But I think Mr. Willie's better now. I was with your mother looking after him last night, and he was just real pert when we left him."

She turned the slices of ham, her face intent and earnest. When she spoke again, it was of another thing altogether.

"I guess Ned's hard to hold, with his Pa coming back."

"I haven't told him yet," Catherine said. "I thought if I did before breakfast, he'd get so excited he wouldn't eat a bite."

It was an explanation not entirely grounded on truth, as both women knew quite well. Had Catherine told the child, he could no more refrain from letting out the news than a sieve could have been prevented from spilling water poured into it. And this, certainly, was something Catherine must pass on to her mother herself. It was a fact both women realized, even as they knew the half-truth of Catherine's answer.

"What's he doing?"

"Dressing. Insists on doing everything for himself— wouldn't even let me tie his shoestrings. He's an independent little piece."

"Takes that from his Pa," Della said.

Catherine flashed her a bright, grateful smile. Suddenly she was young and lovely again, standing on tiptoe, reaching for life. The look deepened on her face as she turned to face the child who came into the kitchen at this moment.

"See, Mama," he said. "I tied them all by myself."

Ned was not yet five, but he looked older. Partly this was because he was tall for his age; partly it was due to his eyes— deeply blue, set off by heavy brows, giving his face a look of maturity and character. He walked lightly, with scarcely any of a child's purposeless, unsteady grace.

"I knew you would, darling," she said. Across his head she and Della exchanged proud, fond glances.

"Hello, Della," he went on. "I'm hungry."

"Of course you are, lamb. And you're going to have your breakfast right away."

"I want oatmeal and an egg and some biscuits. And could I eat here in the kitchen?"

The colored woman hesitated a moment, a hesitation born not of a wish to hurt or disappoint the child, but of some deep, inner reason. Again she and Catherine exchanged glances. The young woman nodded slightly.

"You sure can, lamb," Della told him. "You and your Mama, too. I'll fix it quick as a cat can wink its eye."

"A cat winks slow," the child told her. "I've watched them."

"Oh, you—" Della laughed indulgently. She set a bowl of oatmeal on the kitchen table. "Now you start on this and stop your arguing. You get more like your Pa every day you live."

The child looked at her quickly. For a moment his eyes were anxious and uncertain; then, evidently realizing that she had said a good thing, one meant to make him happy, he grinned and sat down at the place she indicated. She picked up the pitcher to pour cream over the cereal but he took it from her with dignity and purpose, pouring the thick yellow cream slowly over the oatmeal. Della watched him proudly for a moment and then she turned to Catherine.

"You just set down there with him," she said. "I got yours ready, too."

Catherine sat down. Della placed before her a sprigged china plate containing a slice of ham, an egg and a biscuit dripping with butter. She poured a cup of coffee, set it beside the plate.

"It tastes wonderful, Della," Catherine told her. "I don't know why it's always so much better in the kitchen."

"Maybe it's because you don't never get to eat it here," Della was saying when Jessie Montgomery walked into the room.

"Good morning, Mother," Catherine said, half rising from

her place. Ned stopped eating. Della stood still, saying nothing.

"Good morning, Catherine," Jessie said. "My goodness, what are you doing eating in the kitchen!"

"It seemed sort of—cozier—" Catherine explained. The reserve was back on her face now, overlying the warmth that had flooded it when the child came into the room.

"I should think you'd keep Ned in mind—letting him eat out here like poor white trash."

Jessie's high, thinly sweet voice filled the room.

She turned to Della. "I don't suppose Mr. Willie's up yet, is he?" Her face changed subtly as she spoke, making her look older, more vulnerable.

"No'm, his door is closed, so I guess he's still sleepin'."

They were talking now, not as mistress and servant, but woman to woman, friend to friend. A question had been asked and answered after the manner of two people who for a long time have met a problem without ever admitting its real nature.

And then, Jessie was once more the mistress—cool, remote, self-sufficient.

"See that he has a good breakfast when he wakes up, Della," she said. "You can serve ours now. Miss Mae will be down in a moment. Set places for Ned and Miss Catherine in the dining room too."

"But Mother—" Catherine began.

"I'm through," Ned told her.

"You have not drunk all your milk," Jessie pointed out. "And I'm sure you'll want another biscuit and jam. Come now —let's all go into the dining room together."

Ned looked at his mother—a long grave look.

"Come on Ned," Catherine told him. "We'll finish our breakfast with Grandmother and Aunt Mae."

They followed Jessie out of the kitchen . . .

Presently they were all sitting in the dining room, with its

bay window looking out on trees and sloping hills. Aunt Mae
had joined them.

"Good morning, Jessie," she said. "Good morning, Catherine. Ah—Ned."

Light flashed across her face and the child smiled back at
her. Jessie pretended not to notice—as she always did—that although her grandson loved her, he adored his great-aunt.

Mostly it was Aunt Mae and Ned who carried the burden
of the conversation, and they talked with each other. When
the meal was finished, Catherine turned to her mother.

"Could you come into the sitting room awhile?" she asked.
"I want to talk to you, Mother. You, too, Aunt Mae," she
added quickly as the other woman hesitated.

"You want me, too, Mama?" Ned asked.

"Not especially. Wouldn't you like to help Della carry out
the dishes?"

"Oh, yes."

The child ran off to tell Della he was going to help; the
three women went to the sitting room.


They sat down. Outside the window a redbird was singing
in the branch of a maple tree. "Prett-ee, prett-ee, prett-ee," he
trilled. And then, "Come here, come here, come *here*." From
the kitchen came the rise and fall of voices—Della and Ned
talking together as if they were of an age.

"Mother," Catherine began abruptly, "I had a letter from
Edward."

Jessie looked up quickly, but it was Aunt Mae who asked,
"How are things going with him?"

"Fine. The six months are up now. That means he's ful-
filled the first requirements for the claim."

In the nine months since Edward had been gone, she had

always shared bits of his letters with her mother and Aunt Mae. The substance, if not the details.

*I have my claim . . . the land is even better than people said it would be . . . I have built the dugout . . . I have ordered a stove from Dodge City . . . I made some furniture . . . I am missing you, but I will have to wait until spring to come for you.*

She had been glad to pass on these bits, for they were both her strength and his triumph. They gave meaning and texture to her days. This letter she was glad to share, for it was better than any of the others had been.

"Anything of interest?" Aunt Mae asked now.

"Yes," Catherine said, the good news spilling through her voice so that it matched the redbird's song for joy, "he's coming back for Ned and me!"

"Coming back—" Jessie was startled out of her silence.

"Yes, he's catching a ride with the freighters to Dodge City. From there he'll take the train. He says he should be here by the first of May."

"I guess he'll want to be going back right away," Aunt Mae ventured.

"Well, almost at once," Catherine said. "He'll stay just long enough to get the supplies and the wagon ready."

"The wagon—" Jessie repeated. "You mean you are going to Texas in a *wagon!*"

Her shocked voice echoed through the room, gathering nuances, exposing the whole proposition for what it was worth. A woman of Catherine's upbringing driving through the country in a covered wagon, drawn inevitably by bony horses and followed by a mangy dog. Ned, looking out the back of the wagon, yelling retorts to the jibes that home-anchored children called after him. Catherine, wearing a sunbonnet and a no-colored calico dress, her hands and nails grimed and broken with ashes and dirt, her delicate skin chapped and reddened by wind and campfire. The sight of movers, certainly a common one in the hard years after the war, was too familiar to require any elaboration. Catherine herself stirred uneasily, betraying that she saw the whole picture as clearly as her mother meant for her to do. For a moment the young woman let herself wonder whether her going or the manner of it would be the harder for her mother to bear.

"You'll go through in a covered wagon," Jessie went on remorselessly, not content with the picture she had already put into her daughter's mind. "And when you get there, what will you have? A piece of land twenty miles from town."

"It's good land, in a good country. Edward says the Texas Panhandle will be the next great empire to open."

"And so it will, kitten," Uncle Willie said.

He came into the room, Ned at his side. Catherine made her way rapidly to him.

"Hello, Uncle Willie," she said, kissing him on the cheek. It might have been only yesterday, instead of months, since she had last seen him. Always it was like this when he came back. The length, as well as the nature, of his absence was ignored, just as was the nature of the "sickness" through which Jessie and Della must nurse him.

"Edward's taken up a claim in the Texas Panhandle," Catherine told him.

"That's what my young nephew has been telling me. Fine boy you have here, Catherine."

"He's going to make me a willow whistle," Ned said.

"That's nice," Catherine told the child absently.

"Yes," Uncle Willie went on, "that Panhandle land is rich and new. All you have to do is tickle it with a plow, drop in the seed and then just sit back and let things grow."

"I suppose you've been there and know," Jessie spoke up crisply.

"I have." he told her briefly.

"Then you think it's just fine for him to take Catherine and Ned back with him when he comes," Jessie said.

"Oh, Mama," Ned cried. "Is Papa coming home?"

"Yes, darling," Catherine said, wishing she had broken the news to him earlier instead of letting him hear it now as an outsider would do. Everyone else in the family, even Della, knew before Ned did.

"Oh, goody—goody," the child's happiness filled the room.

"They're going back in a mover wagon," Jessie put in.

"Nothing wrong with that, Jessie," Uncle Willie told her.

"He wants to take some things back—seed, a plow, supplies. Oh, he sent me a list," Catherine put in quickly. "He says it will be cheaper to do it this way. We don't have much money," she finished, speaking directly to Uncle Willie.

"You'll have less after this is over," Jessie remarked darkly, speaking with the voice of one who has a clear picture of events, past and present. "Neither one of you seems to be able to keep your hands on money, once you get hold of it."

Catherine lifted her head quickly. She put out a hand in a gesture half protest, half the motion of a child trying to ward off a blow. Every line of her sensitive face showed hurt and anger.

It was Uncle Willie who broke in quickly, seeming to know that if Catherine spoke now it would be to say words she would later regret.

"When do you expect him?"

"By the first of May." Catherine hesitated a moment, then went on. "He'd like to start back as soon as possible."

"Yes—he should. Claim jumpers hang around, waiting to take over the minute a man leaves his land."

"That's what Edward wrote. He said that it would be good if I could do as much as possible toward leaving before he even got here—buying things and so on."

"Good idea. It would be well if you had the wagon all ready to roll, as soon as he arrives."

"Oh, I wouldn't know how to do *that*," Catherine protested.

Uncle Willie regarded her thoughtfully.

"If you want me to, I'll help you," he told her. "I've helped outfit many a wagon in my time."


For Catherine, Uncle Willie's offer went beyond the convenience it offered. The act of beginning preparations made Edward's coming seem a little closer.

She had known when he went away that she would miss him. She found however that she had not been even remotely prepared for the stark and awful loneliness which beset her once she was back in her mother's house.

She did not fit; a home of her own had made it impossible for her to go back to her old room, to the house where she was no longer quite daughter, could never be mistress. She found herself wandering around the rooms, once so familiar and comforting, feeling now only a distaste for them.

Transcending this was the yearning she felt for Edward. Days had once taken their meanings from his comings and goings. She must get breakfast quickly, so he would be on time to open the store. She must have dinner at the stroke of twelve. She must make the house neat and tidy and have supper ready before he came home that evening.

And then, the delight of those evenings. Talking together, rounding out the day so that it could be put away with the other days they had known—complete, perfectly proportioned. The talk that lasted until the final, "Good night, darling."

Now there were no preparations, no need for shaping her days around him.

She took to wearing the locket by day, putting it on the table beside her bed at night. Edward's and Ned's pictures were in it. Touching it seemed to bring Edward a little closer to her. She remembered the time when he had given it to her. "There'll be other dates . . ." The promise helped to sustain her.

The last thing she did at night was to touch it, whispering across the miles that separated them, "Good night, darling."

No answer now. And instead of his arms, the stillness and the lonely dark reaching out to enfold her.

And so she was doubly grateful to Uncle Willie who was taking over the preparations for the journey, displaying energy and purpose and, apparently, an unlimited knowledge of what was required.

"Tell me first of all Catherine how much money you have to spend."

"A little under five hundred dollars," she told him.

"All right—the thing to do is to leave as much of that as we can to take to Texas with you. I'll get the gear as cheaply as possible."

He bought a new wagon. "That's economy," he explained. He found a stout gentle team. "Names are Prince and Lady," he told her. "They're good—they have to be. Your very lives will depend on them."

He took special pains with the wagon bed.

"Needs to be tight as a boat," he told Catherine. "There'll be streams and rivers to ford."

Catherine was glad her mother was out of hearing range. It was a shock to hear him comment casually concerning the absence of bridges on the way to Texas. Had she given the matter any thought she might have known the roads west would not be like those in Missouri, with stout bridges over even the smallest streams.

He had Hiram fasten a wooden box with leather hinges to the back of the wagon, and then directed the dishes and cooking utensils that were to go into it. When Jessie came out with silver and china she thought suited to the trip, he laughed good-humoredly at her.

"No, Jessie," he told her, "those won't do. Catherine won't be asking the minister to dinner on the way down. Find some old dishes—tin plates and cups would be best—and some kitchen knives and forks and an old skillet and coffee pot. If she likes, she can pack a few good dishes and some silver in a box she won't have to open till she gets to Texas."

The plow was bought, fastened under the wagon. The seed was packed inside. A water barrel was fastened to one side of the wagon.

"There'll be plenty of times you'll have to make a dry camp," he told her.

A dry camp! She was confronted with another of the strange hard facts of the new world into which she would be going. In Missouri, water was taken for granted.

"You'll have to take supplies," he told her. "When you get farther down the trail you'll be on your own. For the first two weeks, you can get things from farmers along the road. They won't charge you much—probably will insist on giving them to you."

"I've given hundreds of dozens of eggs to movers in my time," Jessie put in meaningfully. "But I never thought my own daughter would accept them from others."

"All goes to show you never can tell, Jessie," Uncle Willie said. "It's that bread-upon-the-water text you hear about at church."

The man's attitude toward the trip gave the preparations

an air of lightheartedness which helped, in some measure, to offset Jessie's gloom. Without him, Catherine might have felt the necessity to explain things to her mother, to justify, or even to argue. Now she could go calmly about her work, leaving Uncle Willie to answer for her—a chore he seemed glad to undertake, displaying such deft good humor that things were made easier for all.

Jessie got out the atlas to study the route they would take. She took a piece of tape, measured the distance, checked it against the printed scale.

"Why Catherine," she cried, "that is more than four hundred miles from here. It will take you weeks to get there."

"Six of them, Jessie," Uncle Willie broke in cheerfully. "That is, if she's lucky."

"Six weeks—" the woman echoed. It was as if the terrible nature of the long journey had come to her for the first time. "Six weeks—in a mover wagon. What if Ned got sick."

Catherine did not answer. The thought, however, was no new one to her—many, many times that same question had come to haunt her, both by day and by night. She had tried to meet the possibilities by packing a box of remedies she used for his childish ailments, but even this had not made her entirely easy in her mind. While she hesitated, Aunt Mae spoke up.

"There's no guarantee he wouldn't get sick if he stayed here, Jessie," she said calmly.

And then Catherine's answer came clear—to her mother, and to herself.

"It's the chance I have to take, Mother," she said.

Jessie was all for Catherine wearing some of her "second best dresses and a small hat" on the road. Aunt Mae said firmly that this was ridiculous.

"Dark calicoes," she ruled. "I'll make some up for you."

"And I guess you'll make a bonnet to match," Jessie said.

"Of course—and some half-handers, too." Aunt Mae looked at Catherine keenly. "I'll make the dresses real pretty," she promised. "With tucks and ruffles and so on. You'll look a sight better on the way than if you were going all dressed up."

She knows, Catherine exulted. She knows I'll want to look pretty on the road. I haven't seen Edward for almost a year—I don't want to look like a mover woman, even if we are going through in a covered wagon.

She hadn't seen him for almost a year!

Many times, in those long and lonely nights, she had dwelt upon this absence. Her, shut up at home here with her mother; Edward, out in a world of men. And of women. She faced the matter soberly. Edward was young and he was good-looking. And warmly human. Who should know better than she? As a girl, or even as bride, she would have shrunk back from this thought, feeling it both foolish and disloyal. Now the very strength and depth of their own relationship gave her understanding. Edward had been gone for a long time. It was well that he was coming back. When he did, he had a right to find his wife as pretty and as desirable as she knew how to make herself.

Aunt Mae was right about calicoes being the correct thing to wear on the trip. She was right, also, about the sunbonnets to match, and the "half-handers," those little handmade gloves, with the ends of the fingers cut out so that the wearer would have protection and yet would be able to use her hands without difficulty. If these were made from pretty prints, they need not be ugly at all.

Even so, she packed a small trunk with good clothes. A suit and a blouse for Ned. For herself, some becoming dresses, dainty underwear, pretty shoes and a small hat with a single pink rose nestled in a swirl of maline. She meant these things to be worn when she got to Texas. But she put the trunk in a spot in the wagon where she could reach it easily. Privately she was thinking that she wasn't going to be a bit above opening it during the trip and dressing up. Maybe they'd stop some Sunday to go to church. At any rate, the hat was new and very becoming, and it wouldn't hurt for Edward to see her wearing it before they got to Texas.

Della had a gift—a moneybag to wear around her waist, under her skirt.

"It's a real comfort to have it there where you can feel it," she told Catherine.

"Oh, thank you Della—it's sweet of you.".

Catherine thought that of all the preparations being made, Della's was the most useless. Edward himself would carry the money. She let herself think with delight on what it would mean to have him once more—to be able to turn over everything to him. And again she was glad she had accepted Uncle Willie's help and got the preparations started. She hoped he would feel that Uncle Willie had made wise selections. She did not see how he could fail to do so; everything the man had done seemed right.

Things took on a faster pace. Uncle Willie bought the provisions and packed them himself, insisting that Catherine watch so she would know where everything was—beans, coffee, salt and molasses. He also fastened a tin washtub and a washboard under the wagon bed. Catching Catherine's eyes on him he said, "How else did you think you were going to keep your clothes clean on the road?"

To be honest, she hadn't thought about it at all. This she did not tell him, however. She had never, in all her life, washed clothes on the board.

She was more vocal when she saw him driving pegs on the inside of the wagon.

"For Edward's gun," he told her. "You'll see—he won't make the trip without one."

"What for?" she asked.

"To shoot with, of course. There'll be times—lots of them —when he'll pick off some fresh meat. You get mighty tired of cured meat on the road. All the way down you'll be seeing game—rabbits, prairie chicken and such-like."

"But does it have to go right over the *bed?*" she pleaded. "I won't sleep a wink with that thing over our heads."

Secretly she decided that, if Edward insisted on carrying the gun as Uncle Willie seemed to be sure he would, she'd make him see that it was loaded only when he went out in search of game. Sleeping with a loaded gun over one's head— the very idea!

The three women—Catherine, her mother and Aunt Mae —were in the sitting room together. Uncle Willie had taken Ned to town.

"There's just one thing we've forgotten," the man had said gravely, "and that's a bag of striped candy. A boy can't start a trip without something to nibble on. And he must pick it out himself."

Catherine suspected the candy was only an excuse to get away. Now that the preparations were so nearly completed—at least, those which could be taken care of before Edward came —Uncle Willie was showing an increasing restlessness. This was not surprising. Rarely had he stayed here so long. Usually he was gone in less than a week, slipping off quietly, not always remembering to say good-by. Catherine would not be at all surprised to wake up some morning and find him gone. She wished he would stay until Edward came; she wanted Edward to thank him personally for what he had done. She could realize now that Uncle Willie's contribution had been enormous.

Under his direction all of them had worked at top speed for more than two weeks. Each of these days meant one subtracted from the delay she and Edward would have in beginning their return trip.

Her mother's attitude toward the whole venture could not fail to make Edward's visit anything but a pleasant one. She wished with all her heart that Uncle Willie would stay over to bridge the difficult time. Catherine knew that she herself would succeed very poorly at this.

"I'm fixing you a mending box," Aunt Mae remarked, breaking in on Catherine's thoughts. "Needles and thread and buttons and so on. And a good pair of scissors. You put it where you can get to it easy on the road—you're bound to tear things and lose buttons."

"Oh, she needn't bother about mending," Jessie told her. "Movers always let their clothes go to rags. Why shouldn't they—always on the road, never seeing the same people two days in succession."

Oh, she is wrong, Catherine thought. I'll see Edward every day—every single day—all along the trip. She let the loveliness of the prospect flood over her—the sight of the three of them moving along together, taking their world with them, and their love. They would be a unit, a single enduring unit, with no one else around to threaten their unity.

Not long now, she thought. Almost any day Edward should be arriving. It was a good thing her days were so full that she had little time to think; it was a good thing there was so much work to do that, as soon as she went to bed, she fell asleep from sheer exhaustion. Otherwise, she might have found the expectation too happy to be endured.

Each night before she went to bed she got out Edward's letter and read it once more. Partly this was to check and see if she had made headway on the list of things he had said would be needed. But mostly it was because, in reading it, she could see his face almost as clearly as if he were there with her. And now, when she touched the locket before she went to sleep, she no longer felt lost and lonely.

"There," Aunt Mae said, "I have the mending box ready. Better put it where you can get to it easily."

It was at that moment Della came into the room.

"Miss Catherine," she said. "Here's a letter for you—Hiram just come with it."

Catherine took the letter from her. A brightness flooded her face, seeing that the handwriting was Edward's. She opened the envelope eagerly, thinking how good it was of him to write her when he himself would follow so close upon the heels of the letter.

She read it through, the bright expression on her face fading. It was replaced by a puzzled unbelief, as if she did not at all trust the first reading she had given it. From somewhere out of a great distance, she heard Aunt Mae asking,

"Is something wrong, Catherine?"

"I—I don't know," she said slowly.

She looked back at the letter again.

"Well, Catherine," her mother said, "don't just sit staring at it. Who's it from?"

"It's—it's from Edward," she answered in a half-whisper. "He—he can't come for us now."

"What's wrong?" Aunt Mae asked.

"He's—"

She looked from one woman to the other with the puzzled, vulnerable look of a hurt child. How could she tell them what she herself did not want to believe. "It's something about the claim," she explained. "He says he can't get away for three months or more."

She paused, glanced back at the letter.

"He says that if he came right now we might stand to lose the claim entirely." This time she spoke with more firmness and conviction, but with no less hurt and disappointment. Again she checked the letter, skimming through it as if to find more to tell them. No—the rest of it she would keep for herself.

"I can scarcely bear to think that we must wait, Catherine; but there's no other way, believe me. I can't leave now—we have too much at stake—some business concerning the claim, and I must stay here until I clear it up. I'll be there the first of August."

The first of August. Three months! That was a lifetime. The terrible finality of it struck her with all the more force because, just outside the window where they sat, she could see the wagon, packed and ready to go. She looked at it, her face stricken. The other women followed her glance.

"Well," Jessie broke in, "now that you aren't going, we'll just have Willie unpack that horrible wagon."

Catherine stood up quickly, her eyes wide and dark in her white face. She faced her mother and began to speak, and it was as if the words were being drawn from some deep inner part of herself, from a reservoir unsuspected by anyone, even herself. Least of all, herself.

"No." she said. "No—because I'm going. I'm ready, and I'm going on."

Jessie stared at her as if she was convinced the disappointment had made Catherine take leave of her senses.

"How?" She flung the single crisp syllable at the girl, hoping the force of it would bring her back to reason.

"I don't know—Ned and I will go alone, if necessary."

Even as Catherine spoke, she knew she was saying a foolish thing. A woman and a five-year-old child did not travel alone more than four hundred miles overland.

"I'll find another family that's going," she finished uncertainly.

"I suppose you think one will come down the road the first thing in the morning on its way to Mobeetie."

Even in Catherine's upset state she recognized the rightness of her mother's statement. Families going from Grafton to Mobeetie simply did not exist.

"I'll find a young boy to go with me," Catherine said stubbornly.

"A fine scandal that would start," Jessie pointed out. "If he is old enough to be of any help, he'd be too old to travel with you."

Catherine turned wearily. She thought suddenly that it had always been like this. There was no quarreling with her mother's rightness, for it was based on logic. She turned and started out of the room.

"Don't take it so hard, Catherine," Jessie said softly. Once she had gained her point she was always quiet and composed. "He'll be here in a few months. Then you can go back with him. Perhaps by that time things will work out so you won't have to go overland."

Catherine did not trust herself to answer. She walked out of the room.

She made her way to the wagon, its canvas rippling slightly in the late afternoon breeze like a ship straining at anchor. In the lot Prince and Lady stood regarding her with a sort of inquiry on their benign faces. When are we going to be off? they seemed to ask. Even the boxes and trunks inside the wagon had their own questions to ask.

"Well, when do we start?" they seemed to say.

Catherine went around to the back of the wagon. She put her head down on the box of cooking things. She shut her eyes, trying to think.

She would ask Aunt Mae to go with her. No, that was impossible. Two women could not drive to Texas alone. It was as her mother had said—she might as well give up the idea entirely. In another three months or so, Edward would come for her.

Three months! Again the period stretched before her, long and impossible.

"Miss Catherine," a soft voice said at her elbow, "I heard —I'm sorry."

It was Della.

"Miss Mae told me. It's too bad, honey."

Even Della did not question for one moment that the trip was now impossible. Della, who perhaps above all others sensed how much it meant to her. A rebellion rose up in Catherine that Della, too, should fail her.

"Della," she began, a crazy half-formed plan beating in her brain. "Della—why don't you and Hiram go with me?"

The colored woman looked at Catherine, a long, compassionate, understanding look. Finally she spoke.

"You know we can't do that, honey," she said with gentle sadness. "We got to stay here and look after Miss Jessie."

Yes, Catherine knew that. She ran her hand across her forehead wearily.

"Of course—it's just that I can't think straight right now."

"I know, honey," Della told her. "But you keep on thinking—something will come to you."

Catherine was still thinking—a little more calmly now, and with less sense of panic, when Uncle Willie came out to her. Ned was at his side, his eyes filled with tears he had not quite decided to shed.

"Mama," he said, "Grandma says we aren't going—that Papa isn't coming."

"What's happened, Catherine?" Uncle Willie asked. "I couldn't make much sense out of what Jessie was telling me."

"It's Edward—he can't leave now. He can't come for me until August."

She began to cry. She had not cried before, but now the tears came—freely, like a child's tears at a grief too deep for bearing, beyond understanding, beyond help. Uncle Willie watched her a moment. Finally he spoke; very gravely, very slowly—not at all the way he usually talked.

"Catherine," he said, "if you want me, I'll go to Texas with you."

She looked up quickly, light dawning in her face, hope struggling with unbelief.

"You mean?" she asked, as if she did not quite dare to believe what she had heard.

"I said I'd drive you to Texas," he repeated.

They started two days later, early in the morning. Uncle Willie was driving. Ned sat beside him, very straight and proud. Catherine was inside the wagon on a low rocking chair. The latter was Uncle Willie's idea.

"It will be more comfortable," he told her. "A wagon seat gets mighty rough, especially if you aren't accustomed to one."

"I'll find a cushion for it," Jessie said. She went into the house and came back with a small cushion which she placed on the chair.

In the two days since Catherine and Uncle Willie had announced that they were going on anyway, Jessie had settled into a frozen calmness—an attitude born not so much of resignation as of a knowledge that protests were of no avail. Strangely enough Catherine, braced for stormy opposition, found this even harder to bear. Freed of the necessity for answering her mother's arguments against the trip, she had more leisure to think about the manifold hazards of the journey she was about to undertake, to examine her own wisdom in setting forth.

When the time came for the departure, they all gathered around the wagon, even Della and Hiram. The two Negroes were crying openly, the simple unrestrained grief of children. Hiram ran his hands over his hat brim—back and forth, back and forth.

"Good-by, Ned," Jessie said, kissing the child.

"Good-by, Grandma," he said, kissing her. He ran to Aunt Mae, kissed her. Then he went to Della and hugged her around the knees. She bent and kissed him on the top of his head.

"Good-by, honey-lamb," she said.

"Good-by, Della. Good-by, Hiram." Then he went to Uncle Willie. "Lift me up," he demanded, "and let's go." His mind was far too much taken with the journey's promise to waste time on farewells.

"Good-by, Catherine," Jessie said.

She kissed Catherine. The girl put her arms around her mother, could feel the woman trembling as she always did in times of great stress. But still, her eyes were dry. That, too, was like her.

"Good-by, Mother," Catherine said thickly.

Uncle Willie came to them.

"Don't worry, Jessie," he said gravely. He looked at her directly—a message, understood by both of them, seemed to pass from one to the other. "I'll look after her," he said. The words took on more the tone of a vow than that of a simple promise.

"Yes, I know," Jessie told him.

Catherine kissed her mother again. Then she kissed Aunt Mae and Della. She went back to her mother.

"I'll write to you, Mother," she said. "When I get to Texas. Don't expect letters while we are on the road."

"I won't—take care of yourself."

"I will."

"Don't let Ned forget me . . ."

"You know he wouldn't do that . . ."

Words were hard to say, there at the last. Part of her was wanting to go, traveling toward Edward; part of her was wanting to stay here, among familiar things, among the easy safe ways of home and the people she had known and loved all her life. The struggle was an ache in her heart, a constriction in her throat.

"We must be starting, Catherine," Uncle Willie told her, gathering up the lines. He slapped them over the horses' backs. Prince and Lady started off, the wagon creaking after them.

"Good-by . . ." Catherine cried looking back out of the open end of the wagon. "Good-by . . ."

Della waved her apron; Hiram, his hat.

Jessie stood, still without tears, but now the strain showed on her face. It was soft and shapeless, like a piece of crumpled tissue paper—an old woman's face.

Aunt Mae shed no tears either. She stood watching them, a strange expression on her face. Grave it was, yet confident. As if she, of all those people there—the ones who went and the ones who stayed—was able to see what lay ahead. To see it, and not be afraid.

Strangely enough, it was the memory of Aunt Mae's face that Catherine carried with her, above anything else that was said or done that day.

# CHAPTER 6

THE WAGON MOVED SLOWLY, THE CANVAS BILLOWING SOFTLY IN THE BREEZE. NOW IN MID-MAY THE FIELDS AND FENCES OF EASTERN Kansas were emerald green, shot through with the bright design of wild flowers blooming. This was a countryside neat and trim, well ordered and precise almost to the point of smugness— the smugness of a people who, having made their place in life, can feel only condescension at best, impatience at worst, with those who are still struggling or have given up.

Catherine wore a dark calico dress, a bonnet and half-handers. Her hair was neatly combed and she had rubbed the chamois skin with its coating of prepared chalk over her face after she had finished dressing. Each night before she went to bed she had been careful to rub glycerin on her face and hands.

The first day of the trip she had ridden inside the wagon, sitting on the rocking chair. All she could see was the road they had already traveled; it was as if she was forever looking back at things left behind, at experiences not to be retasted. The past, a thin and tenuous web, held to her and would not let her go. It was with her that first night when she and Ned lay on the feather bed inside the wagon while Uncle Willie snored gently in his bedroll beneath it. She looked through the opening at the rear, trying to brush away the thoughts of all that she had left, thoughts that, in the excitement of the journey today, she had scarcely had time to entertain. Now, lying here in the darkness with the canvas curving over her head, she could no longer push them back.

In all her life before she had never been more than a few blocks from her mother. Or, with the exception of the times that she and Mama went visiting to the homes of kin, from Aunt Mae and Della and the house with its great old high-ceilinged rooms. Now she was gone from them. Not for years—maybe never—would she see those loved ones; no more would she sleep in her own bed, waken in her own room. The redbird that perched on the tree outside the sitting room to sing, "Prett-ee—prett-ee!"—she would hear no more.

A great wave of homesickness washed over her; she was close to tears.

She thought of Edward and she sat up, turned herself so that she faced not in the direction of Missouri but the way in which the wagon was headed. She reached out, touched the locket which, during the day, she had worn around her neck, under her dress and which, at night, she had placed beside her bed.

"Darling," she whispered, "I'm on my way to you—"

And then she lay down once more and slept.

The next morning she said to Uncle Willie, "I think I'll ride with you and Ned today—at least, for a while."

"All right. But you better bring up a cushion. A wagon seat gets mighty hard."

She brought the cushion, but even so at the end of an hour she was beginning to ache in every muscle. She made herself stay, however, fixing her eyes with determination on the road ahead. It opened up before them as they moved along—hills gave way, converging fence lines spread apart, turns grew straight. Through the bright spring freshness they moved and a mounting sense of accomplishment, a feeling of deepest content took hold of her.

Ned chattered, chattered, chattered.

"Mama—look at the pretty flowers. Uncle Willie, I want to get off and pick some!"

Uncle Willie obligingly stopped. He did again when they came to another clump the child wanted to investigate. But at the third request he said,

"Now look here, fellow, you want to get to Texas, don't you? We'll never make it if you keep stopping to gather flowers. Tell you what—let's make a rule that we'll stop once in the morning, once in the afternoon. That all right?"

The arrangement suited the child perfectly.

Ned was delighted with camping out.

"It's like a picnic," he exulted. "We're on a long, long picnic."

"That's right, Ned. It's a sort of picnic."

The man and boy had long talks. They discussed the road over which they passed, the possible adventures which might lie ahead. But mostly, Ned wanted to talk about Texas.

"Tell me about Texas, Uncle Willie," the child would beg. "Tell me about Mobeetie."

"Well—let me think. The town clusters around Fort Elliot, like birds around a pile of grain."

The child nodded. That picture he could understand.

"It's a fine sight, all those soldiers in uniform; makes the town look fashionable and gay. Your papa picked well when he chose a place near Mobeetie."

It was good to hear Uncle Willie talk about Papa. Ned did not want Mama to know, but there were times when it was hard to remember what Papa looked like. He had been gone such a long time—almost a year. A lifetime. Mama talked about him and showed Ned a picture of him. Della said he looked like Papa. The times when his father came clearest of all to the boy was when he stood in front of the mirror, trying to trace Papa's features in his own small face. Then it was that he could remember, or fancy he remembered, exactly what Papa looked like. Tall, with dark blue eyes and brown hair, and a quick eager way of speaking.

But even better than he remembered Papa he recalled two other things—the way Mama's face shone when she talked about him and the crisp, sharp tones Grandmother used when she mentioned his name. It was good to know that Uncle Willie was on Papa's side; it was good to hear the warm approval in his voice when he discussed him.

"The town itself is not far from a creek," Uncle Willie went on. "And, as I remember, twenty-five miles or so on beyond the Canadian River. There are trees in the town, but out beyond it things are different. Much of the land is level—like a floor."

He elaborated on the theme. You could see as far as eye could reach, he said. There was nothing to stop you from looking, for here was a land without houses, without fences, without trees. "Almost without people," he finished.

"Why aren't there any people?" the child asked, undecided whether to like this new development or not.

"Haven't got there yet," Uncle Willie explained. "Give them time. They're already beginning to drift in. The land is good, and people always come to good land. It draws them like a magnet. Just a little late getting to the Panhandle, that's all."

"I wish we were getting there tomorrow," Ned cried, his enthusiasm restored. "I want to see it. I want to see Papa!"

"Well, we won't be there tomorrow, nor the next day, nor the day after that," Uncle Willie told him cheerfully. "There are miles to travel and rivers and streams to cross. The horses will take many a step before we come to it; right now, we have to think of a place to camp tonight. Looks like a good one a mile or so ahead. Farmhouse, with a little grove near by. Suit you, Catherine?"

"Oh, yes," she told him. "Whatever you say . . ."

They came presently to the grove which was, indeed, close to a farmhouse. Everything looked neat and trim and inviting. Uncle Willie stopped the wagon, wound the lines around the seat. He got down, reached out his arms to Ned.

"Come on," he said, "let's go ask the farmer if we may camp here."

He took out the wash pan and washed his hands. He combed his hair and dusted off his clothes. Ned went through his every gesture, trying to act grown-up and businesslike about it. He was quite accustomed to this routine: always Uncle Willie asked for permission to camp, and always Ned went with him, and always they went through this cleaning-up ritual first. Catherine thought he did this because he felt farmers would be more willing to have neat, carefully groomed people camping on their place. Uncle Willie said not necessarily.

"The world's on the move these days," he said. "People changing locations for one reason or another. Can't always keep spick-and-span when you're moving and farmers know that."

"Then why are you always so careful to clean up before going to ask?"

"To keep my own self-respect," he told her, grinning as he spoke.

Now he and Ned walked off in the direction of the farmhouse. Soon they were back, reporting that the farmer had told them they were more than welcome—and just to bring the team up to the barn and feed it there.

"And the woman said I was a fine little boy," Ned broke

in importantly, "and if we'd bring back a bucket and some pans, she'll give me milk and strawberries—and things . . ." he hesitated, unable to recall all the richness he had been promised.

"Now wasn't that nice of her," Catherine said. "I hope you remembered to say thank you."

"No," Ned told her practically, "I'll wait and do that when we get them."

"Oh, Ned—" Catherine laughed, highly pleased that the woman should tell him he was a nice boy. That was better than any promise of food.

"I still think we'd better offer to pay," Uncle Willie told her, smiling at Ned's naïve speech.

"Oh, of course," Catherine agreed. "How much?"

"Oh, about fifty cents, I guess . . ."

The smile was gone now and he spoke diffidently, a little patch of color burning on his cheeks. Catherine, who had just turned to go into the wagon so that she might get the money from Della's bag which she wore around her waist, hesitated. She was about to ask him if he felt they ought to pay more. And then suddenly she knew.

Before the trip started, Uncle Willie had made some suggestions about carrying the money through.

"I'd divide it, Catherine," he told her, "in three ways. The part you'll need for the expenses of the trip you should put somewhere so you can get to it easily. Then you should have a second bit—for emergencies. Hope they never come, but even so, tuck away a bit just in case. Finally, put the bulk of the money—the part you want to get to Texas with—in some safe spot where you won't have to touch it until you can hand it over to Edward."

She saw the wisdom of this and acted accordingly. Della's

moneybag was excellent for the trip money. The part for emergencies she tucked away into a small box containing her few pieces of jewelry—a necklace that had belonged to her Grandmother Keith, a ring Aunt Mae had given her when she was sixteen, a brooch or two. This box she packed into the trunk along with her clothes. The greater part of the money had been sewed up into the feather bed, the one which would form her and Ned's bed on the trip down.

They had been on the road a week and true to Uncle Willie's prediction had spent almost nothing for food or supplies. They had brought a great deal from home and the few things needed had been given them by farmers.

For the first time now the question of paying a bill had arisen and Uncle Willie must come to Catherine for the necessary money. Because of this, he was embarrassed. It was a feeling which went beyond the natural embarrassment of a man put into the position of asking a woman for money. It was as if all the pattern of his life was crystallized into this moment—the evasions, the weaknesses, the failures. And, even though they both knew this trip could never have been undertaken without him—that the hopes of the future lay in his hands—he was still ashamed to ask her for money.

In one clear revealing flash Catherine saw this. The next moment she had stepped inside the wagon. When she came outside again, she was carrying, not just the money to pay for tonight's supplies, but the entire contents of the purse.

"Here, you take this," she told him. He looked at her strangely, but made no move to take it.

"This is the money for the trip," she went on. "You're the one who will pay all the bills, so you might as well keep it."

The man's face was a study—pride was there struggling with unbelief, and a rush of gratitude. He reached out and

took the money simply and without further comment. He did
not say "Thank you." He did not need to.

"What time is it, Catherine?" Uncle Willie asked.

"Three o'clock," Catherine told him, checking her watch.
"That's about what I made it."

Usually he could tell, almost to the minute, by looking
at the sun or, at night, the stars. Here on the road it seemed
ridiculous to consult this delicate little watch when they had
only to raise their eyes to see the giant hourglass of the sky.
And yet they made the watch their final authority and at the
end of the day it ticked off Uncle Willie made a mark on the
calendar they carried. The watch and the calendar were symbols
of the ordered existence the travelers would resume at the end
of the journey.

"Never forget," they seemed to say, "this trip is not a
permanent way of life."

Just ahead of them now, perhaps a mile away, lay a little
town. Actually, it was nothing more than a village half-hidden
in trees with its church spire thrusting up into the sky.

"This is Saturday," Uncle Willie said, "so I think we'll
stop there even if it is a little early. We ought to celebrate anyway—the way I figure, we've come a third of the way. Suit you,
Catherine?"

"Oh, yes," she told him.

Two weeks on the road, and they had put a third of their
journey behind them. This was a thing to measure, like the
hours the watch ticked off.

And the difference in Uncle Willie was something to measure, too. It was not just the possession of the money which
was responsible for the change—Catherine knew that quite
well. It was, rather, that her gesture had been an expression of
confidence, something which he was seldom privileged to en-

joy. And, having experienced its joy, he was thriving on it. He dealt with the details of the trip in a way that was nothing short of inspired. So far, they had stopped at places where there were trees and water and friendly people. Their whole route was a chain of friends they had made.

"If you ever come back this way, stop with us again," was the cordial invitation that followed them as they drove off, an invitation which Catherine felt was invariably the result of Uncle Willie's genial conduct.

Moreover he was deft and quick about building campfires and staking out the team to graze and making the campsite neat and tidy. He taught Ned this lore.

"Never build a big fire, Ned," he would tell the child as the two of them bent over the small blaze the man had kindled. "And never leave it burning at night. Might start a grass fire."

Ned nodded wisely.

"And don't leave trash and scraps around your camping place. Clean up before you go."

Ned nodded again. This lesson was well learned, for each morning before they left the child ran around the place like a small hunting dog on a scent, collecting bits of litter.

As a matter of fact, Uncle Willie had taken over Ned as well as the camping routine. He had infinite patience with the child, and yet behind this patience was a good sturdy male discipline, something which Catherine now realized had been lacking in the year since Edward had been gone to Texas.

"Let me drive, Uncle Willie."

"All right—this is a good level stretch."

Then when they came to a place where the road curved, dropping down a steep hill to a narrow bridge, "Give me back the lines now, Ned."

"No, let me. I can drive fine . . ."

"Give the lines to me, Ned. This is not the place for you to drive." Uncle Willie's voice was quiet but firm.

The child handed back the lines, his little lip quivering, his eyes full of tears.

"Men don't cry over the things they have to do," Uncle Willie remarked casually, his eyes on the road.

After that there were no more tears.

Catherine listened, saying nothing. But in her heart she wondered, as she had done so many times on this trip, what she would have done without Uncle Willie.

Now when he pulled up at a small grove, with a creek running close by and the little village companionably near, she knew that his suggestion to camp here had been a wise one.

"Wouldn't wonder if there weren't fish in that stream," the man said as he stopped the team.

"Let's go fishing right away," Ned cried, beginning to clamor out of the wagon.

"After a while," Uncle Willie promised. "Camp chores first."

"I want to go fishing," Ned protested. "I don't want to do chores."

"That's all right," Uncle Willie said calmly. "I'll do them myself."

He set about the work quietly with no further comment. Ned watched him awhile, dark clouds on his little brow. Then he smiled and slipped up to his uncle.

"I want to help," he said. "May I?"

"Sure. Want to start collecting wood?"

Ned ran about perfectly happy once more, gathering wood for the fire.

Catherine watched him, thinking how much the child had changed in the two weeks of the trip. He was more like a child, and happier by far. She thought guiltily that she herself was perhaps most of all responsible for the watchful cautious ways Ned had shown in her mother's house—the way of a child with too much supervision, one who is overly dependent on what his elders think of him. Ned was only reflecting her own uncertainties. There were too many rules in his grandmother's house—too many heirlooms which might be broken if a boy ran or threw a ball in the great, high-ceilinged rooms. There were older heads prone to develop headaches when little boys raised their voices. There were even, God forgive her, certain subjects reserved for discussion when mother and son were alone. Ned was a bright lad; he learned without being told in so many words that his questions about his father were best asked when his grandmother was not around.

With Uncle Willie the child was reverting to normal child-like behavior.

"Want us to do anything for you before we go fishing, Catherine?" Uncle Willie asked now.

"You can bring me some water so I can wash my hair," she told him. "I may want to wash out a few pieces of clothes, too."

The first Saturday they had stopped she had insisted on trying to wash. Uncle Willie helped her but even so she found it a difficult and distasteful job.

"I wasn't cut out for a laundress," she said darkly.

"It's silly to leave it all for one time, anyway," he told her. "Better make up your mind to wash your things out at night, the way I do."

After that she tried his method—rinsing out clothes at night, hanging them straight over bushes to dry. In the morning she and Ned put on those garments, surprised to find they looked neither shabby nor ill-groomed.

"Oh, if mother could see me now," she said the first time she did this. After that she gave the matter scarcely any thought. It was as Uncle Willie said—ironing was not for the road.

But cleanliness was. So that afternoon she washed and aired bedding and, when this was finished, washed her hair and took a bath. From the banks of the stream she could hear the hushed voices of Uncle Willie and Ned as they dangled lines in the water. She couldn't tell which was having the better time, man or boy.

Presently they came back with two small fish flopping on a stick which Ned carried.

"I caught them both," the child exulted. "Didn't I, Uncle Willie!"

"You certainly did."

"Fry them for supper, will you Mama?"

"Indeed I will . . ."

They slept late the next morning and awoke to one of those perfect days—May at its best. This was their second Sunday on the road. Uncle Willie had ruled there would be no Sabbath travel.

"Horses need the rest," he said. "So do we."

This morning, as they had done the week before, they put on clean clothes in honor of the day. Uncle Willie played a hymn on his fiddle; then he told Ned a Bible story.

Catherine, relaxed and content, felt a half-wish to go to the little church whose spire probed the clear bright air, to sit there and listen to people singing hymns, to drop a bit of money into the plate passed by sober decorous men, to hear the words of a minister retelling the story of the faith on which she had grown up. It was strange, here at the edge of the little town where she had experienced the greatest peace she had known since leaving home, that she should also feel a moment of keen homesickness. The thought of Missouri and all its gentle, sure ways was strong upon her.

Home ways and home faces reached out across the miles

to hold her; the beginning of the journey was before her, not the end of it. This town might well be Grafton itself. She sat at the edge of it, a small dot of impermanence among a world of rooted women who lived in neat homes with fences around them and flowers growing in trim gardens. Each morning they looked out on their own land, on the same scene they had gazed at the morning before and the morning before that, and on back through the sure, unchanging years. Catherine was a "mover"—every morning her eyes opened on strangeness, on something that had been only a destination the day before. Her world moved with her—shifting, changing, unpredictable.

While she was in motion, she had neither time nor inclination for such thoughts. Now that she had stopped, doubt and uncertainty caught up with her—those, and some of the old fears that once had been her daily portion. She was glad that tomorrow they would go on again. Some way, it was easier to be sure of the future when she was moving toward it.

Uncle Willie seemed to sense something of her mood. That night he fell to talking. He replenished the campfire several times, poking at it with a stick at intervals, watching the flames shoot up with a warm and steady glow. Catherine listened to him, realizing that a great many lonely years must have been etched into his soul.

Tonight he wanted to talk about Texas.

"It's a wonderful place," he said. "An empire. New country, with all of life ahead of it. It's like a young man. Or a young marriage." He looked sideways at Catherine as he spoke.

She stirred a little. Her marriage with Edward was still young; this new venture was making it seem even younger. Almost as if they were just starting out, leaving behind them all the mistakes they had made in six years, taking only the richness of a love grown more understanding and a son to hold them together even more closely. It was good to bring these things to a new land, where hope seemed right and easy.

"Yes," Uncle Willie said, "it's good to make a new start in a new place. In a way, you are every woman journeying toward her love. Some women make the trip without ever leaving their own fireside; some must go far, as you are doing. It is never an easy journey—this groping one's way toward another. But it is always a good one, if you will make it so."

Catherine reached out and touched his hand.

"You're a poet, Uncle Willie," she said thickly.

As, indeed, he was. Always he had been that. The fact shone clear and bright, above his weaknesses, above his failures, transcending all the lost years that had repeatedly sent him, beaten and ashamed, back to his sister's house to be nursed out of his "sickness." People like him did not always have the strength to stand up to life, to demand things from it. They were easily bruised. But in their very weakness, they sometimes found great wisdom and strength with which to help others.

"As I was saying," Uncle Willie continued, "Texas is a fabulous, unbelievable land. It's the right place to take your dreams. That's because old Sam Houston helped found it, and he was the prince of all the dreamers. Couldn't make his dreams come true anywhere else, so he took them to Texas."

"I'm glad Edward went to Texas," she told Uncle Willie.

And suddenly she knew she was glad. Somewhere down those long lonely months of their separation wisdom had come to her. Now she knew the real cause of Edward's hurt. He did not mind going on without her so much as he was disappointed in her lack of enthusiasm for the venture, her unwillingness to take the risks it involved. He had wanted to feel they were together in the project, if only in spirit.

For her, life had no real meaning without Edward. But

now she knew that meaning must come not only of being in his physical presence, but of sharing his dream as well.

For the first time she understood the strange compulsion which had pushed her into taking this trip even when it might have seemed more sensible to wait. She had wanted to tell him she had been wrong—that she was weak and foolish and stupid. She wanted to tell him she was sorry.

Those emotions had been good enough as far as they went. Actually, however, they were not much more than a desire to be rid of her burden of guilt. Now Uncle Willie had helped her take the final necessary step, to go beyond mere acceptance of Edward's dream.

"I'm glad he went to Texas," she repeated firmly. "There wasn't much chance for him back in Missouri. I can see that. It hasn't been easy for our generation, after the war and all . . ."

"Every generation has its problems," Uncle Willie told her. "If it isn't postwar, it's war itself. Or hard times. Or maybe even times so easy people grow soft. That's about the worst of all."

He was silent for a moment.

"Yes," he went on slowly, "every age has its own peculiar problems. And its own rewards. Too many times we're so busy worrying about the problems that we overlook the rewards entirely. Those very problems in themselves may be rewards—nothing like a good stiff bit of trouble to challenge us."

Catherine was thinking that certainly the problems of this trip had brought out the best in Uncle Willie. She remembered the way he had hesitated before offering to come with her, knew that this was a journey he had not really wanted to take. It entailed responsibilities unfamiliar to him, perhaps even unwelcome. And there must have been another thought in his mind—a fear, an uncertainty, not only of his own actions but of her questioning of them. He must have known that, in

both her mind and in Jessie's, there was the fear, never ex-
pressed but always close to the surface, as to whether he could
see the trip through without reverting to his "sickness." She
was ashamed now that she had ever felt, even in the hidden
recesses of her heart, that Uncle Willie might slip into a saloon
some evening and come back to camp, "sick."

"Yes," Uncle Willie went on, "a challenge is good for us.
Sometimes I think that is the hold the West has on people.
All of them have an inherent spark of nobility and the West
is big enough, and difficult enough, to bring it out."

I didn't need to worry about Uncle Willie, Catherine
thought now. For the first time in her life she rejected the
evasion with which her mother had always met the man's problem. She told herself firmly, letting the word come to her mind
with straightforward honesty, that she need have no worry at
all.

Uncle Willie wasn't going to get drunk on the way to
Texas.

Once more she was glad she had turned the money over to
him. In doing this she had told him, plainly as if she had said
the words, that she had no fears concerning him.

Catherine was in bed, with Ned beside her.

"Mama," he said, moving restlessly.

"What's the matter, honey?" she asked. "Can't you go to
sleep?"

"Mama," his voice was troubled, "do you suppose Papa
will know me? Uncle Willie says I've grown so much—and I
know I have. Wouldn't it be awful if Papa didn't know me!"

"Why Ned, of course he'll know you," Catherine found
herself speaking unusually fast, as if she were trying to ward off
some danger, make up for some grave fault.

"A year is a long time," the child continued.

He was speaking from a real fear in his own small heart. Because at times he could not reconstruct the image of an absent loved one, he was afraid it was a difficulty his father shared.

"A year is not so long for grown people," she explained gravely. "Don't worry. Papa remembers exactly what you look like. He'll know you, never fear, and you'll know him. The minute you see him, you'll know him."

Satisfied, the child fell off to sleep. But to Catherine, sleep would not come.

Ned was right. A year was a long time. A month was long. Even a day, when two people who love each other must, for some reason they scarcely understand themselves, be separated.

They moved along the road, slowly but surely. This was settled country they went through; there were towns, and a railroad followed, more or less, the route of the road. Still, the country was changing subtly. There were fewer trees. It was more level. Houses were beginning to be farther apart.

Uncle Willie brought out his gun and went hunting for fresh meat rather than depend on buying things from the farmers. He was a good shot; he brought down prairie chicken, rabbits, quail and other small game. But always sparingly.

"This time of year, they probably have young at home," he explained to Ned. "We must take no more than we need, and only when we need it."

He tried to teach Catherine to use the gun, but this she steadfastly refused to do.

"I'd be scared to death of it," she told him. "And you be sure it's unloaded before you put it back. What if Ned or I knocked it off accidentally during the night!"

There was another subtle difference in the trip. Once they had stayed off to themselves, deliberately choosing spots where they would be alone. With water and trees becoming more scarce, they really had no choice about stopping with other campers. Catherine was surprised to find she liked things so, to realize each camp was a social experience.

Where once people might have stayed to themselves, now the campfire was no more than a preliminary blaze before men were coming to the wagon to talk with Uncle Willie. Scarcely had the team stopped when Ned was out of the wagon, playing with other children. Women were a little slower, but by and by they came, too, and exchanged greetings with Catherine. It seemed that people inching their way West appreciated their own kind more in proportion to their greater scarcity.

All kinds of people were on the move.

Young couples—grooms still bashful, brides still blushing and shy.

*There wasn't any future back in Indiana farming the old man's place. So we got married one morning and took off as soon as the words were said. Looking to find a place in Kansas.*

Older people—almost, but not quite, beaten by life.

*I declare, Pa did the best he could, back in Ohio. But the house burned and hard times came. We said to each other we didn't have anything to lose—we'd already lost it all. So we thought we might as well try for a fresh start out in the Territory.*

Families, with a wagon full of children.

*It ain't for ourselves we're headed for Texas. It's to give the kids a better chance.*

All of them people with a dream, a hope that could not be realized back where they came from. A few wagons were headed east, but the people in them mostly stayed to themselves. Or, if they mingled, did not talk of dreams.

Catherine found a strange and impelling bond between

herself and those westbound women. Through them, she began to feel the pulse of the road, learned its demands.

"You just put a little vinegar in the water your boy drinks," a lean woman with skin the color of a sallow biscuit advised her. "Not so as he can taste it, but just enough to take away the flatness. That way, he won't want as much. 'Taint good for kids to drink so much strange water."

"No need to cook flapjacks all the time," a fat woman said. "Gets sort of monotonous. You can bake as good bread in a dutch oven as in a regular one—if you're of a mind to fool with it."

"You soak your beans all night and then cook 'em a spell while you're cooking breakfast. Then you cook 'em again while you're getting dinner. By night, it won't take so long to cook 'em, and then you got a batch to last you several days."

They passed their wisdom on to her freely, as they gave their companionship.

Early in the journey she might have instinctively held back from these women, but now she was drawn to them. She had a feeling of kinship with them, even as she knew a faint pity for all the smug homebound women whose homes they plodded by—women condemned to live out their lives in one small spot.

Ned made friends with the children.

"Mama," he said, bringing a little boy to the wagon, "this is Johnny."

The boy was older than Ned but smaller. He had a dried-up look, like a browned and weathered nut. His eyes were sharp and clear but they were also open and forthright.

"Hello, Johnny," Catherine said.

"He says he's from Penn—Penn—Pennsylvania," Ned continued, "and that it's farther away than Missouri. Is it? And can I go play with him?"

The visitor grinned wisely, confident of the corroboration which was to be his.

"That's right, Ned," Catherine told him cheerfully. "And don't you get too far away when you're playing because I'm going to have supper ready in a minute."

The children went off and Catherine turned back to her cooking, remembering how Jessie used to react to the approach of a covered wagon.

"You come into the house this minute," she would call to the small Catherine. "And you stay here until that mover wagon is out of sight. They might be gypsies, and they kidnap children."

In time Catherine overcame the fear her mother had planted in her, but she never quite got over the distaste. Movers were shiftless and dirty—"poor white trash." People who amounted to anything stayed in one place.

And now that she was among them, those people who lived in a wagon, she saw their goodness, their kindness, and their strength. They were not failures, fleeing the scene of their misfortunes. They were people with a hope strong enough to withstand the discomforts of the road as well as the hazards that might lie at the end of the journey. Edward had been blood brother to them—these restless, earnest, seeking ones, bound toward something whose shape and nature they could not quite put into words. But the fact that they were inarticulate did not mean that they were any less sure in their hearts.

And, understanding them, she found herself understanding Edward a little better.

"Just loving a man isn't enough," she thought. "And telling him that anything he wants to do is all right—that isn't enough either. You have to understand why he wants to do a thing and believe in your heart that it is right."

One woman she was sure she could never forget. She was

pregnant, but that did not set her apart, because many of the
women were. But this one was different. She was young and
delicately made. She moved slowly, with infinite caution.

"I'm trying to be very careful," she said. "We lost our
first one."

She looked like a child, yet she had already lost a baby!
Catherine found this difficult to believe, as she found it hard
to understand why the young wife should travel at this time.

"Isn't it dangerous to be on the road now?"

"Well—" the woman hesitated, as if she were unwilling to
admit the truth, even to herself. "Maybe it isn't quite the thing
to do. But it looked like there wasn't any other way. If we
waited, it would mean another six months, and that would put
us into winter. So we just decided to take the chance. And I'm
getting along fine," she finished brightly, not wanting anyone's
sympathy.

She was silent a moment, and then she went on stanchly,
"Even if I wasn't, I'd still be glad we came on. Jim was so set
on getting a claim in the territory that I didn't have the heart
to stop him."

"If you'll excuse me," Catherine told her hastily, "I think
I'll go get supper now."

She walked away, very fast, feeling the young wife's puzzled glance following her as she left.

# CHAPTER 7

<hr>

"WE'LL BE IN CALDWELL THE MIDDLE OF THE AFTERNOON," UNCLE
WILLIE TOLD CATHERINE. "THAT'S ABOUT HALFWAY—A GOOD PLACE
to have the wagon and the team checked over."

Halfway to Texas; halfway to Edward.

"I think we'll stay in a wagon yard," he continued. "Caldwell is a rip-roaring cow town—lots of cowboys coming in with
their herds, and they like to have themselves a time once they
get rid of the cattle."

Then, seeing the involuntary alarm in her face, he went on
hastily, "Oh, don't worry about the cowboys. Mostly they are
just good kids, and you can trust them. But there'll be a lot
of yelling and carrying on in town and things will just be a little quieter in the wagon yard."

"What's a wagon yard?" Ned asked.

"A place where there'll be a lot of other wagons camped,"
Uncle Willie told him. "Maybe children for you to play with."

"Let's hurry," Ned cried. "I can't wait, Uncle Willie."

They drew into Caldwell in the middle of the afternoon
and, as Uncle Willie had predicted, found a real frontier town.
The streets were wide and full of ruts made by the wheels of
the wagons passing west. There was also a railroad and Ned
was entranced with the snorting trains, whistling and tooting
their way to the station. Stockyards, located some distance from

the town, were filled with thousands of milling cattle. Wooden
buildings lined both sides of the streets—many of them bearing
the fanciful names of saloons. "The Golden Chance," "Jake's
Place," "The Nugget." Uncle Willie was right—this was a rip-
roaring town and she would be glad for the shelter of the wagon
yard.

Up until now they had always camped by the roadside,
thus saving the money they might have spent in a wagon yard
even had one been available. This was all to the good—as matters stood, they had spent very little of the money allotted to
the journey. With luck, they should arrive in Mobeetie with a
nice little sum left over.

Still she was glad for this experience in a wagon yard.
Everything was neat and orderly. Other wagons were already
there, drawn up in a loose precision. An attendant, a young
freckled-faced boy, came to meet them.

"Howdy folks," he said, trying hard to be adult and businesslike, "and welcome."

"We'd like to put up a couple of nights," Uncle Willie
told him. "Be leaving Monday morning."

"Stay as long as you want," the boy said. "Fifty cents a
night, including feed for the team. Let me unhitch them for
you, sir." And to Catherine, "You can cook inside in the shelter
house if you want."

He set about unhitching the team, took them off for food
and water. Catherine and Ned got out. Ned immediately started
off toward some children playing by another wagon.

"You come back here," Catherine ordered. "You aren't
going one step until you wash your hands and comb your hair
and put on a clean blouse."

Uncle Willie located a blacksmith just across the street
from the wagon yard and had him come to check the wagon,

and as long as he was there, the condition of the horses' feet.

"Fine shape," the blacksmith said. "Wagon good and tight, horses don't need shoeing. Where you folks headed?"

"Texas," Uncle Willie told him. "We came from Missouri."

"You got the easy part behind you," the man said. "Whereabouts you going in Texas?"

"Mobeetie—or close to it."

"You're about halfway. Still, you got the easiest part behind you. From here on out you won't have so many people, or much water or fuel to speak of. You're sort of on your own after you get past Caldwell."

"Yes, I know," Uncle Willie told him.

"And *she*," he jerked his thumb in Catherine's direction, "is going to raise a terrible ruckus when she has to start cooking with chips. You ever been to Texas?"

"Yes," Uncle Willie said.

"It wouldn't matter if you hadn't," the man went on. "The trail's wore so deep you couldn't miss it if you tried. Looks like the rest of the country is all gone crazy about Texas. I sez to my wife—I'll just stay here in Kansas. Got to be somebody left at home to watch things while the others gad off. They'll be coming back some of these days I'm thinking. Texas is the place that separates the men from the boys."

He gave one of the wagon bows a shake.

"Now you folks are fixed to travel," he said. "Lots of them come through here with the wagon ready to fall to pieces and horses so skinny you can count their ribs."

"We tried to take care of things," Uncle Willie told him.

"Far as I can see, you done it. You ought to get through fine, barring unexpected things coming up. Never can tell about that western country, I always say. For instance, creek or a river can look dry as a bone and then up from nowhere a flash flood will come roaring down and wash you off the face of the map. And that Canadian River—I hear it gets so *quicky* a bird can't fly over it without being pulled in."

"How much do I owe you?" Uncle Willie asked, breaking into the man's dirge of doom.

"Make it about fifty cents. Really hadn't ought to charge you nothing, your gear's in such good shape."

Uncle Willie paid him and the man walked off.

"Now there's a talker," Uncle Willie said when he had gone. "You can't ever believe what one of his kind says. Things aren't so hard from here on. I've been over it, and I know."

He paused a moment, and then went on thoughtfully.

"Of course, he's right about there being fewer people. And about water being scarce, too. Fact is, it might be a good idea to have an extra water barrel. I think I'll go see about one. Anything you need, Catherine?"

She listed a few staples.

"Want to go with me, Ned?"

The two of them set off and Catherine began putting the wagon to rights. Presently they were back, Uncle Willie carrying the groceries, Ned sucking a stick of candy. Following them was a boy pushing a wheelbarrow with the barrel in it.

"Here—we'll fasten it to this side," Uncle Willie directed.

By the time the barrel was in place and the helper gone, Catherine had supper ready. While they ate the town noises came flowing toward them—men's voices and horses' feet and creaking wagons. Snatches of song. Now and then a wild "Yippee!" rose high above the other noises. Uncle Willie turned his head to listen.

"Sounds like they're all in town for Saturday night," he remarked.

"Uncle Willie," Catherine said, moved by some impulse she could not quite analyze, "why don't you go to town for a while? You must be tired of sticking around with Ned and me all the time. Go in and get you a real shave and visit with the men."

He looked at her quickly—a strange look. Not since she had turned the money over to him had she seen such a one. He seemed to lay all his life before her—his failures, his "sicknesses"—and say, "Look carefully. Are you sure you still want me to go?"

What he really said was, "I'll shave here, but I think I might like to go to the barber shop and have a bath. That is— if you don't mind being left alone."

"Of course I don't mind," she told him. "I'm not alone— I'll have Ned. Now you go on and have that bath and don't worry about us. Ned and I will take our baths and go to bed early. I'm so tired I could sleep right there on the ground."

Catherine jerked herself upright in her bed in the wagon. For a moment she did not know where she was, and then the shape of the canvas above her became clear and realization came to her.

Even as she knew where she was, she also knew that something was wrong. Sounds of some confusion, more pronounced and louder than the noises she had been listening to since they camped in the wagon yard, came to her. There were shouts of men and the sound of wagon wheels going very fast and horses running. Then footsteps hollow and loud, echoing on the wooden sidewalks across from the wagon yard. Something was going on out there—something beyond the ordinary wildness of a cow town on Saturday night.

She got up quietly, put on her wrapper, went to the front of the wagon to look out. She saw nothing but the other wagons, doubtless with people sleeping peacefully in them, and under them the pallets of yet other sleepers. Her feeling of

alarm by this time was so real that she decided to waken Uncle
Willie and have him investigate. She bent down, looked at the
spot under the wagon where his pallet was always made.

He was not there.

Then full remembrance came to her. Of course Uncle
Willie was not back yet—there would be a long line of men
waiting to use the barber shop bathtubs. She lighted a match,
looked at her watch and saw that it was just short of ten o'clock.
In her exhaustion, she had slept so soundly that it seemed the
night must be far gone. Uncle Willie would be back in a little
while. Now she felt she knew the reason for her fright. So accustomed had she become to his protective presence that she
instinctively sensed his absence at a time when anything unusual was going on.

She lay down once more but could not sleep. A host of
nameless fears came back to haunt her. She pushed them from
her firmly. But no matter how hard she tried she could not entirely dismiss them. Finally she could stand it no longer. She
got up, dressed and sat on the wagon seat. She was there when
she saw two men, carrying a lantern, coming into the wagon
yard. They stopped to hold a consultation with the attendant,
who pointed toward her wagon. Then the three started in her
direction.

She got down, was standing on the ground when they came
to her.

"Mrs. Delaney?" one of them asked. In the lantern light
she could see how grave his face was.

"Yes—I am Mrs. Delaney . . ."

"You know a man named Willie Keith?"

"Yes—he's my uncle." And then she asked the question
whose answer she already knew. "Has something happened to
him?"

"There's been an accident . . ."

"He's hurt?"

"Mrs. Delaney, ma'am," the speaker went on. "We're sorry to tell you . . ." He paused, looked vainly at the other men, hoping for help in breaking the news. Then seeing that his companions were not willing to speak, he went on. "I'm sorry—but I'm afraid he's been hurt awful bad."

Catherine's stiff lips formed the word the man could not seem to bring himself to say.

"He's—dead?" she whispered.

"Yes ma'am—I'm afraid he is. My name's Jake Hillary, ma'am, and this is Nate Carson, and if you could just come with us to—well, to sort of identify him, and so on . . ."

"Where is he?"

"In Doc Taylor's office, across the street from the barber shop. They took him there when—well, when it happened."

"I'll come," Catherine said. A numbness had engulfed her; she was watching herself from some far distance. "But if someone could look after my little boy—he's asleep in the wagon."

"I'll see to him, ma'am," the attendant said. "You go ahead."

Catherine and her companions walked the short distance between the wagon yard and the doctor's office. As they went, the men tried to give her the story of what had happened.

Some movers had stopped in front of a store to buy supplies. They thought they had tied their team tight enough, but they sure enough hadn't, for when a couple of cowboys started shooting off their guns sort of happy-like, the team broke loose.

"Your uncle had got his bath and had just stepped out of the barber shop door when the team took the corner, the wagon on two wheels," Jake Hillary said. "And there, in the middle of the street was Mrs. Frazier, who washes for the barber shop. She was crossing over to take a basket of clean towels. She's not so young, and can't move very fast anyway. And when she saw that team, she just froze—right in their path."

"Yes-siree, she just froze," Nate agreed.

"Nate and me and some other fellows were standing there, and I guess you might say we froze, too," Jake Hillary went on. "Just stood, like we was made of stone or something. Lasted only a second, I guess, but that's what we did. Then we saw a man jump out in front of the team—it was your uncle, ma'am—and he pushed Mrs. Frazier hard. She went right over against the sidewalk, but she was clear of the horses." He hesitated a moment, then went on.

"But he couldn't jump clear himself, ma'am—he didn't have time. The whole thing went so fast—we didn't hardly know what was going on until it was over."

"We're just real sorry, ma'am," Jake went on. "Too bad it had to happen. We did what we could—took him to Doc's office. Doc tried, but there wasn't anything he could do."

"Was he—was he still alive?" Catherine asked.

"Yes, ma'am, he was. Not what you'd rightly call conscious, but he was breathing. We laid him down on Doc's couch, and then he came to and began to mumble something, a couple of times. I leaned over close, to catch it."

"What was it?" Catherine asked. She had to know—there was some message to her. Of this she was sure.

"He said, 'Tell her I hadn't been in a saloon.' That's what he said, ma'am. It seemed awfully important to him. I wondered maybe if it was you he meant for us to tell."

"It was me," Catherine told him. "And it was important. Thank you for telling me."

A small knot of men were standing together when she and her companions went into the room. She was barely conscious of them; her eyes flew straight to the couch with its white sheet betraying so cruelly the nature of the thing it concealed. A man detached himself from the group, came toward her.

"Mrs. Delaney?" he asked, speaking with ease and authority.

"Yes—I am Mrs. Delaney."

"I am Dr. Taylor. Jake has told you? Yes? We are very sorry. He went almost at once—there was little, if any, pain."

He regarded her with shrewd kindness, taking the measure of her reactions. "He's trying to make things easy for me," Catherine thought, and was grateful for his quiet assurance which had helped to bridge those first difficult moments in the room. He seemed to know this, for now he turned to another man.

"This is Les Clark, the coroner," he explained. "He wants to ask you a few routine questions. Do you feel like answering?"

"Yes," Catherine told him.

Les Clark stepped forward.

"Do you mind—er, just looking at him, ma'am. I have to fill out some papers."

He was awkward and apologetic.

"No." Catherine said. "I don't mind . . ."

The coroner stepped to the couch, pulled back the sheet so that Uncle Willie's face was exposed.

Her first thought was that he looked so peaceful. His body might be broken, but there were no marks on his freshly shaven face. It bore a stamp of complete and inviolate dignity—the dignity of a man placed forever beyond any need for apology or justification. His hair was neatly combed—the men must have done this, hoping to make things easier for her.

She stood looking at the calm face for a long moment. And then the thing she had thought beyond her strength seemed possible.

"Do you know this man?" Les Clark asked, his pencil poised.

"Yes—he is my uncle, Willie Keith."

Her voice was low, but calm. She could feel the men's eyes upon her; she sensed respect and admiration, but most of all relief. They were braced for tears and wailings from her. How could she explain to them that it was Uncle Willie's strength that had come through to help her.

"Where was his home?"

"His home . . ." It was the open road, the trail, the mountain rising dim and blue in the distance. It was everywhere, and nowhere. And then she thought of the Little Room back at her mother's house and the welcome that was always there for him.

"Missouri," she said. "Grafton, Missouri."

"Any immediate family?"

"Only—my mother . . ."

Compassion and sorrow for her mother flooded over her now. And understanding. Perhaps Jessie must have always known death would find Uncle Willie in this way, around the bend of a strange road, far from home and kin. That was why she made no accusations, asked no questions, once her brother was at home.

"That's all—and thank you. We put his belongings here on the table. You'll likely want to take them with you."

She turned to scan the pitifully few possessions that had been Uncle Willie's. A pocket comb. A clean handkerchief. A knife. That was all. Lying on the chair were the clothes he had taken off before he bathed. These, and the things he had left at the wagon, represented his entire holdings—the accumulations of a lifetime. Strangely, their very meagerness seemed as poignant as anything else that had happened.

And then she remembered. The money for the trip. He

had taken that with him, and it was not here with these other things.

They must have sensed that something was wrong.

"Do you miss anything?" they asked.

"When he left," she said hesitantly, "he had some money —I don't see it here."

"Money?" They looked at each other doubtfully.

"Yes—a little . . ."

All the money set aside for the trip. Uncle Willie had taken it with him and now it was gone.

The men exchanged glances full of grave concern. "Well, ma'am," the sheriff said, "if there was any money on him I didn't see it. Maybe he spent it."

"Perhaps," she said, not wanting to imply she was blaming them in any way for the loss. But she knew Uncle Willie hadn't spent the money.

Apparently the men were not entirely satisfied with their explanation either.

"Thad," the sheriff said, speaking to a young man standing a little apart from the others, "you were about the first one there. You know anything about it?"

All the time Catherine had been in the doctor's office she had been dimly conscious of a man who, while he said nothing, continued to stare at her. It was to him that the sheriff directed his question. Catherine turned to face him, saw a young man with a small mustache and a nose that looked slightly on the bias. At some time or other it must have been broken and then set poorly, or not at all, so that not only was it crooked but had a small white hump halfway up the bridge. When he caught her eyes on him, his glance slithered away like drops of water on a hot stove.

"No," Thad said, "I don't know nothing about it. Wasn't no money around that I seen."

The sheriff turned to her again.

"You know how it is—a crowd gathered around so quick there's no keeping up with things. Hope it wasn't too much."

"Oh, no—" she told him. "Not too much. Please don't bother about it."

"Well, I'm glad it wasn't much. And now, we were wondering what you wanted to do about the—er—funeral."

The funeral! She had not thought of it, had not yet realized there would be a need beyond this frozen nightmare she was enduring at the moment. But the end was not yet—death, like life, continued to make its demands.

Della had used to say that people died the way they had lived—wild and no-good, or decent and respectable. Uncle Willie had lived his life among strangers and he had died among them. He had given his life for a woman he had never seen before and, for all these men knew, this was the final heroic gesture of a man whose life had been a pattern of greatness. Maybe that was right, after all. Perhaps Uncle Willie had always had a touch of greatness about him, unrecognized and unheralded. Perhaps that was why in that one instant where he might have chosen life for himself or for another, he had not hesitated.

"We'd be proud to see to everything for you," Jake Hillary told her.

"I will be very grateful to you," she told him simply.

"The thing for you to do now," Dr. Taylor told her, "is to go back to the wagon yard and get some rest."

She turned, walked steadily toward the door. Jake Hillary fell in step with her.

"I'll go with you," he said.

They walked the few blocks in silence. When they came to the wagon, he said,

"Sure there is nothing else I can do for you?"

"Nothing—and thank you."

"We'll come for you tomorrow, when it's time. Just try to rest, now."

"Good night, and thank you."

"Good night . . ."

Funeral services for Uncle Willie were held the next after-noon. Only a few people were there—Catherine and Ned, wearing the good clothes which she had taken out of the trunk so that their appearance would be a last tribute to Uncle Willie; Dr. Taylor, Nate Carson and the coroner, Les Clark. The minister and his wife and Jake Hillary. And, surprisingly enough, the one with the crooked nose, the young man they called Thad. She wished he had stayed away. The others were a different matter—their kindnesses had helped to make this difficult thing easier. Apparently all Thad did was to stand around and look at her, averting his glance when she caught his eye.

There were no flowers except one bouquet of crepe paper roses, faded by sun and time.

"Mrs. Frazier sent them," Jake Hillary explained. "She would have come herself, but she was hurt pretty bad. Got a broken hip. She wanted you to know she was real thankful to your uncle, and she hoped you'd understand why she couldn't come."

"A broken hip—" Les Clark said. "Now ain't that too bad. And her with that bunch of kids to take care of."

The services were simple and, in as far as it was possible for them to be, comforting. The minister read some scripture, something about "Greater love hath no man . . ." He spoke briefly and offered a prayer. The minister's wife sang in a reedy, thin soprano.

Then it was over, and the minister's wife stepped forward to offer condolences.

"You certainly have my sympathy, Mrs.—er—Delaney," she said piously. "But remember—it is the Lord's will. He took your father to his eternal reward and you must not grieve or be rebellious."

Catherine mumbled something she hoped would be correct, not bothering to explain Uncle Willie's real relationship to her. "And thank you for singing," she added.

"Oh, that was nothing—I was glad to do it."

Now Jake Hillary, evidently elected or appointed by the group to do the next part on the program, stepped forward to Catherine. He cleared his throat.

"Mrs. Delaney, ma'am," he said, "seeing as how your uncle saved the life of one of our own town people, and seeing as how his money disappeared some way and, well, you being a woman alone and all, we thought we'd just like to make up a little purse to help you get back home. So we did, and here it is."

He spoke very fast, as if he hoped he'd get finished before he forgot or she interrupted. Then he held out a purse toward her.

Catherine's face went red, then white. They were offering her money. To them she was just another one of the many cases with which they doubtless had to deal—shiftless families headed West, so poorly equipped for their journey that the loss of even a small sum was a tragedy. Either that, or they thought she had secretly suspected them of taking Uncle Willie's money.

"We'd be real proud if you'd take it," Jake Hillary said softly.

She looked at him; she looked around at the small circle of people, there on the level, lonely prairie cemetery. Not a face that did not mirror the kindness of the man who stood holding the purse in his hand. The goodness of their intention came through to her.

But even so, she could not bring herself to take the purse. Not alone because it smacked of charity, which certainly it did. But more because to do so would, in some obscure way she could not put into words, be an admission that she had been wrong in turning the money over to Uncle Willie. In her heart she knew that had been right, and she would continue to think so.

The man still held the purse to her, but now there was uncertainty on his face and the beginning of hurt. She looked at him, knowing that she could neither take the gift nor refuse it. And then suddenly the way was clear.

"It is very kind of you," she said, and took the purse from him. "You have all been kind—and I thank you."

She could feel the ripple of relief going over the little group.

"Didn't you say, though, that Mrs. Frazier was a widow, with children? I know Uncle Willie would want me to turn this over to her. She won't be able to work for some time. Would you see that she has this—for Uncle Willie's sake?"

They looked at her strangely. They looked at each other. Finally Dr. Taylor spoke. "If that is what you want to do, Mrs. Delaney, it can be arranged. Mrs. Frazier will be very grateful to you."

She handed the purse back to Jake Hillary. She was conscious of Dr. Taylor's eyes on her, regarding her shrewdly. He knew what she had been thinking—he knew and approved.

They began to move away from the newly made grave.

"Is there anything else we can do for you—or him," the sheriff asked.

"Oh, yes—if you would see about a marker."

"Sure. We'd be real proud."

"A very simple marker," she stipulated.

"Yes, ma'am, I understand. And what shall I have put on it?"

"Just his name, and the dates of his birth and his death."

"Yes ma'am, and if you'd just let me write it out . . ."

He got a stub of a pencil, a bit of paper, waited for her to go on.

"Willie—" Catherine began, and then stopped. All his life he had borne that boy's name, and it had not seemed incongruous. But in death, he had come into the dignity and stature of a man.

"His name was William Ellery Keith," she said.

Catherine and Ned got into the buckboard with the minister and his wife. The man touched the horses with the whip, drove away with a look of bland cheerfulness on his face.

"I guess you'll be going back to Illinois now," he said to Catherine. "You can sell your gear and go back by train you know."

Catherine thanked him without feeling the necessity to explain she had not come from Illinois in the first place, and, therefore, could scarcely be expected to go there now. Again the terrible irony of it all swept over her—that she should experience this thing here among people who knew so little about her, about Uncle Willie, that they should assume their roles with almost impersonal kindness. Yet, they had been kind— that she must not forget. Perhaps the very impersonal quality of their kindness was, in its way, an antidote to sorrow.

They came to the wagon yard; she and Ned got out.

"Thank you for everything," she said. "You have been kind—more than kind."

"Oh, that was nothing. If there's anything else we can do please feel free to call on us."

"Yes, please do," the minister's wife said.

"Thank you, there is nothing I can think of."

They drove off.

Jake Hillary had followed them on his horse. He came to the wagon now.

"If I may be so bold, ma'am, what do you plan to do?" His good middle-aged face was furrowed with concern.

"I don't know—" Catherine told him dully.

"Well, it's like this. The sheriff is sending me up the trail tomorrow on some business for him. If you cared to go along that would be a couple of days' start toward your folks."

He assumed without question that she would be going back to Missouri.

"Thank you," she said, "but I don't know exactly what I'll do."

"Of course it would probably be more sensible all around for you to sell your stuff here and take the train."

"Perhaps," she agreed.

"Well, if there's any way I can help, you call on me. You can just tell the wagon yard man and he'll get in touch with me."

She extended her hand.

"I don't know how to thank you for what all of you here have done for me," she said. "If I need you, you may be sure I'll call on you."

"Oh, thank you, Mrs. Delaney, ma'am . . ." His face was relieved. It was as if, at long last, he felt he had really been of some help to her.

He went off leaving Catherine and Ned alone.

"Mama," Ned said timidly, "what are we going to do now?"

It was the question they were all asking her—the minister, Jake Hillary and now Ned. In one way or another, they were asking her the question whose answer she herself did not know.

"We'll manage, honey," she told the child. "Don't you worry."

What, indeed, would she do?

She could sell the team and the wagon with its contents. That should not be difficult in this town whose streets echoed constantly with the sound of the wheels of movers. In all likelihood, she would not have to touch the money realized from the sale, or the sum sewed up in the feather bed, for the amount Uncle Willie had suggested she put aside for emergencies would buy her ticket back to Missouri, in case she decided to go there. Again she thought of the purse that had been offered her, but now the thought gave no hurt. She had done the only thing possible for her to do and the men understood.

She was brought back to the present by Ned, tugging at her sleeve.

"Mama, I'm hungry," he said.

"Of course you are," she told him. Actually, they had eaten scarcely anything all day. She had not had the time—or the heart—for thinking of food.

"I'll cook you something right away, darling," she told him.

But before she could so much as start the women from the other wagons began edging toward her.

"I cooked some bread today, Mrs. Delaney. I thought you might like some."

"Thank you—" she did not even know the name to call. She took the bread from a stranger and said, "Thank you."

"Here's a couple of fried pies—the little feller might relish them."

"Thank you—you are very kind."

"Here's some roast prairie chicken. It's real tasty, if I do say so myself."

"Oh, thank you—thank you so much."

"Is there anything we can do? Anything at all . . ."

"No, no thank you. You are very kind."

They slipped away, back to their wagons, back to their husbands, back to their children.

She spread a meal.

"Here, Ned, eat what the kind people brought us."

She forced herself to eat some, was surprised to find it tasted good.

"As soon as you finish, darling, you must go to bed. You are very tired."

They washed dishes, set things to rights. The familiar routine calmed her, gave her strength.

"Mama," Ned said, his lip trembling, "I want to see Uncle Willie. Mama—won't I ever see him again—ever?"

She gathered him into her arms, wondering how one comforted a child in the face of death. A thing so final that you cannot say, "There, there—don't cry. It will be better tomorrow." She did not know what to say. She did not know at all because she had not found the answer for herself.

Ned was sobbing now in grief brought on as much by exhaustion as anything else.

"I didn't want Uncle Willie to die," he cried. "I want to see Uncle Willie."

Catherine tried to soothe him.

"Don't cry, darling," she said. "Just try to remember how fine it was to have him with us this far on the trip. Think of all the good times you had with him—like when you went fishing . . ."

And even as she talked to the child, she felt her own grief taking possession of her. Uncle Willie had died in trying to help a woman he had never seen before. Indirectly, he had died in trying to help Catherine. It did not seem right that he should have to pay so high a price for his generosity.

"I loved him," Ned sobbed.

"We both loved him."

"And he loved us."

"Yes—he loved us."

There was her final answer. He loved and was loved. Perhaps more on this journey than ever before in all his strange and lonely life. Remembering this, some of the weight of her sorrow began to slip from her.

"Yes," she said firmly, "he loved us and we loved him. That is why we mustn't grieve too much. He wouldn't want the people he loved to be unhappy. Come now—it's time you went to bed."

"You going to bed, too, Mama?" he asked, still catching his breath in half-sobs.

"Yes—I'll be right there, honey . . ."

By the time she was undressed and beside him, Ned was fast asleep. But for her sleep would not come.

All day there had been the need for action which had mercifully kept her from thinking too much. Now she could no longer push her problem from her. With Uncle Willie gone, what was she going to do?

Sell the wagon and team and equipment here—as everyone seemed to expect her to do—and go by train either back to Missouri or on to Mobeetie, taking with her the knowledge of her own defeat and humiliation, as well as the admission she had been wrong to start in the first place? And the realization that by her stubborn insistence she had been indirectly responsible for Uncle Willie's death.

If she decided to sell, how would she go about finding a buyer? She had no knowledge of values—anyone could take advantage of her ignorance. And that could mean a loss of money, something she and Edward should not have to suffer. Besides, there was no train to Mobeetie, even if she wanted to travel on that way. With the wagon gone, she would have to go by stage, if she meant to go to Edward.

Edward—she whispered his name, trying to invoke his presence. She reached out to touch the locket, found it gave her no comfort. She wanted his actual presence, wanted to go into his arms and there sob out her guilt and grief and fears, to turn the burden of her decision over to him. She was half way to him now—she wanted to go on.

To continue by wagon, then? Just she and Ned? Alone?

Panic swept over her. She had been frightened last night when she awakened and sensed Uncle Willie's absence. Those fears were as nothing to the ones which beset her now. She turned restlessly, trying to push them from her, but they would not retreat. How did one make camp? Care for horses? Follow a trail, even one as well marked as the blacksmith had declared this one to be? What about food? Water? She had heard of travelers dying or going mad from thirst. Did she have the right to take Ned into possibilities of this sort?

There must be other, unsuspected, dangers in this wild and uncertain country which lay between herself and Edward. People—well, face it—men who were not safe for women to be around. Uncle Willie had said she could always trust cowboys, but all men were not cowboys. For no reason at all she remembered the crooked-nosed man, the one named Thad. She pushed the thought quickly from her, but at the same time she wished that she had let Uncle Willie teach her to use the gun. How foolish she had been in her sublime confidence that the trip would continue to be as easy as it had been since they left Missouri.

Missouri! A great nostalgia swept over her. She could see

it plainly as if it were there before her—the green and gentle landscape, the safe, well-traveled road. Home, sitting white and serene among the great trees. Her Mother—Aunt Mae—Della. They all seemed to stretch out their arms to her, beckoning her to come back to safety and comfort and love.

The road back to Missouri was familiar to her. Besides that, for the first two days she would have the escort offered by Jake Hillary (which she suspected was something coming out of his own kind heart rather than of the need for taking care of any business). After that she could make the same camping places Uncle Willie had selected each night. People, hearing her story, would be kind and thoughtful. In this way she would be able to get the wagon back with most of its supplies intact and then wait for Edward to come for her the first of August.

Again she turned restlessly. The first of August! More than two months away. Two months to wait when, only last night, she had thought it would be a matter of a few weeks. To be half way to Edward and then turn back!

No. She must not turn back. She must go ahead. She must deliver the wagon and its precious contents to Edward. Only by doing so could she overcome the guilt she felt in letting him go without her in the first place. For a moment she even welcomed the thought of the hazards which might lie ahead of her, feeling that Edward's pride in her would increase in direct proportion to their difficulty.

But even as this thought occurred to her, she discarded it hastily. Her reason lay beyond a desire, great as it was, for Edward's approval, his reassurance that she had not, after all, failed him. The fact of his need for the things she was bringing, and, she urgently hoped, his need for her presence, her love, rose above her doubts and fears, her sense of guilt.

Edward needed her. That was why she must go.

Having made her decision, she fell into a half-doze, something between real sleep and an awareness of her surroundings.

She awoke, to find that the people in the wagon yard were stirring. She got up, dressed.

The attendant came to her, the same snub-nosed freckled boy who had met them day before yesterday—a lifetime ago.

"I'll just harness your team when you want it," he said.

She thanked him and went inside the shelter house to cook an egg for Ned, coffee for herself. When she came out, the boy had the team harnessed and waiting for her. Prince and Lady looked back at her, as if they, too, were wondering what she meant to do.

She got up on the wagon seat, Ned beside her. She took the lines. The sun was just coming up—the sky was bright with the colors of it. The day was new and fresh and beautiful.

She drove to the exit, out into the street. Then she halted the team. She sat there quietly, making no effort to move on. She might have been a statue carved in stone sitting there— a woman on the seat of a wagon, a little boy sitting beside her. Waiting—thinking.

Last night she had made up her mind to go on. It was a decision from which she had no intentions of drawing back. But now that she sat here on the verge of carrying it out, she wanted to examine the compulsion which was pushing her forward. Was it only a sense of guilt at having failed Edward so that for her own satisfaction she must do this as penance? Was it vanity, wanting him to think well of her? Was it his need of her, certainly not to be denied and commendable enough reason in itself.

Or was it a deeper more fundamental issue—something she had never really faced before?

Finally Ned spoke.

"Mama," he asked timidly, "what are we going to do now? Are we going back to Grandma or on to Papa?"

Catherine looked at him quickly. And then it came to her that the decision was as simple and as clear-cut as that. She squared her shoulders. She bent and dropped a kiss on the top of his head.

"We're going on to Papa," she said.

She turned Prince and Lady west. Toward Texas. Toward Edward.

# CHAPTER 8

CATHERINE SAT ON THE SEAT OF THE WAGON, THE LINES LOOSE
AND EASY IN HER HANDS. SHE HAD PUT ALMOST A WEEK BETWEEN
her and Caldwell, between herself and the tragedy of Uncle
Willie's death—a week so different from anything she had ever
experienced that she might as well have been another woman
living in another world. She had come into this new life with
scarcely any knowledge to carry over from the old one. But,
she had come on. That was the thought to cling to. She had
kept her hands on the lines, and she had guided the horses
forward.

The first day she held the lines in a grip so tight that by
noon her whole body ached with the strain. She would make
a conscious effort to relax, but the first thing she knew she
would be tense again, rigid as iron. Her state of mind communicated itself to Prince and Lady. They shook their heads,
they shied at nonexistent obstacles in the road.

As for herself, she was hardly conscious of anything they
passed, real or imagined. In the back of her mind was the one
thought—what will I do when night comes? She should have
asked the attendant at the wagon yard concerning camping
sites ahead or wagon yards.

Some way she got through the day. There was the need
to keep driving. There was the need to look after Ned.

163

"Mama, I'm hungry."

The thought of food had not even occurred to her. Now she looked at her watch, was surprised to find it was noon. She stopped the team, brought out food that had been left from yesterday. She got water from the barrel, made Ned wash his hands. The child ate, but she could make only a pretense of tasting something. They got back into the wagon and started off again.

Ned leaned against her, slept. Already he had accepted the fact that Uncle Willie was gone, an acceptance which both surprised and relieved Catherine. She was afraid that he would continue to be irreconcilable for days.

It was good that this was so, for she had had small experience with death and people's reactions to it. After all she had been only two at the time of her father's death and remembered nothing about it.

"We had been married only five years when your father died," Jessie had told her.

For Catherine, inching her way now toward Edward, the statement took on added significance. Her mother and father had had less time together than she and Edward had already put behind them. What if Edward, instead of being in Texas, were gone forever beyond any hope of seeing him again! Hard though this journey might be, it still had its bright promise at the conclusion.

And suddenly it occurred to her to wonder what her mother would have done, had she been in Catherine's place. Jessie's face was before her and across the miles the answer came, too.

"I would have gone on, Catherine," she seemed to say. "Most assuredly, I would have gone on."

As, indeed, she would. She would have felt it her duty, and clear and unmistakable above all else her devotion to duty had arisen. Something must have died inside her when her husband died, just as part of Catherine would have died with Edward's death.

Now her mother would have another sorrow in Uncle Willie's death. Catherine considered how best to break the news. Her mother had loved her younger brother dearly, in spite of his weakness; maybe *because* of it. If she wrote her mother at the next stop, which was what she had first thought of doing, she would not have herself sufficiently under control to break the news as carefully as it needed to be told. Moreover, she could not conceal the fact that she and Ned were going on without him. The first would bring great sadness to her; the second would be a worry that might be great enough to make her ill.

I'll wait, she decided. I'll write her when I get to Mobeetie. That will be best.

In the wish to shield her mother there came, also, a rush of protective love. It was as if she and her mother had reversed roles now so that she, Catherine, was the strong and guiding influence, her mother the weak, dependent one.

I'll write her a good long letter as soon as I get to Mobeetie. I'll tell her exactly what happened and why. I want to make her see just how brave Uncle Willie was at the last—she will be proud.

Toward the end of the first day out of Caldwell she sighted a small town. When she drove into it there was, thank God, a wagon yard. Not a good one, like at Caldwell, but at least there were other wagons and water and a boy to care for her team. But best of all there were people—blessed, comfort-giving people.

"There's a stove inside the shelter house—you can cook your supper on it," the attendant told her.

She cooked their meal and afterward went out to the wagon. The people camped next to her wagon—a man and a woman—talked with her, easily and casually.

"You folks traveling alone?"

"Our Uncle Willie came with us," Ned began, but Catherine broke in hastily.

"This is a nice wagon yard. Do you suppose there is another one tomorrow night?"

"Which way you going?" the man asked.

"West—"

"Yes, fifteen miles or so from here. A good day's drive. No town the next night, but there is a fine camp place with water and wood. You can make it the second night, if your team's good."

"Mine is," Catherine told him.

"Fine. You got a long hard stretch ahead of you. Up hill a lot of the way. Dry, too. Better carry plenty of water."

"We have an extra barrel," Ned put in wisely. "Our Uncle Willie got it for us."

"Come on, honey," Catherine said. "It's time for you to go to bed now."

Ned went without protest, and Catherine put him to bed. No need to let people know she was traveling with only a small boy for company. Thank goodness he had put in his innocent contributions about Uncle Willie. For all the other people knew Uncle Willie might be asleep in the wagon.

The attendant had her team ready the next morning when she was ready to leave.

"That will be fifty cents," he told her.

"Oh, yes—just a moment."

She stepped back into the wagon, took the money from the emergency fund in the jewel box. She paid the boy, then went back to consider the sum left. She counted it—a little over thirty dollars. She had no idea of the expenses that lay ahead of her—she could only hope this would cover them. She transferred the money to the purse that Della had made her, tied it around her waist. This done, she took her place on the wagon seat again, gathered up the lines.

"Good-by," the attendant said.

"Good-by . . ."

She drove off.

That day went easier. She knew now what was ahead of her—another wagon yard and more people. She would stay there, paying fifty cents for the privilege. Tomorrow night she'd camp out, but tonight she needed to be with people, to have help in caring for the team. The numbness began to leave her brain just a little; her hold on the lines relaxed.

The wagon yard was small, but it served her purpose. She was so grateful for it that she did not question its accommodations. At least the team was taken care of; the next morning the attendant harnessed it for her and hitched it to the wagon. She paid him and drove off.

Even before she got to the campsite that evening she saw two other wagons were already drawn up there. At the sight of their white tops a great surge of gladness came over her. She pulled up—not too close to them, but close enough for comfort—and set about making camp.

She got off the wagon, Ned at her heels, and began to unhitch Prince and Lady. She was able to unfasten the tugs, and then stood looking at the straps and buckles and all the intricate fastenings. Tonight she wouldn't even try to unharness them. It wouldn't hurt them to stay harnessed one night. She'd feed them from the emergency bag she carried in the wagon rather than staking them out to graze.

"But Mama," Ned protested, "Uncle Willie always took the harness off the horses."

"I know, honey. After tonight we will. Mama's tired tonight."

She built a campfire; it roared up, big and hot.

"But Mama, Uncle Willie said you needed just a little fire."

"I know. Tomorrow night I'll have a smaller one."

A woman strolled over to the wagon.

"You folks going far?"

"Not very."

"We ain't neither. Should be there by noon tomorrow. We got a place about ten miles off the trail. You got a claim yet?"

"My husband has already located one," Catherine told her.

"That's good." She looked at Catherine curiously. "He sick or something?" she asked.

"No," Catherine said. "He's quite all right."

The woman went off, shaking her head. Catherine saw her conferring earnestly with the woman in the other wagon. Once or twice they looked in her direction so that she knew they were discussing her and, no doubt, her husband's strange actions. Let them—she didn't care what they said about Edward, so long as they didn't know he wasn't with her.

The next morning Catherine started off following the other wagons, but not close enough to get their dust. About ten in the morning they turned off and Catherine waved to them, feeling very lonely as they disappeared into the distance.

Ned must have sensed her mood.

"Mama, I'll drive awhile."

They were on a good level stretch of road, so she turned the lines over to him.

"Mama, I'm here to take care of you. Uncle Willie's gone, but I'm here."

"Yes, darling. I couldn't get along without you."

Nor could she. It was more than the fact that she had someone with her—a voice to speak to her, a hand to touch in the loneliness of the night. Because he was with her she must display a courage she did not feel, put on a cheerfulness that was not really hers. And because she must do this some actuality of courage, some genuineness of cheer, came through to help her.

Again that night they camped near people. This time she unharnessed the team, trying to memorize where things went so that in the morning she could put the harness back on without difficulty. Almost it was as if Prince and Lady knew her problem, they stood so patient and still while she worked. Finally she had the harness off and took the team down to the water to drink. They drank deeply and shook themselves with a relief, glad to be rid of the harness. She took them back, staked them out to graze.

She built a campfire.

"That's as good as Uncle Willie's," Ned said. And then, loyally, "Well, almost . . ."

It was not as good as Uncle Willie's, but it was better than her first effort. She had done that and she had cared for the team. She had been adequate to the demands of the day.

That night, for the first time since Uncle Willie's death, she slept soundly and well.

When she set about harnessing Prince and Lady the next morning she found that she did not know how to go about it in spite of the care she had used last evening in removing the harness. She looked at the welter of lines and straps, the great clumsy collars, and she did not know where to start. If she had only made Uncle Willie teach her this most fundamental of camp chores.

She worked so long and fruitlessly that she was exhausted. The other campers began to pull out. Just as the last of the wagons was leaving, a man stopped, got off the wagon seat and came to her.

"You seem to be having a mite of trouble, ma'am. You traveling alone?"

Catherine was beyond pride now, beyond the fear of having him find out.

"Yes," she said simply.

"Mebbe I could help you."

"If you only would!"

He began harnessing the horses easily, throwing the heavy gear over their backs with a man's skill and a man's strength. Catherine watched him carefully—every move, every intricate joining. Finally the team was hooked to the wagon.

"Oh, thank you," Catherine said. "Thank you so very much."

"Nothing at all. Glad to help."

He walked back to the wagon, with its tattered canvas and its bunch of unkempt children peering out of the back. His wife, who had been holding the lines while he helped Catherine, moved over. The man took her place, and they drove off.

Catherine mounted her own wagon seat, watched them for a moment or two, finding it in her heart to envy that drab untidy woman in the wagon ahead. She had her husband with her. She did not have to make decisions about camping; at night she did not lie, tense and fearful, trying to trace each noise. She did not spend her days in deep concern as to whether that evening there would be other campers near. She carried her certainty with her, her shield against fear. She might travel in a tattered wagon, but at least she did not travel alone.

And then the thought came to Catherine that she had not needed to travel alone, either. Even when Edward was saying good-by to her she could have cried out, "Listen, Edward, we'll go together. You promised. Money doesn't matter. Let Ned and me go with you. We'll work things out—together. You promised, Edward."

That was what her heart had wanted to say that morning when he left. But she did not let the words cross her lips. She let him go, with all the wishing left inside her.

He would have protested, if for no other reason than because he thought it was his duty. But he would have given in. Perhaps he had half-expected her to beg, there at the last. And when she didn't he was disappointed. Maybe that was why he kept telling her he'd come back as soon as he had things worked out. He thought that was all she wanted—things made smooth and easy and sure.

"We went on and took the chance," the young wife had said, back on the trail. Catherine had taken a different kind of chance—she had let her husband go off without her.

She thought of how close she had come to turning back, even after she started. There at Caldwell. She shivered a little, as one does at the remembrance of some grave danger, narrowly missed.

"You cold, Mama?" Ned asked.

"No, honey, I'm fine."

That night it happened—the thing which had cast its shadow of fear across her path ever since they left Caldwell.

They camped alone.

She knew she would never, as long as she lived, forget that night. There was terror lurking in the very trees that gave them shelter, in the sound of the stream from which the team drank. The wood in their fire snapped; the sound was thunder in her ears. Her voice and Ned's were eerie wails, high and unnatural in the darkness. She made Ned undress but she kept her clothes on, slipping off her shoes. She lay beside the child, tense and nearly numb with fear each time Prince and Lady stamped, each time a night bird called.

She looked at the spot where the gun was supported on its pegs. It gave her small comfort, however. It was empty but even had it been loaded, she would not know how to use it.

A twig snapped. She sat up straight, listening, straining her ears for a greater sound to follow. There was only stillness— and she did not know whether she feared that or noise the more. The silence was terrible—a great relentless vacuum, threatening to pull her down into it.

She dozed off and then awakened with a jerk. Surely the sound she heard was not just the wind. There was something— somebody—slipping up to the wagon. She sat up straight again, her hands icy cold, her heart beating so hard that the intruder —if there was one—must hear it. She sat still a long time, then decided the noise was nothing to be alarmed about. She lay back, a little ashamed of her terror.

When she awoke again, dawn was streaking the sky. She thought she had never seen anything more beautiful than its multicolored pattern. By daylight things came into focus once more. She could see the horses, still grazing where she had staked them out last night. She could see the ashes of the campfire she had made.

She got up, removed the rumpled clothes in which she had slept, took fresh ones from the little trunk. She washed her face and hands, combed her hair carefully. She even rubbed the chamois skin over her nose. When she was dressed, she wakened Ned.

"Get up, Ned," she said. "There are some clean clothes for you. Dress while I'm getting breakfast."

"But Mama—my clothes aren't dirty."

"Change anyway."

Today she sat straighter on the wagon. She had camped alone last night and nothing had happened to them. She had faced the thing she most feared and because of that she was a little stronger, a little more able to face whatever might come next. If she had to camp alone tonight, she could do it. Not willingly, but of necessity.

But that she would not face until it came.

I will not let myself think beyond this stretch of miles— these miles I can see ahead of me, she told herself. I will not run ahead to meet the problems that may come up—camping alone or making dry camp or anything else. I will go as the horses go—a step at a time.

They plodded along, Prince and Lady, their feet making a tune as they went.

Every step is forward, Catherine thought. Every step is one toward Edward.

It was really too early to stop that afternoon when she saw the house silhouetted against the afternoon sun—a small, dirt-colored rectangle retreating back into the earth as if it were part of it, as she found out later it was. She knew instinctively that she was looking at her first sod house—slabs of sod fitted together the way people fitted stones together in other regions.

The house was small; it could not have had more than two rooms. But there was a well near it and a few trees. There were other marks of civilization—a clothesline with small garments and several women's dresses hanging on it, some outbuildings. A cow was in a lot and chickens were scratching about in the yard. A family lived here.

Catherine decided that she would ask permission to camp near the house. If the family proved friendly, she might even lay over a day in order to rest the team and herself. Besides, she ought to wash and air the bedding. Now with the terror of those first days behind her, she could turn her attention to some of the routine needs of their lives.

Catherine stopped the team about a quarter of a mile from the house. She looked at herself in the little mirror—she smoothed her hair and ran her finger around the neck of her dress, making it neat. She tied her bonnet strings straight. She washed her hands and made Ned wash his; she combed his hair. This finished, she took up the lines and drove on. When she got to the house she stopped the team, climbed over the side of the wagon and, with Ned by the hand, walked up to the door.

A woman answered the knock. Seeing Catherine, her face lighted up with surprise and delight.

"Oh, hello," she said. "Come in—do come in."

She was a tall, strong woman who must have been young, but looked old. Her hair was a dun color, faded out from its original light brown by sun and wind. Her face was thickly freckled—protection built up by a sensitive skin against the unmerciful force of the weather. Her hands were large but well shaped and capable looking—worn by hard work, chapped and with broken nails. Her eyes, so blue they made a spot of startling brightness in her face, had small delicate laugh-wrinkles at their corners.

"Do come in," she urged again.

"I wondered—" Catherine said. "Well, would it be all right if we camped here? My little boy and I . . ."

The woman reached out and took Catherine's hands in her own. "Why of course it would," she said. And then she went on uncertainly, "You mean—there's no one else with you?"

"Just the two of us," Catherine told her.

"You get yourself right into this house," the woman urged. "You aren't going to camp—you're coming in the house and stay with me. My husband's gone for a couple of days."

Catherine hesitated.

"Oh, if you knew how starved I was for company, you'd come right on," the woman told her. "Men have it easier out here—they go off for supplies and things and they trade work, so they get to see each other. But sometimes it's months before us women can get together. Now stop holding back and come on."

Her speech was a torrent of sound, loosed at the sight of another woman's face.

"All right," Catherine told her. "I'm as anxious to stay as you are to have me. I'm Mrs. Edward Delaney—Catherine Delaney and this is my son, Ned."

"I'm almost five," Ned said gravely, as if that were an item of greatest importance.

"Well, now, you are a big, fine boy," the woman assured him. "I bet you and my boys will get along fine."

By this time two boys had slipped up to join their mother, staying close to her like small wild animals who made no move until their mother's attitude assured them it was safe to do so. One seemed slightly older than Ned, the other was a little younger, although it was hard to judge for, like their mother, their faces had been bleached by the sun, their bodies toughened to sparseness by the force of the wind. They stood regarding Ned with unblinking eyes.

"This is Hugh and this is Jack," the woman told Ned.

"Hello," Ned said.

The boys mumbled something that was meant for a greeting.

"I must say I think you're just real brave," the woman continued, speaking to Catherine now. "I don't know as I could have done it myself—travel alone, with even the two boys."

And then suddenly she began to laugh.

"If I'm not the crazy one," she said. "I haven't even told you my own name. I'm Lola Hardy. Now why don't we put that team of yours in the lot, so we won't have to think about it any more, and then you can come in the house for a good rest—and a visit . . ."

The team was cared for and the little boys, now over their first shyness, had taken Ned off for a look at the baby chickens. Catherine followed Lola Hardy into the house.

It was small, but neat and clean. There were two rooms: a kitchen-living-dining room and a bedroom with two beds in it. These were covered with patchwork quilts.

"John—that's my husband—" Lola Hardy explained, "well, he made those beds for me. They're forked branches, driven into the ground. He's that handy. Look . . ."

She lifted the covers to show Catherine the strong and sturdy invention.

"And he wove rope across, for slats," she went on. "And he helped me stuff the mattresses with dried grass. Oh, we have to do the best we can," she said.

She spoke with quick, nervous eagerness, as if she felt she must talk fast or Catherine would go off and leave her before she had half finished with all she wanted to say.

"And I'm just real proud of my carpet—it's made of tow sacks. We sewed them together and then put a layer of dried grass on the floor and spread it down. Did we ever have a time figuring a way to fasten it to the floor! Finally John thought of cutting wooden pegs and driving them all around the edge of the room."

She caught Catherine's look of puzzled wonder.

"The floor's dirt," she explained.

"Oh—" Catherine could not suppress her amazement. Dirt, for a floor. Then it occurred to her that the house Edward had made for her probably had a dirt floor. The woman seemed to guess her thoughts.

"You'll most likely have one of your own if you're going to Texas," she said. "But you shouldn't be looking at my house —you're tired. I'm so anxious to talk to you, I haven't even given you a chance to sit down and rest. How long have you been on the road?"

"Almost a month."

"Well, you *must* be worn out. Now I tell you what, I want you to lie down and rest while I fix us some supper. Your little boy is playing so nice with my boys. He's such a fine child— such good manners. I'm glad for my boys to be with him."

We're not movers to her, Catherine was thinking. We are human beings. People she likes to be with. She was delighted that Lola Hardy should sense that she and Ned were different from the others who rode in those tattered wagons. Then it came to her that the woman would, in all likelihood, have treated anyone the way she now treated Catherine. Loneliness was a common denominator which made all people look alike to her. Or maybe it went deeper than that. Loneliness had given her the ability to look beneath the surface and see the real goodness, the essential dignity and worth of every one. Catherine herself remembered all those people in shabby wagons who had helped her on the road—the man who had helped her harness the horses, ones who had spoken to her in kindness, even the families who had done nothing more than to be camped close to her during nights that might have turned to terror had she spent them alone. And she was ashamed that she should want to be thought better, or even different, from those others on the road.

"I'll bring some water and a tub and you can have a bath," Lola said. "You can take a nice bath, and a rest, and you'll enjoy your supper more."

Presently she came back into the little room with a tin tub, a bucket of water and soap and towels.

"The soap's got perfume in it," she announced with a child's delight. "Ma gave it to me when I got married—just to use for special."

Catherine did not protest. This, she knew with a wisdom rooted deep within her heart, was "special." She said,

"Thank you, Lola. You are so very good to me." And then she reached out impulsively and took the woman in her arms. "I can't tell you how much this means to me," she went on, "having you take me in like this."

Tears were in Lola Hardy's eyes.

"How much it means to you . . ." she said. "What a way to talk!"


When Catherine walked out into the kitchen an hour later she felt like a new person. She had taken a bath and put on clean clothes. She had even lain down on the patch work quilt and rested awhile, so that the shadows were gone from beneath her dark eyes, the lines smoothed out of her face.

"Well," Lola said, "you look just lovely. Not like a woman that's been traveling overland." She put her head on one side, the better to regard her visitor.

"That's a real pretty calico you got on—all those nice tucks and ruffles."

"My aunt made it for me," Catherine told her.

"And that locket—it just sets the dress off."

"My husband gave it to me," Catherine explained proudly. "It has his picture in it. See?"

She opened the locket and Edward looked back at them. Lola gazed at him intently. "My," she giggled, "I don't blame you for rushing out to him if he's that good-looking."

"He's even better looking than that," Catherine assured her. She held the locket, still open, reluctant to close it. She studied each dear familiar feature of Edward's face, as if she, and not Lola, were seeing it for the first time.

"And those dates carved on the back?" Lola asked.

Catherine explained the pretty fancy, a delicate flush coming to her cheeks.

"Now that's real clever," Lola said. She looked at Catherine shrewdly. "It ain't only because he's handsome that you're pushing through to him," she went on. "It's because you're just crazy about him."

Catherine looked at her quickly, and then back at the locket with its carved dates and the smooth surface beneath.

"Yes," she said softly. "Yes—that's it."

"I know," Lola told her. "That's why I came West with John, when everyone said it was a foolish thing to do. That's the way it is out here. The men come because they love the country and the women come because they love the men. But," she cried, "here I am letting my supper burn while I talk!"

She turned quickly to check the pans on the stove.

"You call the children," she told Catherine. "They'll have just time to wash their hands before it's ready."

Presently they were all sitting down at the table to cured meat, homemade bread and home-churned butter and sour plum preserves. There was a dish of beans, a platter of fried eggs and glasses of milk for the children.

"All right, boys," Lola said.

At the signal the two Hardy boys ducked their heads; the

oldest said a few words of blessing, the younger followed him. Apparently their shyness was forgotten in this familiar routine.

"Wouldn't you like to say a blessing, too, Ned?" Lola asked generously.

Ned looked around, frankly puzzled. This was something he did not understand at all. His grandmother said the blessing back in Missouri; he said his prayers at night. This was a blessing, yet the children said it. His mind struggled with the complexity of the problem. Then he closed his eyes, bowed his head.

"God bless Mrs. Hardy," he intoned, "and Mama and Papa—" He raised his head and then seeming less than satisfied, ducked it again.

"God bless *all* the Hardys," he added.

"Why you little darling," Lola Hardy cried. Catherine found her own eyes were misty with tears.

Lola Hardy made pallets on the floor for the children, dragging out clean comforts, pillows and bedclothes from a chest under one of the beds.

"The three boys can sleep here," she said. "Then you can have a bed all to yourself."

She turned down the covers of the bed intended for Catherine, showing the white sheets and pillow cases.

"And from the looks of you, you'd better turn in right away. You look just real worn out."

Catherine helped Ned get ready for bed. Then she undressed, put on her nightgown and slipped into bed. She remembered thinking, "These sheets are ironed!" And after that, she was asleep.

She awakened the next morning to the smell of coffee and of bacon frying. For an instant she thought she was back in

Missouri—that presently Della would call her to say that breakfast was ready. Then she was fully awake and knew where she
was. She looked around—she was alone in the room. Even Ned
had slipped out without awakening her. She jumped out of
bed, dressed hastily, combed her hair and went into the kitchen.

"Oh, good morning," Lola Hardy said. "I was hoping you
could sleep late."

"I slept—my goodness, I don't believe I even turned over,"
Catherine told her. And then, "Where's Ned?"

"Out with the boys, feeding the little pigs. They are having the best time. You know," she said soberly, "sometimes I
hate to think of how my children have to grow up without
ever seeing others their own age." She turned a piece of bacon,
her blue eyes serious and intent as she worked.

"But there," she finished brightly, "I sound like I'm com-
plaining. And I'm not. Not at all. We don't have things like
we want them, but we didn't have them perfect in Illinois,
either."

She turned toward the table, a plate of bacon and eggs in
her strong, capable hands. She set it down, placing it on a clean
cloth. The dishes were set on neatly, the silver was placed correctly. She caught Catherine's eye on the table.

"I try to do things right," she said. "Sometimes you get to
thinking it doesn't matter how you act, way off out here. But
I always tell John that if you know your manners, there'll come
a time when you can use them. Besides, who is better to use
manners on than your own family?"

"Who, indeed," Catherine laughed.

Just then the children came in.

"Mama," Ned cried, "I fed the pigs. I fed them myself.
I'm having the best time!"

"I tell you what," Lola Hardy said, "there's no need for

you to rush off today. Stay on another day or so. It will be grand for us to have you."

"If you can put up with us, we'd love it. And—would you mind if I washed?"

"Why of course—we'll get at it as soon as breakfast is out of the way."

Lola put on water to heat, Catherine began gathering up the soiled clothes. Lola watched her as she started washing.

"My goodness," she finally said, "you aren't going to put those dark things in ahead of the white ones, are you?"

Catherine looked at her uncertainly.

Suddenly Lola threw back her head and began to laugh. She laughed until the tears ran down her freckled cheeks.

"You've never washed a lick before," she said. "Now don't try to tell me you have. I know better."

"I washed things out on the road," Catherine said, feeling herself flushing.

"That's not real washing. I might have known. You have the look of a woman who's never had to work."

Once Catherine might have known pleasure at her words. Now she felt only embarrassment.

"Oh, don't feel bad," Lola comforted her. "That's what makes it all the more wonderful. You, starting out to Texas by yourself."

"I didn't start by myself," Catherine told her.

And then, while the wash water cooled, she told Lola Hardy the whole story—about Uncle Willie and the way he died. She went further back than that, to herself and Edward— of his wish to go West, and of the final going, and the way she came to decide to follow.

She told it all, the words coming from her in torrents. She needed to talk—she needed to get these things out of her mind, to crystallize them into a pattern of speech before she met Edward. Telling them now would, in a measure, rid her of the past. Once she came to him there must be only present. Present and future.

The woman listened, alert, absorbed. When finally Catherine finished, she said,

"All right, first we'll put this washing out, and then we've got a lot of other things to do."

That day, and the one which followed, duplicated those last ones in Missouri. There was planning; there was checking, discarding, organizing.

"Your next real stop is Camp Supply," Lola told her. "That's four long, hard days away, with not much between but sand and wagon tracks. Rough country, too—hills and breaks and scrub oaks. You'll probably have to make dry camp every night."

"That's what Uncle Willie told me—that's why I have the extra barrel."

"You'll need it—we'll fill them both before you leave and you should make out fine."

She considered a moment.

"Of course you have a gun," she finally said.

"Yes, but I'm scared to touch it."

"You mustn't be. You have to know how to use one on a trip like this. Thing for you to do now is to learn how to use that gun. Maybe you can shoot some fresh meat . . .'"

She looked a little to one side of Catherine when she spoke. Catherine knew she was not thinking of fresh meat alone. There were other dangers awaiting a traveler on the road— dangers having no connection with the food they must eat.

Catherine got the gun off its peg and Lola showed her how to load, how to aim.

"You hold it tight against your shoulder," Lola said. "If you don't, it will kick something awful. You've got to let it know who's boss and you'll do all right."

Catherine tried to follow directions.

"Here," Lola cautioned her. "Don't act so scared. And don't shut your eyes. You have to look where you're aiming. Let me show you."

She took the gun herself, raised it, held it firmly against her shoulder.

"Like this," she said. "Now you take it back and try again."

Catherine took the gun once more, felt a little more sure of herself. Just then a jackrabbit sprang up from a small bush close to them.

"Shoot him!" Lola cried. "Shoot him!"

Catherine fired. The sand spatted up around the startled rabbit, covering him with dust and pebbles. He leaped high into the air, tore off unhurt into the distance. The women stood watching him, laughing too hard to take aim again.

"If ever I kill anything it will be by scaring it to death," Catherine said.

"You'll learn. At least you know now how to load and fire. The hitting will come later, with practice."

They went back into the house—talking, talking, talking.

"I must leave in the morning," Catherine told her. "I hate to go, but I must."

Lola's face became still, clouded. But she made no protest.

"I know," she said. And then, "We better begin getting things ready to pack. I'm going to make some sugar cookies for you to take along. You'll like that, won't you, Ned?"

Ned grinned his approval.

"And I'll pack some eggs and butter and bacon—I'll roast a chicken so you'll have meat that first day."

She busied herself with the cooking. And while her hands

were occupied with this, she tried in other ways to make Catherine ready.

"Once you get to Camp Supply, it will be easier. There'll more than likely be other people going on down to Mobeetie—they all seem to go through Camp Supply. Maybe people coming down from Dodge or even from Caldwell."

She tried consciously to paint a bright picture.

"You'll have to cross the Salt Fork of the Arkansas and the Cimarron, but they won't be too hard. Probably will be someone there to help you. Better wait, if the water's high enough to make the horses swim across. But if it ain't swimming-deep, you can manage by yourself all right, if no one's there to help."

"Uncle Willie had the wagon made watertight," Catherine told her.

"That's good," Lola said.

She took her finger, drew a rough map on the floured dough board on which she had been rolling out cookies.

"You'll sort of angle all the way from here to Camp Supply, going southwest. There'll be the North Canadian to cross, but it ain't much problem. You'll be leaving Kansas soon, going into The Strip."

"The Strip?"

"Yes—the Cherokee Strip."

"Didn't that belong to an Indian tribe?"

Her mother's warnings came back to her. *You'll be scalped by Indians. There'll be Indians lurking behind every bush.*

"Now don't you worry about the Indians," Lola told her. "They're a dirty, thieving lot, but they won't hurt you. You probably won't even see one—they're all supposed to be on reservations. Anyway, lots of them are a sight better than some of the whites you'll meet."

And then, realizing that she had said the wrong thing, she

continued hastily. "But don't you worry about them—don't worry about *anything*."

"I'm not worried," Catherine assured her.

"Only thing," Lola mused, "when you get to the Canadian, you better not try to make it yourself. Especially if the water's high, the way it's likely to be this time of year."

The blacksmith had warned them about the Canadian. As far back as Caldwell—perhaps even farther—it was known and feared.

"Even if it's low, you best wait for someone to help you over," Lola went on. "It's easy to get in the quicksand there. It might look safe as anything, and still be quicky."

And then, at Catherine's look of alarm, she added hastily, "But you wait—there'll be someone coming along to help you. The cowboys now, they can go back and forth across that river without never a bit of trouble. And there'll sure be some cowboys drifting along to help you. Just you wait for them."

"I will," Catherine promised, wondering what she would do if no cowboys showed up. Would she just sit there waiting, camping indefinitely? It was annoying that the barrier, the one most dreaded, should be so close to her destination—perhaps two short days' travel. Well, that was something else she would wait to face until the time came. A day at a time—that was enough for a trip like this.

They packed the wagon the night before so that Catherine could get an early start the next morning. They put in the clean clothes and the food, making a separate package of the cookies so Ned could get to them easily. They filled the water barrels. They checked the gun; this time when it went back on its peg it was loaded.

"Sure you know which end to point?" Lola asked. "I wouldn't want you to scare any more little rabbits that bad!"

They were making sorry jokes as they worked.

She got up into the wagon, helping Catherine to put her washing into the trunk.

"My goodness," she said, "you're taking a rocking chair. It's real pretty, too."

She ran her hand over it musingly, a far off look in her blue eyes.

"I had a couple of real pretty rocking chairs, back in Illinois," she said. "I wanted to bring them the worst way, but there wasn't room. Seems like a wagon just fills up before you know it with things you *have* to bring. John tells me not to fret—that some day he'll buy me rocking chairs by the dozen. Now who," she finished laughingly, "would want a dozen rocking chairs!"

The next morning, very early, Catherine started off. She and Lola kissed each other, clinging together for a moment.

"I know this will be the last time I'll ever see you," Lola said thickly. "Seems like I can't stand to have you go!"

"Oh, maybe we'll see each other again," Catherine comforted her, although she knew in her heart this was not so.

"No, you're not the kind who'll turn back. And I'm not the kind to leave."

Which was the truth. The woman would stay here, bound by the love she had for her husband. And Catherine would go on, bound by the same love she felt for Edward.

Catherine went back into the wagon. When she came out, she was carrying the little rocking chair.

"Here," she said to Lola, "this is for you!"

For a moment a flash of light went across the woman's face. She half reached out to take it, and then she drew back. But the hunger stayed on her face.

"No—" she said, "I couldn't take it. I'd always feel you thought I was—was asking for it!"

"I want you to have it," Catherine told her. "I don't need it—not at all."

Nor did she. The rocking chair belonged to another part of her life, to the days when Uncle Willie drove and she could sit in the shade of the canvas, rocking if she wished. To the days when she was protected, cared for. Now she was a different woman, with no one to stand between her and all the problems of the road. She did not even want this symbol of other, easier days.

"I want you to keep it to—to remember me by," Catherine said.

"I wouldn't need it for that," Lola told her softly. "I'll never forget you—never. But I'll keep the little chair. That way I'll feel a part of you has stayed with me and it will help me when I get lonesome or discouraged."

Catherine put her arms around her once more.

"And I'll take you with me, too," she said. "I can't tell you what this has meant to me—being with you. I couldn't have gone on, without these days here."

"You'll be all right," Lola said, as if she had not already said this a dozen times. "People go to Camp Supply all the time."

"I know," Catherine said.

A strange look came over Lola's face. Courage was there and resolution.

"I've been trying all along to tell you that there isn't any danger," she said, speaking clearly and with firmness. "And we both know I've been lying. It's a hard trip, and all sorts of things can happen. They have happened. But—well, I've lived out here long enough not to expect things to be safe and sure. All I want is strength enough to stand up to them when they ain't easy, or even safe. I couldn't let you go without telling you this," she finished simply. "I thought I could, but now I know I couldn't."

"I know," Catherine said thickly. "I know about—about those things ahead. And I'm not asking for—for anything more than you ask for."

"Then you'll make it," Lola said. "You'll make it . . ."

Catherine got on the wagon seat. Ned crawled up beside her. She cracked the whip over the horses' backs. The wagon began to move.

"Good-by," she said. She drove forward a little. "Good-by," she called again. "And thank you—oh, thank you."

Her voice floated back, across the distance that was widening between them.

"Good-by," Ned called.

Lola Hardy stood watching them go, the two little boys beside her. Twice Catherine looked back and she was still standing there, exactly where she had been when they left. The last thing Catherine saw before the turn in the road hid the place was Lola Hardy, standing there watching. The little boys had gone back to their play, but she was there. She must have sensed that Catherine had turned to look, for she took off her apron and waved it.

That was the last Catherine saw of her—a woman in the dun distance, waving her apron.

# CHAPTER 9

CATHERINE DROVE ON. WHERE FOR DAYS SHE HAD BEEN TRAVELING WEST, STRAIGHT INTO THE FACE OF THE AFTERNOON SUN, NOW SHE angled southwest. She liked this—it made her feel she was cutting off corners and so, shortening the journey.

As Lola had warned her, this was rough and desolate country. She did not mind overmuch; she had fortified herself with courage and companionship as well as food and water. Things Lola had said kept coming back to her—small things, but ones to hold to.

*You aren't the kind that turns back. . . . I don't ask for things to be safe and sure—all I want is strength to meet them.*

The woman's words were like a tune to march by.

"Mama," Ned said, "we're getting closer to Papa every day, aren't we?"

"Indeed we are, darling. Every single day."

The first night she made a dry camp by herself. She did not even need a fire—Lola had packed food sufficient, and more, for the day. She drew water from the barrels and gave the horses their portion; she staked them out to graze beside the wagon. Then she went inside and pulled down the canvas flap. After she had lain down, she reached up to touch the gun, drew comfort from the solid coolness of it. Perhaps she could not hit what she aimed at, but at least she knew how to load, how to aim, how to fire. The sound of her gun need not betray her lack of skill.

For a while she lay there thinking she could not possibly sleep, but by and by she dropped off. She woke up several times during the night, alert and listening. When morning came, she felt rested and triumphant. She had passed the night alone, and she had done so without the terror that had been hers on other similar occasions. This morning she was a little stronger than she had been the day before. A little stronger, and a little nearer her destination. Once she was on the road she began to sing. Ned joined her. And so they traveled on, leaving a trail of song behind them.

It was as if Lola had sent her blessings along with them as well as her courage and her strength, willing that good fortune should accompany them. When Catherine reached the Salt Fork of the Arkansas River, there was a wagon waiting to cross.

It was an old wagon and the team hitched to it was thin and bony. Catherine's first thought was that all those children —there must have been eight of them—could not belong to one wagon.

A man came up to her.

"Howdy, ma'am." He looked at her doubtfully. "You and your little boy traveling alone?"

"Yes," Catherine told him.

"My name's Jule Graham, and this here is my wife. Dulcey, step up and meet the lady."

Dulcey came around the corner of the wagon. She was rail-thin and tired looking. All the lines in her face sloped downward; even her hair, parted in the middle and scalloped around her forehead, carried out the same descending motif. It was hard to guess her age—she might have been anywhere from thirty to fifty.

"Howdy," she said.

"Hello," Catherine said.

"And these are the kids—Bub, Henry, Maggie, Lily . . ."
He called off the names and they looked at her with solemn
shyness, either too timid to acknowledge the introduction, or
feeling it was not necessary to do so. The one named Lily, however, grinned at Catherine and Ned, her head hanging down
a little, tangled brown curls falling around her face.

"Hello," she said.

"Hello," Ned answered her and walked to where she stood.

"How old are you?" he asked.

"Almost five."

"I'm almost five," Ned told her proudly.

"Look how them two have made up," Jule Graham said
with pleased complacency. "That Lily, now, she's different from
our other kids. Never sees a stranger." Dulcey's eyes gleamed
with a bright, engulfing pride.

Jule turned back to Catherine.

"We are just a-fixin' to cross the river," he said. "My boy
Bub would be proud to drive your wagon acrost if you want."

Catherine hesitated.

"Now, don't be scared to have him do it. He's fifteen, and
strong for his age, and he's driven us acrost many a river since
we left Indianny. It's kind of hard for a woman to get a team
acrost a stream."

"Oh, I wasn't afraid of his driving," Catherine assured
him hastily. "I didn't want to be any trouble to you."

"No trouble at all," he assured her gallantly. "People jest
naturally have to help each other in these parts. Bub, come
drive the lady's team. You kids—crawl back into the wagon
now—we're about to roll."

Catherine looked at their wagon. It was nothing more
than a shell—like an autumn leaf, or a locust's cast-off skeleton.

She looked at the children—eight of them, counting Bub. How could the wagon possibly carry the load! What if it came apart in the middle of the stream?

"Why don't you let some of the children ride with us awhile," she suggested. "They'd be company for Ned."

"Well, that's real kind of you," Jule Graham said, making no objections at all. Dulcey looked at Catherine quickly, on her tired face something like relief.

Bub, snub-nosed, shy and barefoot, mounted to the wagon seat, took the lines in his hands. Once this was accomplished, he became a man—confident, sure of himself, capable. Five of the children including Lily got into Catherine's wagon. They settled down like little quail, scarcely seeming to breathe—as if only in this way would the wagon be able to bear their weight. Catherine felt that they had done this ever since they left Indiana—had helped, with their own deep wishing, to pull their rickety wagon across the hills and streams.

They crossed the river—left its blue line behind them. They continued, traveling south by west, two plodding blobs of whiteness etched against the sky. Catherine continued to keep some of the children in her wagon. And always she felt, even though they were with her, they were helping their own wagon across each difficulty which came to it. And always when the hill was steep, they rolled out as of one accord in order that they might walk and save the horses.

At night they camped together. Catherine had first thought that she would cook extra food and give the children a real meal for once. And then something stopped her—a look of inviolable pride on their faces. She wound up by cooking less than usual for Ned and herself. She could not offer the Grahams charity, nor could she enjoy her own meal knowing they were hungry.

"We're stoppin' here in the Strip," Dulcey said. "We don't

have far to go. We'll put in a crop—we'll be getting there in good time. They say the soil is mighty rich."

"The Strip," Catherine said. The Cherokee Strip. The Grahams would leave her, and she would drive on, alone, into country that only recently had echoed to the war whoops of Indians. "That used to be Indian country you know," she said.

Dulcey Graham looked at her keenly. "You're scared of Indians?"

"Oh, a little—maybe," Catherine admitted reluctantly.

"Well, you needn't be. They ain't free to bother you— they've all been put on reservations."

Almost Lola's exact words.

"Do you suppose," the woman went on kindly, "that we'd settle there if we thought there'd be trouble with them?"

She's trying to help me, Catherine thought. She's trying to give me courage to go ahead with what I must do. And she felt a great rush of tenderness for this thin drab woman.

"Oh," Catherine said, "I don't know about that. I think you'd go ahead and do it, no matter how dangerous it was. You're not the kind that scares easy."

The woman's sallow face flushed with pleasure.

"Well, a body can't give up," she said stanchly. "And that's sure."

A body can't give up, Catherine thought. And was ashamed of her fears.

They drove on, Bub still holding the lines. They crossed the Cimarron.

That night when they camped, Jule Graham said,

"Well, in the morning we leave you—taking off due west. You can make it to Camp Supply by night, if you keep driving."

"I'll keep driving," Catherine assured him. "I don't like camping out by myself. I'll certainly miss you people."

"Oh, pshaw, we've been just real proud to have you," he told her.

They were going about the business of breaking camp the next morning when Ned came to Catherine.

"Mama," he said, "today is Lily's birthday. And she says she's never had a cake, and she doesn't know what a birthday party is. Mama, can't we have a party for Lily?"

Catherine looked at Lily, standing with the toes of her left foot hooked around her right ankle, peeping out from a shock of tangled hair like a small wood sprite. A terrible kind of wishing was on her face but pride was there, too. She would not ask for this thing, even though with all her heart and soul she wanted it.

"Mama, can't we have a birthday party before Lily leaves?" The wish on Ned's face was almost as ardent as the one on Lily's.

Catherine hesitated. If she went on now, right now, she could make Camp Supply by night.

"She's never had a birthday party," Ned reminded his mother.

Something gave way inside Catherine—she did not know whether it was Lily's great wish or Ned's that moved her.

"Why of course, honey," Catherine said. "If Lily's folks aren't in a hurry, we'll have a birthday party for her."

"Now see here," Jule Graham broke in, "you hadn't ought to fool with this party. If you go on now, you can make Camp Supply by evening. No need for you to spend the night on the road just to wait to give a kid a party."

Catherine hesitated. Of course he was right—it was foolish for her to delay when she could so easily make a wagon yard by night if she started at once. She was almost ready to drop the idea altogether when she happened to look at Dulcey Graham.

The wish the child had shown was nothing compared with that mirrored on the woman's thin face now. All her frustrations were there, and her hopes, and the great dreams a mother has for her children. She was thinking that maybe—sometimes in ways quite foreign to her understanding—things will be better for them than they have been for her. Lily's disappointment, should the party fail to materialize, would be a fleeting thing, something time would heal. Dulcey's would represent just one more burden added to what must already seem, at times, too great to be borne. The woman said nothing; she simply stood there, patient and enduring, making no demands of Catherine, as she had made no demands of life.

"I've camped out before," Catherine heard herself saying, "and it won't hurt me to do it again. I'm going to have a party for Lily."

Whatever reluctance Catherine might have felt vanished at the look of gratitude Dulcey Graham gave her.

And now that she was committed to the party, Catherine began to think of ways she might achieve it. A cake. Could she bake one in a dutch oven? She could try. Candles? At the last minute she could light matches and set them upright in the cake. A gift? Here she could enlist the aid of Dulcey, who wanted humbly to be of help. Between them, the two women could fashion a doll of sorts out of the scraps of cloth Aunt Mae had put into the mending box.

"You children go gather some flowers," she said, mostly to get them out from under foot. "Fix a little table out of a box and put the flowers in a vase. Wash your hands and comb your hair." She gave them a list of errands. And then to Dulcey, "Now you can help me, if you will."

It was almost noon when Catherine finally drove away. The party had been all anyone could have wished. Ned, his face very clean, had presented a quite passable doll to Lily while all the other Grahams, so happy it was almost past enduring, looked on. Then Catherine carried in the cake—a little flat and lopsided but a real cake with match-candles sputtering bravely.

"Oh—" Lily let out her breath in one great, glorious sigh. "Oh—" the other Grahams, no less delighted, joined her.

"Happy birthday to you . . ." Ned sang, off key—a matter which bothered him very little and the Grahams not at all. This accomplished, Ned said to Lily, "Now, you cut it."

Lily was so overcome she could not move. She stood there, her eyes fixed on the cake as if it were a product of her fond imaginations and would vanish if she so much as lifted a finger.

"Say 'thank you,'" Dulcey Graham prompted her daughter, scarcely able to speak herself so great was her happiness at the sight of the child's delight.

Lily still could not speak. Her silence, however, was a greater tribute than any words could have been.

Catherine held the knife toward her. "Do you want to cut it?" she asked. "Or do you want your mother to?"

"I want to," she said. She took the knife, she brought it down through the cake. Then she stopped. She looked at Catherine. She dropped the knife and ran to her. She put her arms around Catherine's knees. "I've had a cake," she said. "*You made me a cake.*" And then the words came. "Thank you," she said.

All that afternoon Catherine traveled through broken country—hills and small streams stretched on every side. A

profusion of scrub oak grew on both sides of the trail. She
pushed the team ahead, knowing as she did so that it would
be impossible to reach Camp Supply before dark even with
the days as long as they were now in early June. Because of the
birthday party, she must spend the night on the road. Remembering Lily's happiness and the even greater joy that had been
Dulcey's she could not feel too regretful.

She began to watch for a suitable place to stop, saw one
before too long. Ashes of dead campfires—always an encourag-
ing sign—proved that others before her had used this spot. She
pulled off the trail into a little clearing that ran down to a small
stream. Water was there and the grass was good and wood was
available for the campfire.

"Mama," Ned said, "I want to go down to the little creek."

"After while, Ned. I'll take you down. You play around
the wagon until supper's ready."

His face showed his disappointment.

"Look," she said, "there are some pretty little flowers growing at the edge of the clearing. Why don't you gather them so
we'll have a bouquet on our supper table?"

He went off, content enough with her suggestion, and she
set about making camp. This done, she took off her bonnet
and half-handers, laid them on the ground beside the wagon,
began to prepare a meal. The breeze ruffled her hair. The little
stream lapped lazily against the bank. A bird started to sing.
Once or twice she raised her eyes, saw Ned playing contentedly.
Presently she had supper ready and called him. He came, carrying a small bunch of flowers.

"Go wash your face and hands," she said, taking the flowers. "Supper's ready."

He obediently went to the washpan, then came back and
sat down beside her. She handed him his plate.

The food tasted good—she began to eat immediately. Then she realized that Ned was not even tasting his meal.

"What's the matter?" she asked. "Don't you like your supper, honey?"

"I—I don't feel so good," he said thinly.

Catherine put her plate down, looked quickly at the child. He did look sick. He was pale and his little mouth was outlined with a ring of perspiration.

"Where does it hurt?" she asked.

"Here—in my stomach."

"Let me see your tongue . . ."

He stuck out his tongue. It, as well as the inside of his mouth, was brightly purple.

"Ned," she asked sharply, "what have you been eating?"

"Just those little berries—they looked so pretty. Oh, Mama, I'm sick."

He ran to her, crying. She gathered him into her arms, panic overtaking her. Those little berries! This went beyond the ordinary sicknesses which had come to Ned on the trip— the little stomachaches and colds that were to be expected, and against which she had fortified herself with remedies before leaving Missouri. This was—she faced the word. This could be *poison.*

Frantically she tried to recall the antidotes for such cases. By now Ned was in real distress, his little face contorted with pain. Perhaps if she could induce vomiting he might be relieved. Della's method had been warm soda water.

"There, there, darling," she told him. "Mama's going to give you something to help you."

She grabbed a quilt from the wagon, spread it on the ground.

"Lie here, honey," she said.

He lay down. She ran to the cook box, got some soda,

measured it into a cup. She poured a little hot water from the pan on the campfire, put cold into it until, testing it with her finger, she thought it was the right temperature. She ran to Ned, put the cup to his lips, her hands shaking so that some of the liquid spilled over him, down on the quilt.

"Here, honey, drink this."

He took a sip.

"It tastes so bad . . ."

"Never mind, try to drink it. That's my fine big boy."

He tried. The cup was only half empty when he sagged against her, began to retch violently.

She gathered him into her arms, wiped his face with a damp cloth.

"Feel better?" she asked.

"I hurt," tears were rolling down his little cheeks.

The soda water had not helped. What could she do now? Somewhere she had heard—or thought she had heard—that lard was effective in such cases.

She put the child back on the pallet, ran once more to the cook box. In a moment she was back with a spoonful of lard.

"See if you can swallow some of this, darling," she pleaded.

Ned took some. He really tried to swallow it, but could not.

"Try," Catherine urged, terror sweeping over her. "Try!"

"No!" Ned screamed. Her panic had communicated itself to him now.

Catherine did not know what made her look up. Certainly it was not noise, for there had been no sound at all. It was, rather, the consciousness of something more terrifying than Ned's condition, fearful as it was. She turned her head a little, and the thing she saw brought an involuntary scream to her lips.

There, almost directly behind her, stood an Indian.

He had on a pair of ragged pants, a filthy, tattered shirt,
its tail hanging outside the pants. A black felt hat, the crown
uncrushed, sat straight on his head and from under it two long
black plaits of hair hung across his shoulders. Back of him was
his horse, a bony, mangy-looking animal. Both horse and Indian
were perfectly immobile.

An Indian! Her mother had warned her. Lola, in her way,
had also tried to prepare her. They were supposed to be on the
reservation, but occasionally they got off and when they did
they sometimes vented their hatred against the white people
who had put them there. This one had got away. And even in
her terror, she could see the spark that glowed in his black and
piercing eyes, recognized it for what it was—real dislike for her.
She drew Ned close to her in a convulsive movement of protection.

"Him sick?" the Indian asked.

"Yes," she said, almost in a whisper. "He ate some berries
—I didn't know—he was down at the creek."

Surely even he would be moved by the illness of a child,
an illness as grave as this.

Without a word he melted away into the bushes. So quietly
he left that Catherine, but for the presence of the bony horse
still standing where the Indian had left him, might have felt
she had dreamed up the whole thing.

She put aside the spoon of lard. It was no use—Ned would
not take it. She sat there holding the child, wondering what
to do next, when another light noise made her turn and there
was the Indian back once more. He had some sort of roots in
his hands. These he threw into a pan sitting by the campfire.
He poured some water over the roots, put the pan over the fire.

The firelight glanced across his face. It was hard and in-
scrutable—like a carving made out of wood. He looked up,

caught Catherine's eyes on him, and returned her glance with a smoldering, arrogant look.

"He's ragged and old and dirty," she thought. "And yet he feels superior to me."

"Eat?" she said, pointing to the food spread out—her own supper which she had barely tasted.

"Huh," he grunted.

Ned began to twist about in her arms once more. The pain was apparently growing worse.

"It hurts," he screamed. "Mama, Mama—I'm sick."

"Honey, honey—" she tried to soothe him.

There was castor oil in the medicine chest, and paregoric. Perhaps the paregoric.

She put the child down on the pallet, ran to the wagon. When she came back with the paregoric and a spoon, there was the Indian at Ned's pallet, a cup in his hand. He bent over, put his other hand under Ned's head, lifted the child.

"Drink," he said.

Catherine ran to them. "No," she cried, remembering the smoldering look of hate on the Indian's face. "No!"

"Drink," the Indian repeated, as if she were not there at all.

Catherine knelt by the child on the pallet. She had some sort of crazy notion of grabbing the cup away, dashing its contents on the ground. She even reached out her hand, making the first motions. The Indian looked at her—a cold, quiet look. He had not moved a muscle, he did not say a word. And yet Catherine felt he had willed her to stop, had broken down her own impulse with the stronger, better one of his own.

Ned's dying, Catherine thought. How will I tell Edward. *Edward—our baby's dying. It's my fault. I didn't watch him— Forgive me, Edward . . .*

Tears streamed down her face. She took one of Ned's

limp little hands in her own, sat holding it. The Indian did not speak, did not even seem to notice her. When the last drop was gone from the cup, he laid Ned back down on the pallet, got up and walked over to the campfire and squatted there on his haunches.

Catherine took Ned in her arms. The child was a dead weight against her. The Indian threw a piece of wood on the fire. Then he took something from his pocket—a dark brown, strangely dry-looking substance—and began to chew on it. He might have been a rock or a tree or a bit of scrub oak for all the noise he made or word he said. Behind him the bony horse bent its head to graze.

Ned shuddered. This is the end, Catherine thought.

She held him tighter, dropped her face against his head.

The child grew quiet. His eyes were closed. For one awful moment Catherine's own breath ceased to come. And then she saw the front of his little blouse rise and fall—rise and fall. He was breathing. Naturally, easily.

It may have been an hour—it might have been a lifetime that passed. Catherine sat, still holding the child. The Indian sat, too, now and then replenishing the campfire. Finally, he got up, walked over to Catherine. He looked down at Ned.

"Good," he said.

As quietly as he had come, he walked over to the horse, mounted and rode off into the night.

Catherine continued to sit with Ned in her arms. He did not move; his sleep seemed peaceful and untroubled by pain. She felt his pulse; it was regular. His skin was cool. She got up, still holding the child, and carried him to the wagon. She put him to bed, left him long enough to make things safe for the night. This accomplished, she ran back to the wagon, lay down beside him.

Then reaction set in for her. She began to shake; she could

not stop. The bed under her, the very wagon itself seemed to rock. Tears ran down her cheeks. She let herself cry—why not? And by and by she grew calmer. After that, she dropped off into a half sleep.

She was awakened the next morning by the sound of Ned's voice. He had not spoken a whole syllable before she was sitting upright, looking at him.

"Mama," he said. "I'm hungry."

"Honey," she cried. "How do you feel?"

"Fine," he told her.

She looked at him, searching for signs of last night's ordeal. There were circles under his eyes, and he was a little pale around the mouth. But there was little evidence of the ravages one might expect from the experience he had undergone.

"I'm hungry," he told her again.

"You shall have something to eat, soon as ever Mama can fix it," she promised.

She boiled him an egg, watched with delight while he ate it. She was surprised to find how hungry she was herself. As soon as breakfast was out of the way, she finished the chores, hitched the team to the wagon. Then she turned to look for her bonnet and half-handers.

They were gone.

She searched the camp, even looked in the wagon. They simply weren't there. They could have blown away—no, there had been no wind last night. And then she remembered.

"They're a dirty, thieving lot," Lola had said.

The Indian had taken them. He had seen them lying there, was attracted by them, and had carried them off.

He didn't have to steal them, she thought. I'd have given them to him if he had only asked me.

The thought of his picking up the articles, small as they

were, made her feel uncomfortable. She was grateful to him—oh, how grateful she was. But she still wished he hadn't stolen from her. It gave her a shivery feeling just to think of those dark hands reaching out, taking what they wanted.

What would he have wanted with them? she wondered. And then she thought, Probably for his squaw.

That made her feel a little better. She had a quick vision of a dark face looking out from the bonnet Aunt Mae had sewed so carefully, of dark fingers encased in the matching half-handers.

"Even so, I wish he had asked for them," she said, half-aloud.

"What did you say, Mama?" Ned asked.

"I said I would have to get me a fresh bonnet and a pair of half-handers out of the trunk before we left," she told him.

She felt she couldn't get out of this place fast enough.


She pulled into Camp Supply in mid-morning. At first she thought she would stay here only long enough to have the team and wagon checked, buy some needed supplies and ask information concerning the road ahead. According to her own reckoning she was a little less than two weeks away from Mobeetie. An excitement took over at the thought, an eagerness.

She turned to look at Ned, sleeping on the pallet in the wagon. He still looked a little pale, but that was no more than natural. He had slept much of the morning; of course, that was good for him, but still she was not entirely easy about him.

The wagon attendant came to her.

"Howdy, ma'am," he said. "Unhitch your team for you?"

"I'm not sure—I may go on in a few hours. I wonder if there is a doctor close by."

"Yes, ma'am, Doc Langley. Office right across the street. You sick?"

"My little boy was—well, he's been sick. I thought I might like the doctor to check him before I went on."

"If you'll go across to his office, I know Doc can help you. He's a mighty good doctor, and that's a fact. Your little boy does look a bit peaked, if you ask me."

Catherine's mind was made up. She'd take Ned to the doctor.

Catherine, wearing a good dress, a hat and gloves and her locket around her neck led Ned, also dressed in his best, across the street to the doctor's office. She opened the door and walked in. A voice from the back of a partition called, "I'll be there in a minute. Just sit down."

She and Ned took chairs and presently a man walked out. He was short and limped a little and looked tired. But his eyes were keen and alert—the eyes of a kindly man, an understanding one.

"I'm Dr. Langley," he said. "Did you want to see me?"

There was a certain brisk astringent quality in his voice—the speech of a man who dealt mostly with the great realities of life and death and had little time, and less patience, for any pretenses in between.

"Yes," Catherine told him. "I'm Mrs. Delaney. My little boy, Ned—" she hesitated, not quite knowing how to go on.

"Yes," Dr. Langley encouraged her. He inclined his head to listen, his face patient and interested.

"He ate some berries," Catherine began.

And then she found herself telling him the whole story—the strange story she scarcely believed herself. About the berries, and the remedies she used, and the Indian who came out of nowhere and saved Ned's life.

The doctor let her talk on, as if each word she said was an important symptom.

"I don't know what sort of berries he ate," she said. "I never thought to check. I was too frightened."

"Could have been any one of a half dozen kinds that would have produced those results," he told her. "There's no way of telling now."

"Anyway, I thought before I went on I wanted a doctor to check him and see if he is all right."

"Good idea." He turned to Ned. "What you say, young fellow, if we just go back here and have a look."

He performed the examination with care, poking and probing Ned's small stomach and then asking a few questions. Finally he looked at Catherine. "Seems all right," he said. "At least, as far as I can tell. Might be a good idea to let me have a look at him before you leave. Where did you say you were going?"

"Mobeetie," Catherine told him, not mentioning that she had not, as yet, told him anything about her destination.

"Driving through?"

"Yes."

"In that case I'd certainly like to have one more look. When did you plan to leave?"

"As soon as you think it advisable."

"Suppose I check this evening, and then if he's all right— and I'm sure he'll be—you can start in the morning. In the meanwhile, I'll give you some medicine for him."

"That stuff the Indian gave him," Catherine said. "I still don't understand . . ."

"Oh, they have an amazing knack for healing," Dr. Langley told her. "Especially the older ones. The younger ones are beginning to lose that skill, along with a lot of other things their ancestors once possessed."

"I was scared to death," Catherine admitted. "He was so

dirty, and so—well—menacing. He looked at me as if he hated me. His eyes simply smoldered."

"He probably did hate you. No, not you, exactly, but the race you represented. We haven't done too much for his people, you know."

"Then why would he want to help Ned? For he did help him. Ned would have died if the Indian hadn't given him the tea. I feel sure of that."

"And you are probably right. Why did he do it? Because Indians are very fond of children. His kindness to Ned, like his dislike for you, was an abstraction."

Catherine smiled. The doctor had put her at ease; he was helping her to make some sense out of the thing that had happened. She wanted to tell him, also, about the sunbonnet and half-handers.

"I would have given them to him," she finished. "I would have given him anything he wanted, if he had only asked. Why did he have to—well, steal them?"

"To him it wasn't stealing," Dr. Langley told her. "They were just lying there for the taking. He was an old Indian. Before he was put on the reservation that was the pattern of his life—taking the things that nature put before him. To him, carrying off those things wasn't any more stealing than it was to take the roots he needed to save your child's life. Do you understand?"

"Yes," Catherine said. She did. Dimly, but after a fashion. It was as if another milestone in her growth had been reached. She had overcome one more aversion, had reached out toward one more understanding.

"White men make strange distinctions," Dr. Langley mused. "They take land from the Indian, which was his home. They take the buffalo, which was his food. But worst of all, they take his freedom—his right to roam the land he still considers his. That is the greatest theft of all, but the white man thinks nothing of it. Then let the Indian reach out and take something—even a small thing—and in the white man's lexicon, that's stealing."

"Thank you for talking to me as you have," Catherine said. "I feel better now. I didn't want him to steal. He was so —well, so dignified," her voice trailed off, and she looked at Dr. Langley uncertainly. "And so sad."

"And well he might be," the doctor assured her. "He and his kind, they are all children of despair. It is to their great credit that they bear their condition with dignity rather than with self-pity."

He got up briskly, went behind the partition once more. In a short while he was back with a bottle of medicine.

"Give him a teaspoon of this every two hours. Keep him as quiet as possible. I'll look in on him before bedtime."

The interview was at an end. Catherine paid him and she and Ned walked out of the office.

The doctor, true to his promise, came to the wagon yard that afternoon. He checked Ned again.

"He's all right," Dr. Langley told Catherine. "Just see that he eats lightly for a few days and gets plenty of rest." And to Ned, "You feel all right, don't you?"

"Sure," Ned told him. "I feel fine."

The doctor looked curiously at the wagon and then at Catherine.

"Are you and the little boy traveling alone?" he asked.

"Yes," she said, knowing she should not bother him with explanations.

"Uncle Willie started with us," Ned piped up. "But he got killed."

The doctor looked at Catherine keenly.

"Where?" he asked.

"In Caldwell—we had come from Missouri. He was in an accident. He saved a woman from being trampled by a runaway team."

It was good to be able to speak so proudly of Uncle Willie.

"And you decided to come on—alone."

"Yes, my husband is in Mobeetie. He couldn't come for me, so I am going to him."

The doctor regarded her for a long moment.

"Mrs. Delaney, I think that, above all other qualities in man or woman I most admire gallantry. May I tell you that I consider you a truly gallant woman."

"Thank you," Catherine said. "I must admit I do not feel at all gallant. Most of the time I am just—well, just scared."

"And yet you go on."

"Yes."

"That is what I mean by gallantry. Good evening, ma'am, and a safe trip to you."

He turned and walked out of the wagon yard, very fast, before Catherine could ask how much she owed him.

It rained that night. The sound of it was a steady pit-pat on the wagon top. There was thunder and lightning. Catherine, who was afraid of both, found that she must quiet her own fears in soothing Ned's.

"Why, honey, don't be afraid of thunder and lightning. It's just a big light and a big noise—like fire crackers on the Fourth of July."

This from Catherine Delaney, who had used to crowd close to Edward during even a minor storm—cowering at each crash, wincing at every flash of fire across the sky.

Now, in reassuring Ned, she grew quiet herself and slept.

When she woke up the next morning the rain had ceased, but the sky was still overcast. The wagon canvas over their heads was a soggy transparency. She dressed, dug out Uncle Willie's old slicker for herself, made Ned don warm clothes. She went inside the shelter house to cook breakfast.

"How's your little boy this morning?" a woman asked.

"He's better, thank you."

"Tell you what. I've got an extra lot of beans cooked up and I'm going to give you some. It ain't always easy to stop along the road and cook beans. I got more than I need."

"Thank you," Catherine said. "You're very kind."

"Your team's ready," the boy told her when she came out of the shelter house. "Everything's in fine shape. I checked."

"Thank you," Catherine said again, thinking how often she had need for gratitude on this trip.

"You say you are going to Mobeetie?"

"Yes."

"You head straight south from here—it's a good, open trail. You'll cross Wolf Creek, but that won't give you no trouble. Four, five days—depending on the rate you drive—you'll come to the Canadian . . ."

"Yes, I know," Catherine interrupted him. She did not want him to add his warnings to those she had already heard. She'd wait till she got to that treacherous river before she tried to solve the problem of how to cross it. A day at a time—that was the way she must travel. A day at a time . . .

"Hope your little boy gets along all right."

"He will. The doctor says he'll be fine. You've been good to me, and I thank you."

"Nothing at all, ma'am. It was a pleasure to have you. If ever you come back this way, be sure to stop with us."

"Thank you. I will."

She paid him, got up on the wagon seat. By now the sun was struggling to come out; the day might be a good one after all.

"Good-by," she said, and drove out into the street.

The rain had washed the whole world new and clean. There was a zest in the air, a winelike quality. She drove on, past the inevitable saloons. A man on a mud-spattered horse had reined up in front of one of them. He turned to watch her as she drove up even with him; she had the vague notion that she had seen him somewhere before. She turned to look at him, and when she did so he looked away quickly.

His profile turned toward her had a disturbingly familiar look. The quickly averted glance. The little mustache. The nose, sitting slightly aslant on his otherwise ordinary face. The nose!

And then she knew. It was the man whose appearance she had liked so little back in Caldwell, at the time of Uncle Willie's death. What was it the men had called him? Thad—?

A sense of foreboding came over her. She tried to put it from her. Perhaps he had not even noticed her; even if he had, she did not need to feel it would mean any harm would come to her. She was going out of her way to imagine things.

"Mama," Ned asked, "does that man know us? He keeps looking at us."

She might as well face it. He had seen her and knew her, even as she knew him. Judging from the mud-spattered horse he had just ridden in, possibly from Caldwell. Lola said people made the trip all the time. If so, he would be more interested in the pleasures Camp Supply had to offer than he would be in following her, even if he recognized her.

Don't be ridiculous, she told herself.

"Does he know us, Mama?" Ned asked again.

"Oh, honey," she told the child, "he's just watching us the way he'd watch anybody passing by."

But in her heart she only half-believed the words.

# CHAPTER 10

THE DAY PASSED WITHOUT INCIDENT. THE COUNTRY WAS BEAUTI-
FUL, MADE FRESH AND LOVELY BY THE RECENT RAINS. FLOWERS
bloomed beside the trail. Birds sang from the branches of the
scrub oaks. The sky was brightly blue; the air was soft and
sweet. Surrounded by so much loveliness, Catherine began to
feel that her concern had been unwarranted and foolish. Just
because she saw a man she distrusted did not mean he would
follow her. Especially that he would follow her to do her harm.

Again she thought of Dr. Langley's words, ". . . a gallant
woman." And the memory of them made her feel ashamed of
her uneasiness.

She made a dry camp, went to bed early. Even though
she had convinced herself her fears were groundless, she had
the gun handy during the night, and at the sound of each
noise, no matter how faint, she was awake and alert. The next
morning found her hollow-eyed and weary, scarcely able to
stay awake in order to drive. But the trail was so well marked
she could not have missed it had she wanted to. Wheels of
freight wagons had cut deep dashes in the road as they went
to and from between Fort Elliott and Camp Supply. It came to
her that Edward had traveled this very road, and the thought
was sweet, bringing him very close to her.

"Let me drive, Mama," Ned begged. "I want to help."

"You help me, darling. I couldn't go on without you."

Nor could she. Not alone because he was companionship, although certainly he was that. But more because he was her need for courage, her strong defense against fear. Since she must keep him from knowing terror, she must first remove herself from it; he would feel secure only if she had that feeling in her own heart. Dangers she would have ridden into thoughtlessly, had she been alone, she now sized up with caution. Chances she might have taken by herself, she dismissed at once with him beside her. Yes, she was right. Without Ned the trip would have been impossible.

This day went better. She had seen the night through, had convinced herself of the groundlessness of her fears. Once or twice she saw wagons ahead of her, but she did not overtake them. By afternoon she lost sight of them entirely.

All day she had been traveling parallel to the course of a small stream—not close enough to see it except at intervals. But the line of trees following it and the broken land were refreshing to her eyes, reminding her of the gently rolling hills of home.

Ned seemed entirely well—apparently not even a trace of discomfort remained. Now she let herself think of that awful experience, there in the fading daylight. It seemed incredible that she, Catherine Montgomery Delaney, brought up in the gentle ways of Missouri, should have her child fall desperately ill in that lonely, distant spot and have relief come in the person of an Indian who hated her kind and whose race she, in turn, had been brought up to fear and discredit. For a brief, strange interlude their paths had crossed and each had taken from the other something desperately desired—she her child's life, he a gift doubtless destined for his squaw.

"Mama," Ned interrupted her thoughts, "let me gather some of those pretty flowers."

She stopped the wagon and helped him down, remembering how Uncle Willie had let the child gather flowers, ages ago. Then it was the delicate wild rose of Kansas or late blooming violets; now it was blossoms whose names she could not even pretend to guess.

As always, in remembering Uncle Willie, she tried not to blame herself too much for his death. She was beginning to be able to think about him now without the great pain she had felt at first. She held fast to the words she had spoken to comfort Ned,

"He loved us, and we loved him."

That night she came to what looked like a very good camping place. A stream was near by and trees and evidences to show that others before had used it—dead campfires, grass worn down. If people had been here, that meant they would come again. Perhaps later on in the evening she would have company; the thought added to the attraction of the spot.

Last night she had been too concerned to cook food worthy of the name—all day today she had traveled on without bothering much about eating. Both she and Ned were hungry; she would cook a good meal. She made the campfire, started preparations. She got out the beans the woman at Camp Supply had given her. Those she would heat. She would scramble eggs because Ned liked them. There was a can of peaches left from the box of fruit and preserves her mother had sent along—she'd open them. She'd make this a real feast.

"I was foolish," she told herself, "foolish indeed. To ruin a whole day and a night, worrying about something that didn't happen, couldn't happen."

That was one of the best meals they had eaten on the road.

"Here, Ned, eat another peach. Grandmother sent them with us, from Missouri."

She dawdled over supper, went to get herself another cup of coffee from the pot still heating over the campfire. She considered a second serving of beans, bubbling away in a tin pan, but put that idea aside in favor of a peach.

"Somebody's coming, Mama," Ned said.

Sure enough, there was the sound of a horse approaching. Catherine felt instant relief. She had told herself she did not mind camping alone, but nevertheless she was glad to know others would be near her.

She took another sip of coffee, and then suddenly she grew tense. That was a *single* horse approaching—one horseman, riding alone. Involuntarily, she turned to look back at the wagon where the gun hung. Then she relaxed.

This was a main traveled trail. The rider was probably on some errand to Mobeetie. Seeing her wagon, he would have no way of knowing that there was not a man inside—maybe several—armed with the gun without which no one traveled. A man riding alone would not dare to molest a wagon. Everything would be all right.

The sound of the horse's feet drew nearer. Prince and Lady, staked out to graze, raised their heads. Then Prince gave a neigh, a sound meant to welcome an approaching horse but it shattered the night air and Catherine's nerves as well.

And close upon the sound the man rode into sight.

Catherine saw him, and seeing, felt no real surprise. She had known he would come—all along she had known it. She had tried to talk herself out of the knowledge, but it had stayed with her all those miles since she had left Camp Supply.

It was the man named Thad.

She stood up.

"Let's go to the wagon, Ned," she said.

"But Mama . . ."

"Come on."

Together they started. But before they could get to it, the man rode close to them.

"Get into the wagon, Ned."

Some quality in her voice carried through to the child. He turned and without protest crawled up into the wagon.

"Hello," the man said. "What's the matter? Ain't you glad to see me?"

He wouldn't dare do anything to me, she thought. He'd be afraid—he's a coward. He'd have to be drunk or crazy or both before he'd try it.

He swayed a little on his horse. Oh, he was drunk all right—he was plenty drunk. All this time he had been in Camp Supply, getting drunker and drunker. It was only because he was so drunk that he had thought of following her.

"Can't you speak to a fellow?" he asked. He spoke thickly, slurring his syllables together.

She did not answer him, realizing the delicate balance of the moment. The man was a bully, and weak. His courage was born of drink; right now, he was enjoying the knowledge that he had frightened her. If she stood calm and collected, he might go off and leave her.

But the next moment, she knew this had been a false hope. He got off his horse, linked the reins through his arm and walked close to her.

"What do you want?" she asked. No trying to put on a pretense of bravery now. He knew she was afraid; he knew it and gloried in the knowledge.

"To see you, you little minx."

He laughed, apparently very much pleased with himself.

"I'd forgotten how pretty you were until I seen you, back there yesterday morning. I knew then I ought to come on and look you up. You must get awful lonesome, traveling alone. Come on now, give us a little kiss."

He reached toward her.

"Don't you touch me!" she said. She spoke very low, but her eyes blazed in her pale face, dark and terrible with something that went beyond fear. Even reeling drunk, he must have recognized it as a force not to be ignored.

"My, what a temper you've got," he said a little uneasily. "Ain't right for anyone so young and pretty. Now stop pretending you ain't glad to see me. You know you get mighty lonesome sleeping alone all the way."

She looked around her for some sort of weapon, wishing she were close enough to reach the gun. But if she got it, what could she do? Her hands were trembling so she could not hold it steady enough to convince him she meant business. She saw the wagon whip lying across the tongue. She reached, picked it up, held it gripped tightly in her hand.

"Don't you come near me," she said.

He stopped. The look in her eyes, as much as the weapon she held—perhaps more than the weapon—sobered him a little.

"Well," he said, "stop acting so high and mighty. I ain't really wanting you—not the way you're acting, anyway. I'd rather try to pet a she wildcat. What I really want is the money."

"The money—" the words fell from her lips quickly, too quickly. She had not said, "What money?"

"Yes, the money you got in that wagon. You never would have turned down the purse if you hadn't been carrying plenty with you. I've thought about that a lot since you left Caldwell. Now you get it, and quick."

Catherine's mind worked with a terrible clarity. This time he meant what he said. He would take the wagon apart, piece by piece if necessary, until he had found what he was looking for. She knew something else—he had taken Uncle Willie's purse; he had robbed a dead man. If he had done this, he would not stop short now of getting what he wanted.

With this knowledge came a hot and searing anger, and also, a great determination. He would not get the money she carried with her—the money which represented her and Edward's future. Not without a fight would he get it. And she knew, too, that here was danger. All those other things—the noises in the night, the fears, the terrors—those were but shadows, things to laugh at when dawn came. Here was a real menace—cold, ruthless, deadly serious.

"Get it for me," he said.

"All right," she told him.

She started toward the wagon.

"Just leave that—er—little switch on the ground," he ordered.

She dropped the whip, began to climb into the wagon.

"Now you're acting with some sense. I'll just pour me a cup of coffee while you're getting the money. You ain't very polite to visitors—haven't even asked me to have a bite to eat."

He walked over to the campfire, evidently much pleased with himself and the way things were going. He poured himself a cup of coffee, stood by the fire to drink it.

Catherine got into the wagon.

"What's that man want, Mama?" Ned asked, fear on his face, in his voice.

"Hush," she said.

She worked her way toward the back of the wagon. She laid her hand on the gun—the gun Uncle Willie had insisted she bring, the one Lola had taught her to handle. Almost it was as if they were on each side of her now, supporting her, helping her to put her trembling hands upon it. She moved to the rear of the wagon, crouched down with the gun across her knees.

"Get back of me, Ned," she said softly.

The child obeyed without question.

She lifted the gun, held it against her shoulder.

Just at that moment the man looked up from the cup of coffee he was drinking. Looked, to see the gun pointing straight at him.

"You little fool," he snarled. "Put that gun down. I'll go . . ."

He turned slowly, acted as if he meant to mount. Then suddenly he faced her, and now there was a gun in his own hand. He took a step toward her—a single step, his body silhouetted against the red coals of her campfire so that he was a figure of menace, of terror.

Catherine herself did not know how it happened. There was the roar of a gun—her gun. She saw the campfire go up in a spatter of sparks and flaming pieces of coals, like rockets exploding on the Fourth of July. There was a hiss of steam. She must have hit the coffee pot, sending its contents in all directions. There was a shattering sound of tin. That must be the pan of beans plastering the area with their searing heat. There was a yell of pain, and over it all a burst of oaths.

"You . . ." the man's words filled the air as he rolled off the list of names that, in his opinion, best fitted her. They were words with which she was entirely unfamiliar, but she did not fail to grasp their meaning, nonetheless. The man was beating at his clothes as he screamed at her, wiping his face. She had a hysterical desire to laugh, watching him scrape beans off his crooked nose, his whole face which was red now, and pain-distorted.

Her shot had missed him, but it had not missed its purpose. It had hit the campfire, spattering it over him, showering him with boiling coffee, with scalding hot beans, with searing bacon grease. She remembered the rabbit she had once spattered with sand and again she wanted to laugh.

She was a little more in possession of herself now. She realized that in her trembling, inept haste she had fired off both barrels of the gun—a single shot would not have created so much havoc. The man must know this—any minute he would have the worst of the mess scraped off, would start toward her. With shaking hands she broke her gun, reached for two more shells. Hastily she reloaded, put the gun back against her shoulder, holding it tight, trying to control her trembling.

She was conscious of Ned whimpering, but still staying behind her as she had told him to do. She was conscious of the horses—Prince and Lady—who, at the sound of the shot, had neighed wildly and lunged back on the ropes with which she had staked them. They were beginning to quiet down a little, but were still moving about nervously.

The man's hands were empty of the gun. He had dropped it to beat out the sparks that had flown up on his clothes, perhaps even lodged there; to scrape off the beans and the coffee grounds. Now that she had reloaded, she could fire at him again—he was unarmed. She would have no compunction about that any more than she would at shooting a mad dog. But if she fired again, the shot might go entirely wild. As things stood, he had no way of knowing she had not actually meant to shoot as she did. She decided to hold fire unless he started toward her.

"Get on your horse and leave," she told him, feeling that her words might come closer to the mark than any bullet she would fire. "If you don't, I'll shoot to hit next time."

She hoped she sounded convincing.

He looked directly at her, no sliding glance this time. She thought she had never seen a human face so twisted with evil

—the slanting nose was only a part of the distortion made greater by pain and hate and frustration and a dark engulfing evil. She trembled a little at the sight of him as she had not trembled before, even when he seemed most ready to carry out his threats.

"I'll fix you," he said. He spoke with a deadly, cold certainty. Instinctively Catherine tightened her grip on the gun. This time, he meant what he said. Pain had both sobered him and made him wild with anger and desire for revenge. He was dangerous now, as he had not been dangerous before.

He swung on his horse. He started off toward her team which was pulling nervously on their ropes. They neighed shrilly again at his approach, drawing back until the ropes were taut.

There was a flash of steel—Catherine saw a huge knife in his hands. Once, twice, the knife came down. Then both horses stood free, their ropes cut through.

He leaned forward. Horrified, Catherine saw him take his riding quirt, lash the horses—first one, then the other. Again he hit them with lightning-like swiftness. Prince and Lady, who had never known the cut of a whip before, were frenzied with pain and surprise. They began to run. He rode behind them, yelling as they went.

Catherine was conscious of Ned's screams: "Mama—Mama —he's driving Prince and Lady away . . ." She was conscious of the sound of horses' feet, running off into the night, dark now. And above all, she was conscious of her own terror, sharp and clear and not to be denied, rising up to engulf her.

Her first impulse was to jump out of the wagon, to start running after the team. It was all she could do to force herself to sit still, listening to them running farther and farther away, out into the blackness of the night. At last the sound of their running feet was swallowed up in the distance, and the only noise that came to her was the chirping of the birds in the trees under which they were camped; of the water, lapping the shore of the little stream.

And then Ned touched her hand—timidly, as if he was loath to break the trance that held her.

"Will the horses come back, Mama?" he asked. And then he began to cry. "How can we go on to Papa if they don't?" he sobbed.

From somewhere deep within herself, from some unsuspected reservoir of strength, she found the courage to answer him.

"Don't cry, Ned. By morning they'll be back."

He brightened up at once.

"And now," she told him, "you must go to bed. It's late."

"All right," he agreed. "And when I wake up, Prince and Lady will be back."

She did not answer that. She was glad he settled down almost instantly, beyond the need of comfort which she would find hard to give.

As for herself, she knew she could not sleep, should not sleep. There was no assurance that Thad would not come back. Having driven the horses off, he might have a wish to return, feeling that now he would be able to take his full revenge. This night she must keep watch, her gun handy. She would not even dare to get out of the wagon to replenish the camp-fire. Fortunately there was a moon—not full, but enough to enable her to see anyone who came too close to the wagon.

She put a warm coat over her dress. Then she sat down on the trunk inside the wagon, facing so that she could see out, her gun across her knees. Sitting there, she tried to size up the situation that confronted her.

The horses would not come back of their own accord. That was nothing more than a story to quiet the child. Thad

had driven them before him as he went. Even when he ceased to do this, as he probably would before long—for work horses could not keep the pace he set for them—even then they would have no instinct that would guide them back to this camp they had never seen before tonight. No, the horses were gone. That she must face.

She must face, also, the gravity of her situation. Horses were a mover's bulwark against disaster. Without them, the wagon was a ship becalmed, the people in it helpless as castaways on a desert island.

Not only was it a terrible thing that had come to her, but the location at which it had occurred could not well have been more unfortunate. Even if Thad had caught up with her that first night out of Camp Supply—when she had both expected and feared him—it would have been better. For there, she would have been closer to a place where another team could be bought. She would have paid for it, but even so, it would not have been impossible. She thought again of the money in the feather bed. Too bad some of it must go for a team now; but, at least, she had it. That much she had saved. With the thought, a measure of courage came to her, an ability to think a little more clearly.

Perhaps she could buy another team from some settler. But then she realized that she had seen no houses all this day. No, that was out. She was in lonely, sparsely settled country.

Her one salvation lay in the fact that this was a road which movers traveled, going to Texas; which freighters used on their way to Mobeetie; which Uncle Willie had said, cowboys rode back over after having delivered their herds to market. By tomorrow someone might happen along. Perhaps even people with an extra team to sell.

She discarded that hope almost as soon as it came to her. If people did come they doubtless would be kind, but they would have no extra team. Or, having one, they would need it themselves. The best she could hope for would be that someone would take word back to Camp Supply concerning her need. Then, a new team would be sent out to her. This however she must not expect too soon. Not tomorrow or even the next day. But in time, it would happen. She must believe that.

She and Ned were due for a session of camping here. Thank God there was enough water. She mentally checked supplies. She could hold out for days, if necessary. She would cook sparingly, watch every morsel. But more than the need for food was the one for courage. She must hold her own fears in check; she must be calm and strong.

She was aware of a curious sense of detachment, a numbness. Almost it was as if nature provided her own anesthetic to deaden the pain and terror she felt. She was not sleepy. Her ears were keenly alert to the slightest sound; her eyes saw clearly objects she would have overlooked on ordinary occasions.

All night she sat there, watching the stars wheel across the sky, feeling no cold, no real weariness. She saw the sky take on a pale light, watched it grow brighter until the first hint of day stained the east. Only then did she feel it was safe to lie down. She put the gun back on its peg, slipped into bed beside Ned who was still sound asleep.

Her first thought, when she jerked herself to a sitting position, was that she had overslept and must hurry to break camp. Then remembrance came to her and, with it, a wave of terror that refused to let go. She looked at the tree under which the horses had been staked, saw the blank bareness of it. She saw the dead campfire with the cooking things scattered all around the ground.

Ned sat up beside her. He rubbed his eyes. And then he, too, remembered.

"Is the team back, Mama?" he asked.

"No, dear."

"But Mama—*you said they would be back.*"

The child's accusation was a hard thing to bear. She shouldn't have told him that—not even to quiet him, she shouldn't. It was only delaying the hard, inevitable truth. Nothing was ever gained by refusing to face facts with children any more than with adults.

"I was wrong. Don't worry, though. We'll manage for another team. Maybe not today, but some time."

Now she was sure of what she said. Daylight had brought her courage. Besides, this time she had not promised the impossible. She would manage. The way was not yet clear; only the fact was sure.

"Come on," she said. "We'll eat breakfast, and then we'll go fishing. Won't that be fun?"

Ned was immediately cheerful once more. She went to inspect the damage done by her shot of last night.

The coffee pot was bent, but would still serve. The shot had not pierced it—had only upset it. The pan in which the beans had been cooking was peppered full of holes. She picked it up, sailed it across the bushes. She began to clear things away, making the place shipshape once more.

After breakfast she and Ned went fishing. The boy caught one scarcely larger than a minnow, but it served to divert his attention from their plight. Catherine cleaned and cooked it for his midday meal, and after he had eaten, suggested that he take his nap on a pallet under the trees. This he thought was an adventure.

Once he was asleep, a great unrest came over her. She knew she must keep busy—in that direction sanity lay. She dragged out bedclothes to air. She washed clothes, thinking of Lola as she did. She washed her hair.

The clothes were dry now, and she got out Aunt Mae's sewing box—found the scissors and thread and buttons the woman had packed for her so long ago. She began to sew on buttons, set patches, mend rips.

Slowly, slowly, the long day dragged on. Ned awoke from his nap, looked around eagerly.

"They haven't come back yet, have they?" he asked.

"No, honey, but don't worry."

And she wondered again, as she had done so many times during this day, where they were now—Prince and Lady, that strong and gentle pair who had brought her this far on the trip. They had grown to be real individuals to her. She knew ahead of time when Prince was going into a lazy spell, pulling less than his share, just as she knew that Lady, impatient with his shirking, would reach out and give him a warning nip. When she really needed them however, there had been no foolishness, no holding back. They had marched stanchly up the steep hills; and when they came to the Arkansas—the first stream too deep for walking across—they lifted their heads and swam, strong and sure and without hesitation. And there at the first when she had been awkward and inept, they had stood patiently while she harnessed and unharnessed them.

Now two good friends were gone, not just a team of horses.

But she must not let herself think about this.

"I'm going to cook supper now," she told Ned. "I'm hungry, aren't you?"

"I wish I had another fish to eat—"

"We'll get another one tomorrow—"

She set about preparing supper—mentally weighing each bite she cooked against the supply that was left. The meal was almost ready when she heard—or thought she heard—the sound of horses approaching.

She stood perfectly still, straining her ears toward the sound. She tried to tell herself she was mistaken—that she heard only what she so much wanted to hear. Then it came nearer. There was no mistake—there were horses, several of them, coming toward her. Again she listened, thinking to hear the creak of the wagon they would be pulling. Then it dawned over her that there was no wagon—just horses.

"Let's go to the wagon, Ned," she said.

The child followed her without question, but she could see that her own uneasiness had carried over to him. He never took his eyes off her. She started to reach toward the gun, and then at the look on his face let her hand drop. She sat still, every nerve tingling.

And then two riders came into sight—two men, each leading a horse. Catherine looked at them, wanting to believe what she thought she saw, afraid to believe it.

They rode closer.

"Mama—" Ned's voice was a cry of purest joy. "Oh, Mama —it's Prince and Lady. They *have* come back—"

"Hello," the men called. "Anybody home in that wagon?"

"Yes—" Catherine called. She worked her way to the back, looked through the opening.

"Hello," one of them said, seeing her. "Would these be your horses?"

"Yes—" she said again. She could not trust herself to say more. All the terrible hours she had passed through came back to her; all the fears of what lay ahead, fears she had tried to push back from her. It was strange that now, with the horses standing there before her, the danger past, the future once more secure—it was strange she wished only that she might break down and cry.

"Good. We thought they might be yours when we saw

the wagon here. Want us to water them and then tie them up for you?"

"If you would . . ."

Catherine got out of the wagon. No place for tears now, no time for them. Ned followed her. Once they were out of the wagon, the two men got off their own horses. One was very young, with dark close-cropped hair and the snub-nosed look of a boy. Even his mouth was young and boyish, his chin smooth. He squinted up his eyes a little, so that he looked like a child just up from a nap.

The other man was older, more thin and wiry. He had a bleached-out look—hair, eyes, clothes—so that he was one with the dunness of the country. There were lines in his face, etched in by wind and sun.

"Well," the older one said, "here they are. Looks like the bridles is torn up pretty bad, but I reckon your husband can fix that."

"I don't know how to thank you," Catherine said. Her voice was ragged and uneven. She was going to cry in spite of all she could do. And she mustn't. Not here, not now. "I mean, I don't know how to thank you—"

"Oh, that's all right. We found them grazing in a thicket five-six miles up the trail. We figured they would belong to someone camped around here, because there weren't no houses around. So we just decided to bring them on and look for the owners."

"Yes, they're mine," Catherine told them. And then she saw them looking at her campfire—at the coffee just coming to a boil, at the bacon sizzling in the skillet.

"Wouldn't you stay for supper with us?" she asked. "I was just getting ready to cook something. We'd love to have you."

"Well, ma'am, don't care if we do. It's hard, finding good grub along the road."

They took the horses off to make them secure. She set about finishing the meal. No need to be careful of supplies now. No need to skimp. Her hands moved with skill and swiftness. Everything went right. Before long she had things ready—coffee, flapjacks, bacon. She opened another can of fruit from her mother's supply, and one of preserves. These she had meant to save for Edward, but now she sacrificed them joyously to the great delight of the occasion. Prince and Lady, whom she had thought lost, were back once more. It was a wonder too great for believing.

"Supper's ready," she called to the two men.

They came toward her.

"Now, ma'am, that sure does look good," the older one told her. And then, remembering,

"But we ain't told you our names. I'm Cliff." It was the older one who spoke. "And this here is Scoop."

The boy grinned, blushing to the roots of his hair.

"I'm Mrs. Delaney," Catherine told them, handing each a full plate and a cup of coffee. "And this is my little boy, Ned."

"Pleased to meet you, ma'am," they made a duet of it.

They took the plates, sat down to eat. Ned got his and moved over by them. The one called Cliff reached out and roughed his hair. Ned grinned; he was enchanted with both of them.

They began eating. Catherine joined them, finding that she was hungry herself, very hungry.

"Where are you boys going?" she asked.

"Mobeetie."

Here it was, her help across the Canadian. Lola had been sure it would arrive. It had come even sooner than she had expected, but certainly not before it was needed. She said, trying not to let her wish show in her face, waiting for them to make the offer.

"Mobeetie—ah, that's where we are headed, too."

"Yes, we've been up to Dodge trailing a herd of cattle. Sort of drifting back to the ranch, now."

She had noticed that several times while they ate they looked toward the wagon. Finally the one named Cliff cleared his throat.

"I have to tell you, ma'am," he said, "that you gotta be awful careful about tying a team up at night. It was just luck we found 'em; they could have wandered off in some other direction. Now if your husband is sick, or something—and, well if he leaves it to you, just remember—"

Catherine was opening her mouth to tell them she didn't have a husband—not one with her, that was, when Ned broke in quickly.

"Mama did tie them. She tied them tight. But the man cut them loose."

"The man—" they repeated the words after him.

"Yes, he got mad because Mama shot at him."

"Shot at him?" Cliff echoed the words stupidly.

"Listen," Catherine said, "it was like this . . ."

She told them the story, bit by bit, piece by piece, trying to sort out the events so that they came in sequence, trying to make some order out of the blur of horror she had gone through. It was necessary to go back as far as Uncle Willie's death and the man who had come to bring the news with the others.

"You mean, you and the little tad have come alone from Caldwell?"

"Yes."

"Well I'll be danged," Scoop broke in, almost the first words he had uttered.

"And then he followed you?"

"Yes."

"And—er—bothered you."

"He was drunk," Catherine explained hastily. "He was crazy drunk—"

"Mama shot at him," Ned broke in, "and the beans flew all over him!"

There was laughter in camp, sudden and quick—saving laughter. When they came back to the subject, there was a little less tension in their voices. But there was, now, a great grimness, a cold questioning.

"He cut the team loose? You are sure they didn't just break their ropes because they was excited?"

"No. I saw him cut them loose. And then he whipped them. Otherwise they wouldn't have run. They're gentle. He whipped them and drove them off ahead of him."

"Well, the—the ornery skunk," Cliff finished lamely. He was apparently far from satisfied with the term he used.

"That's why it was so lucky you boys found them," she said. "I didn't know what I was going to do."

Yes, they admitted she was lucky.

"You know, we almost decided not to bring them on. Goes right hard for a man caught horse-stealing out here."

"It's God's mercy you did," Catherine told them.

"Well, we decided we better take the chance," Cliff said. "We never once dreamed you was a woman alone, here waiting for them."

They polished off their plates in silence. Something was on their minds—an idea, a matter of great import. They moved restlessly as if impelled by a single motive.

"The man who cut them loose," Cliff asked, clearing his throat, "what did he look like?"

She described him.

"Did you get his name?"

"They called him Thad, that's all I know."

"You seen him first in Caldwell, and folks there seemed to know him?"

"Yes," she said. And then, "Why? Do you know him?"

"No, ma'am, we ain't never seen him."

They continued to look at each other, meaning in their glances.

"Well, thank you for the supper, ma'am," Cliff finally said. He stood as he spoke and Scoop stood, too. Automatically, as if they both worked from a single decision. "We watered your team, and we fixed the bridles. Now, if you'll excuse us, we better be going."

"Yes," Scoop agreed, "we gotta be going. Good-by, kid," he said to Ned.

"Going—" Catherine repeated after them. She had assumed that, since it was night, they would camp near by. She did not know how much she had depended on this hope until now, when they announced their intentions of leaving. And she had been so confident that here were her guides across the Canadian, perhaps even into Mobeetie itself.

"Thank you for the supper," Cliff said again. "It was mighty good. We hate to eat and run, but we just remembered a little errand we got to take care of, back Caldwell-way."

"Yes, ma'am," Scoop said. "A real important errand."

Catherine looked at them. And then something came to her. They had said the errand was at Caldwell.

"But you were headed west," she told them, suspicion dawning in her mind. "You were going toward Mobeetie, not Caldwell."

Scoop shifted uneasily from one foot to the other. He looked at Cliff, nudging him with his eyes to make the answer.

"So we did," Cliff said innocently. "But we had forgotten. Now we gotta go back to Caldwell—or at least, up that way."

And suddenly she knew what the errand was, as clearly as

if they had named the nature of it. She knew, too, that they must not do this thing. It was for their sake she must try to dissuade them.

"Don't do it," she said.

They looked at her quickly.

"I mean, don't go back after him. He's not worth it."

They thought about the matter; she could see them turning it over and over in their minds. Finally Cliff spoke.

"He didn't ought to get by with it. That's the worst thing a low-down skunk could do—to drive off a man's team. Excuse me, ma'am, a *woman's* team."

"It's even worse than a *man's*," Scoop added.

"That's right, it is," Cliff agreed somberly.

"He ought to be shot for it. Shooting's too good for him."

"You may be right," Catherine agreed. "But you two are not the ones to do it. It wasn't your team. The law wouldn't take any excuse if you were caught."

"Oh, the law—" they dismissed the word with careless disregard as something which had neither threat for, nor appeal to, them.

"And you would get caught," she went on confidently. They would ride out after the man named Thad, counting it a kind of adventure. They would keep on until they found him, and once they did, they would dispose of him as carelessly as they now dismissed the law about which she had reminded them.

But the law would not dismiss them that lightly. She was sure of this, just as she was sure she could not let them go back and do the thing they had in mind. She would feel responsible —to the last day of her life she would feel responsible—not only for what came to them but for whatever vengeance they finally wrought on the man named Thad. Oh, he deserved it—

there was no question about it. But bringing him to justice was not a job for these two cowboys.

"You mustn't go back after him," she told them firmly.

They did not look at all convinced.

"You have no way of knowing where he went. He may even have doubled back, may be waiting for me farther down the trail."

They considered her words and for the first time she had the feeling that she was winning them over—against their will, against their inclinations. Pressing her advantage she went on hastily, "Instead of trying to find him, why don't you ride on to Mobeetie with me? I—it would mean a great deal to me to have company the rest of the way."

They looked at each other, considering the matter. She waited for their answer, every nerve in her body tingling with the great hope she had.

And as she waited, she thought, Isn't it strange? I'm not thinking of myself at all, now. It's for their sakes I want to take them on to Mobeetie instead of letting them go back to Caldwell.

Which was true. Earlier she might have begged—or wanted to beg—them to go with her along those last, hard, desperate miles. To help her across the Canadian, that treacherous, undependable river which stood between her and the end of her journey; between her and Edward. But now it was for their sakes she asked.

"Come on with me to Mobeetie," she begged. "Come go along with Ned and me. We need you."

They looked at her uncertainly.

"I couldn't cross the Canadian by myself and you know it," she reminded them.

That was her trump card; she played it without regret. It was the truth she spoke and they knew it.

"Well, ma'am," Cliff finally spoke. "Maybe you're right. Oh, I don't mean about letting him go, but about needing us to help you across the Canadian."

"Yes, ma'am," Scoop said, grinning shyly. "You'll need us there."

"And there ain't nary a cowboy between here and Dodge that knows the river better'n we do," Cliff bragged.

"There sure ain't," Scoop agreed.

"Then you'll go with me?" Catherine asked.

"We will. Early in the morning, off we start."

# CHAPTER 11

———◆———

THE LITTLE CARAVAN MOVED ALONG, BUT WITH A DIFFERENCE. WHERE ONCE THERE HAD BEEN ONE WOMAN AND A SMALL BOY IN a wagon, now there were two horsemen riding with them. Cliff and Scoop reined in their horses, accommodating them to the slower pace of Prince and Lady, who, either glad of company or happy at being back after their adventure, stepped along more briskly than they had done before.

Catherine, holding the lines loosely, wondered if she had really gone through all the dark days behind her or if she had dreamed them. Surely there had not been a time when she had driven the team, harnessed and unharnessed it as well, cooked the meals, and acted as a shield of fear between Ned and the hazards of the road. She had not, by herself, selected camp-sites, built and extinguished fires, and checked the camp to see that all was neat before leaving.

Now Cliff and Scoop took things over—making and breaking camp, caring for the team. In fact, she did nothing but drive the team and cook the meals—chores which, had she consented, they would also have assumed. Even so, there were times when one of them insisted on driving the team while Catherine rested.

They also took over almost the sole care of Ned.

239

"All right, Hot Shot, you want to ride with me?"

Usually it was Cliff who asked the question, for he and Ned had formed the most steadfast of friendships. The child would immediately signify his willingness. Then Cliff would reach out and pick him up, placing him in front of the saddle horn. This was not accomplished, however, without a few admonitory words to the horse.

"Now Jimbo, you behave. Savvy?"

Jimbo, thus warned, walked along sedately, like a magician's blindfolded helper treading a path among eggs.

Much as Catherine was enjoying the turn things had taken, she thought they were having an even better time. As for Ned, he had almost entirely deserted her, going over to them as wholeheartedly as he had gone to Uncle Willie during the first half of the trip. Watching him, she could not help feeling a little twinge of jealousy. After all, who was it that had brought him on from Caldwell!

The second day the boys freely turned the cooking over to her. They could not say enough in praise of the food she prepared.

"Tell you what, ma'am, if you ever run into hard times, you can just start a boardinghouse. Usually we don't get food fit to eat on the way back."

Usually you don't have to poke along waiting for a wagon to keep pace with you, she wanted to tell them. Had it not been for her, they would already be in Mobeetie. Long ago Uncle Willie had told her she could trust cowboys. Certainly his words were true. Cliff and Scoop were tact itself in the various emergencies, as well as the necessities, of travel. She was grateful for their thoughtfulness. But, more than that, she was glad because they were willing to talk about the land into which she was going—Mobeetie—and the surrounding territory.

"Now Mobeetie is quite a town, ma'am," they told her.

"Fort Elliot is still there, although it isn't really needed. It was built to protect the country from the Indians, but they ain't bothering anybody these days. All backed off onto reservations, tame as tabby cats."

"Indians," Ned said. "Indians are good. I was awful sick and one came and gave me something to drink and I got better, didn't he, Mama?" He evidently believed the tale was one which would need corroboration.

The cowboys looked inquiringly at Catherine.

"That's right, Ned," she said. And she told them of the incident.

"Well, it ain't so surprising," Scoop mused. "A lot of Indians are better than the hombres that took their places around Mobeetie."

Then, seeing her concern, he added hastily, "Oh, ma'am, that town's all right. It's as civilized as—well, as Caldwell." This, he knew, was scarcely a correct stick to measure by, so he went on quickly, "It's as civilized as whatever that town is you come from."

Catherine tried to follow them as they talked about Mobeetie. They might tell her it was like Grafton, but she knew better. Mobeetie was a mixture of frontier outpost and cosmopolitan culture. Because of the presence of Fort Elliot wives of army officers were there, giving the town a society of its own. And, even without them, the picture was not one she had anticipated.

"Got some fine goings-on in that town," Scoop told her. "Our boss now—the man who owns the Circle K—well, him and his wife, they drive in seventy miles to Mobeetie now and then, just to go to a party. And the old lady—excuse me, ma'am, I mean his wife—she orders her clothes from Dodge or Fort Worth or Kansas City. She packs them up and takes off to Mobeetie to a dance and stays maybe a week."

Seventy miles to a dance!

Then there was Court Day.

"There's a fine courthouse. I reckon it draws cases for a hundred miles—maybe two hundred," Cliff said. "Got a bunch of lawyers in Mobeetie. When court's in session, people come in for a real to-do."

There was more to the picture—a rock hotel which was really "something." Houses out on "Toney Ridge." These belonged to people who were "real toney," if she knew what they meant.

She did. Mobeetie was no wild gun-toting town. She was glad for the two good dresses in the trunk, the hat with its pink rose, the little high-buttoned shoes. She was glad she had also brought good clothes for Ned. She would not go into this town dressed in such a way as to shame Edward. She would send the cowboys on, once they crossed the Canadian. Then she and Ned would take their time and, before they came to town, they would change into the second best clothes she had packed in the trunk.

But, however much the place might fascinate Cliff and Scoop, it was the surrounding country which really drew their love.

"Nothing else like it," they said. "Big, and broad and—free."

"You mean it was until it began to clutter up," Scoop put in sadly.

"That's right," Cliff agreed. "It ain't what it used to be, and that's a fact."

"What's wrong?" Catherine asked.

"People moving in. First they came, just settling where they wanted. Then a bunch of men came with some little three-legged dinkuses and began squinting through them and said here was where people could move in. Called themselves surveyors."

"Yes," Scoop grinned, "it was right funny. That little business was supposed to tell us to get off our water spots or take down our fences."

"Did you?" Catherine asked.

"Sometimes." They looked at each other and grinned.

"Well, most times," they added honestly. "Because, as fast as them surveyors got through squinting, nesters came in and said they'd bought up the part that had been squinted at. Bought it!"

There was infinite distaste in the words.

"Isn't that the way it's supposed to be?" Catherine asked.

"No, ma'am, it ain't. Grass is supposed to be free. It was made for cattle to eat, not to be plowed under for stuff to grow on."

They considered the matter a moment—seriously, as one looks back over a past too far away for touching.

"Ma'am," Cliff asked suddenly. "What is your husband doing in Mobeetie?"

"He's taken up a claim—out from the town."

"Oh." They were polite, but something had come over them—a light shadow over the face of the sun, a reserve.

"Isn't that all right?" she asked quickly.

"Oh, yes. Sure, ma'am, sure it's all right. There are lots of them coming in now. Coming every day. Just a sitting in each other's laps and that's a fact. Them surveyor boys got things a little mixed up there for a while, and now and then more'n one person claimed a piece of land. But they settle it amongst themselves and one stays on."

"But you don't like them to be there," she said.

They looked at each other, evidently trying to decide which

one must answer. Strangely enough, it was Scoop who drew the assignment.

"Ma'am, it ain't that we don't like them. It's just that they are playing—" he stopped, looked at Cliff for help. Cliff grinned, but did not supply the word he sought. "Well, they are ruining the free range," he finished and then lapsed into embarrassed silence.

"It was like this," Cliff continued. "For a long time all the ranchers could run their cattle out on the range. There it was, just made for cattle. No fences, nothing to stop them. Then all of a sudden a law got passed down at Austin that people could come up and buy land. First thing you knew, people were there, each one fighting like mad to get a little section for himself. And of course he wants to fence it off, once he gets it. Can't run cattle with little spots fenced off all over the place."

"Looks to me like those people down at Austin were putting into something that was none of their say-so," Scoop said somberly.

"I'm sorry," Catherine told him. Some way she felt responsible for the whole thing—for the death blow to a way of life, for bringing an era to an end.

"Oh, that's all right, ma'am," Cliff assured her. "Everybody's doing it now. When the law went through, even a few cowboys weren't above grabbing themselves a section here and there."

"Personally, I wouldn't fool with one section," Scoop said. "Don't know what you'd do with it, out here."

Catherine wanted to tell them that one section was a big piece of land. Edward had considered it enough to come all the way to Texas for. He had thought it of sufficient importance to prevent his coming for her, when something came along to threaten his ownership. It was important enough to

make her willing to push on by herself, after Uncle Willie's
death. For a moment she let her mind run over the things she
had endured—both of real dangers and of those only imagined
—and something like indignation rose up in her that these two
should dismiss so casually the prize for which both she and
Edward had suffered so much.

"It's fine for them that wants it," Cliff told her, sensing her
feelings. "And it's bringing a lot of good people down—like
you, ma'am." He smiled engagingly at her. "Yes, a lot of people.
That land office at Austin must be busier than Court Day."

"No wonder Mobeetie's full of lawyers," Scoop said, not
without a faint distaste in his voice.

Catherine laughed. "I don't think you boys believe much
in law, or lawyers," she accused them.

They pondered her statement, neither denying nor affirm-
ing it. Finally, Scoop spoke.

"The way I see it," he said, "they just go at things all
wrong. For instance, not long ago we caught a man rustling
cattle. Now us boys out at the ranch could of settled that right
fast. But no, they had to take him over to Mobeetie for a trial.
Bunch of men rode in for maybe a hundred miles or better to
sit on the jury. Couple of lawyers got up and jawed for two
days steady. Then the jury said the man was guilty and rode
back home."

"We knew he was guilty all along," Cliff told her earnestly.
"We caught him with the iron smoking and the old cow bel-
lering her head off with a fresh burn on her. We didn't need
no jury to tell us he was guilty. And we knew all along what
to do with him, too."

"But a man—even one caught in a crime—has a right to a
trial," Catherine reminded them. "That's the way our country's built—on law."

"Maybe you're right," Cliff admitted reluctantly. "First

we had the soldiers at Fort Elliot keeping the Indians in order, and now that the Indians are calmed down, we got the lawyers, telling us how to keep straight."

"But you still don't like them," Catherine said.

"It ain't that so much," Cliff told her sadly. "It's that lawyers don't seem to go with our way of life. Ranching is sort of free, like—at least, it's been the way we've known it. Now with all these new people coming in, I guess there's got to be lawyers—but, well, it just looks like the old days are gone."

They drove on. Here was broken country, with tall grass and a bright wash of flowers. Slender, graceful spikes lifted toward heaven, on them a mass of waxy white cuplike flowers.

"Yucca," the boys told her. "Mexicans call it 'Candles of the Lord.'"

There was the sage, silver green and delicate, lending its faint pungency to the clear, bright air.

"When you see that, you know you're back home," they said.

They crossed Wolf Creek. They were climbing now—sometimes it seemed to Catherine her wagon tongue was pointing straight up, probing heaven. The horses needed to rest often. Then in the late afternoon, they came to the Canadian.

It was a thread of silver, winding its way through the dun earth. At first she felt only disappointment. Was this the danger everyone had warned her against, almost since the day she left home? Here was only a small skeleton of a river, trickling along through a wide canyon. It did not look in the least formidable.

Cliff and Scoop rode down to inspect it.

"It's not high," they said, evidently relieved.

It certainly was not high. Catherine had crossed the Arkansas and the Cimarron—both real rivers, not a small stream of water snaking its way across a sandy gash in the earth.

"You don't cross this man's river when it's high," Cliff explained. "Current gets to thirty-forty miles an hour, and that could drag you off downstream."

Well, here they were. All the way down there had been a chant, "Look out for the Canadian." It was here at last—the one real barrier standing between her and Edward. An excitement came to her, intense and strong. Della had used to sing, mournfully, and in a minor key, "There's one wide river, there's one wide river to cross!"

Here was the last river. Not wide, but holding something more menacing than width. And after that, no more barriers until she came to Edward.

Edward! Her heart beat quickly, and she touched the locket she wore under her calico dress. In just a few days now she would no longer have to turn to this little trinket; she would have Edward himself. Her heart ran ahead, covering the distance between them.

"As I was saying, ma'am," she heard Cliff's voice. "I think we'll just camp here. In the morning we'll cross."

"Oh, sure," she said. "That's fine."

The next morning they were astir very early. The cowboys conferred together, appraised, checked. They went down to have a look at the river.

"Yes, ma'am," they said, "it's a right good time to cross."

They inspected the team, the harness, the wagon.

"They are in good shape, ma'am," they told her.

The river, and two days' journey, and then she would be in Mobeetie. Again excitement ran through her; she felt like a child planning some wonderful surprise for his elders. She tried to picture Edward's amazement, his delight, when he discovered she had really come on instead of waiting for him to return for her. It seemed to her that, at long last, she had canceled out her former hesitations, her weak indecisions. Once he had stayed home because of her; once she had let him go off without her. Now, she had made up for both these times.

"You aren't to be one bit upset about crossing," Cliff told her. "We've gone across here hundreds of times. There's a ford as good as a bridge, if you know where it is, and we know."

"All you got to do is to sit there on the wagon seat and keep your team moving along right after us."

"Yes," Catherine said. And from somewhere in the back of her mind came the blacksmith's words: "So quickie a bird can't fly over it."

In spite of herself, the question was on her lips.

"What about the quicksand?" she asked.

"Oh, that—" Cliff dismissed the word airily. "It's there but the way we go—well, it's all right. I've crossed this river hundreds of times and always got over."

"But you cross it on horseback," Catherine reminded him stubbornly.

"Yes, ma'am, and I drive bunches of cow critters over it, too," he told her patiently.

Suddenly she was ashamed of her questions, of the fears that prompted them. These boys knew what they were doing.

"Breakfast's ready, come on and get it," she said.

While they were eating they heard the distant sound of thunder, reverberating continuously in the morning.

"They must be getting a dilly of a storm over on Red Deer Creek," Cliff said.

"Glad it's there, not here."

"Sure thing. It's a dandy."

They finished eating, began to break camp. Once more they checked the wagon.

"Somebody sure saw to it that this little boat was ready to travel," Scoop told her.

"Uncle Willie—" she told him.

The man's thoughtfulness was following her, even to this last stage of her journey. Strange wasn't it, she was thinking, that some people are fated to have little personal joy of their own but must be, instead, the bridge across which others cross to their own happiness. Such was Uncle Willie. He had made her trip possible. Before his death he had given two priceless gifts—life to a woman he did not even know, reunion to Edward and Catherine. Men have lived their long lives out in their own home town with less to show.

Catherine got on the wagon seat, Ned beside her. She took the lines.

"Get up," she said, slapping the horses. They started off. Down the bank they went, the wagon swaying and lurching over the uneven path.

Ahead of her the two cowboys rode, their eyes fixed on the river.

"Set your brakes," Cliff called, without even turning around.

She obeyed. She could hear the cooking things, in the box at the back, rolling around with the tilt of the wagon. She could hear the creak of the wagon itself. They came to the bed of the river.

"Take 'em off," Cliff called back to her.

She released the brakes.

Now she was driving on the bed of the river itself. Here was nothing but sand—they had not yet come to the stream of water in the middle. At first the sand was dry; a little farther along it grew damp. Now she came to the water, but it was shallow, scarcely knee-deep on the horses. Prince and Lady stepped into it without hesitation.

Cliff and Scoop veered a little. Catherine turned the team to follow them. Everything was going fine. The water was a little deeper.

She looked at the shore toward which they were going. It was difficult to gauge distances out here. The water was beginning to grow shallow once more. Sand, damp and water logged, was before them. She saw Scoop's horse begin to tremble nervously.

"There, Hap," the boy said, patting him gently, "there's nothing to be afraid of . . ."

"Quicksand," Catherine thought, watching it as it quivered and trembled in the light. A chill swept over her. What if the team shied off, what if . . .

The cowboys rode on, their horses stepping daintily, moving as fast as they could go without leaving her team behind. Prince and Lady did not really need much guiding. They followed the other horses.

She began to be conscious of a dull roar. The thunderstorm over Deer Creek—it must be moving this way, she thought.

The roar continued, louder now. It didn't sound like thunder—that would die down, flare up again. This was constant, unending. And it was coming nearer, moving directly toward them, apparently following the course of the river. She saw Cliff turn to listen; he said a single word to Scoop, who turned, too.

For one split second they all sat there, listening. Then the horses neighed suddenly. Jimbo reared, some ancient instinct surging up in him, so that he knew, almost before his rider did, the awfulness of the thing that threatened.

And at that moment it came in sight.

A wall of water, a crest, a flood. It filled the stream, spreading out to the banks. Gray white it was, and mist covered and it rolled toward them, faster than doom. On its surging crest great trees rode, carried along as easily as if they were match sticks.

"My God," Cliff whispered. And then, as if the sound of his own voice loosed the spell that held them, he swung his horse around. "The river's flooding—"

Catherine could never have told, afterward, how it all happened—the speed with which the cowboys worked, the awful sound coming nearer, the wild and frantic lunging of the horses, terrified now and beyond control. There was a swift flash of knives—Cliff's and Scoop's—on each side and then the team was loose. Prince and Lady, their heads high, neighed wildly, running down and across the river, back toward the bank from which they had come, angling to be out of the path of the swirling, raging thing which rolled toward them.

There were Cliff and Scoop, one on each side of the wagon.

"Come here, Hot Shot," Cliff called to Ned. Catherine passed the child into the cowboy's arms just as Scoop called to her,

"Here—quick, ma'am."

The roar was closer. She felt—or fancied she did—the icy, terrible spray on her cheek. She was on the wagon edge, she was back of Scoop, on his horse. The horse, frightened by the thing which menaced, by the unaccustomed weight upon its back, reared, struggled.

"There, Hap," Scoop said.

She held to the cowboy's waist. She could feel his young body tense beneath her arms. He leaned forward, as if his own eagerness, his very will, would push them forward.

The water was rising higher now, closer . . .

She had always heard that, at the moment of death, people looked back and saw all their past life spreading out before them. For her, this did not happen. It was only the future she saw, the future that never was to be.

"I'll never see Edward again," she thought.

It was the vision of her and Edward growing old together that she saw now, with the fearsome wall of water bearing down on her. He, with thinning hair and glasses, and stooped shoulders; she with thickened waistline, brown hair turned quite gray and fine wrinkles webbed across throat and neck. Two of them, old people, walking along sedately together, their steps slow and cautious. Young people watching them would think only that here was an old couple who had once been young and ardent but now had settled down to nothing more than content and companionship.

They would not know, these watchers, that love grows stronger with the passing years, and deeper for its quietness.

But she and Edward would.

No, they would not. Now, they would not.

She closed her eyes, keeping Edward's face before her.

Then she heard Scoop speaking, words she had never thought to hear again.

"Well, we'll make it."

His voice shook a little, but it was real enough.

She opened her eyes. Scoop's horse was clambering up the bank; Cliff's, with its lighter burden, was ahead. Ned rode, high and safe, in the cowboy's arms.

"Thank God," Catherine said. Her lips began to tremble.

She looked back. The wall of water covered the ford entirely now. They had escaped, but with only seconds to spare. It had reached the wagon, was turning it over, as a child would roll a hoop. Over and over and over—until there was nothing left of it, not even the canvas.

"The wagon," she said. "It's gone."

The wagon with all the things she had packed into it. The plow and the seed. And the money. Everything was gone, those treasures she had guarded so carefully all the long hard way.

She had brought them so close, only to lose them. If she had only saved the money. A few seconds, that's all it would have taken. She could have ripped it from its hiding place. Why hadn't she remembered to do it?

"Don't you think about that wagon, Mrs. Delaney," Scoop told her gently. "You and Ned are safe. That's what counts."

And so they were. The few seconds necessary to save the money—that might have cost all of them their lives. Now they were safe. She must remember that. They might have been down there where the wagon was now—rolling, rolling . . .

She shuddered, turned her head away.

"Mama," Ned cried, "Mama, they're gone. Prince and Lady. And the wagon."

"Don't cry, Hot Shot," Cliff comforted him. "The team got across safe to the other side. When the water goes down, we'll come back and look for them."

"But how'll we go to Papa?"

"Don't you worry, you'll get to your papa all right. You and your mama, too."

"But how?" Ned wailed.

"You'll ride back of me and Scoop, that's how. You'll ride right to Mobeetie. Now stop your crying and let's get going."

# CHAPTER 12

———————•◆•———————

THEY CAME TO MOBEETIE IN THE MIDDLE OF THE AFTERNOON.
THEY FORMED A STRANGE MOTLEY LITTLE GROUP—TWO COWBOYS
riding more slowly than their kind was wont to go, and with
good reason. Behind one rode a woman; behind the other, a
small boy.

For Catherine, this long-anticipated arrival had little reality.
She was conscious only of a great numbness, both of body and
of spirit. In spite of all Scoop could do to make her comfortable, the ride had been, at times, almost pure physical torment.
And in her mind was the one churning thought—I've lost everything. Everything I started out to bring.

"You are lucky," Scoop reminded her, as if he knew her
thoughts. "Those flash floods, they sure can catch people quick."

"Oh, I know that," she told him. As, indeed, she did. The
talkative blacksmith back at Caldwell had mentioned them.
Strange she had given his words no thought, either then or
later, remembering instead the warnings about the quicksand.

"That must have been a real cloudburst up Red Deer Creek
this morning," Cliff said. He was both embarrassed and apologetic, as if, in some way he could not quite define, the whole
fault lay on his shoulders. "I should of known. A rain like that
pours down these creeks into the river and first thing you get—
well, what we got."

255

"My goodness, Cliff," she said, forgetting for the moment her own desolation in trying to comfort him, "you couldn't help it. You saved our lives. Think what would have happened if Ned and I had been alone."

"Well—" he considered the matter. And then he went on, grinning at her shyly, "I guess it's a right good thing you wouldn't let us go back after that Thad fellow."

"Oh, I don't know," Scoop drawled. "We could of brought him along and pushed him in when the water came."

Catherine joined in the cowboys' laughter. Having done so, she felt a little better.

It was still light enough when they rode into Mobeetie for Catherine to see the courthouse and the rock hotel. They were just as the boys had described them to her.

"Would you like to go to the hotel?" Scoop asked her.

"I—" Catherine hesitated. Certainly she was in no condition to go to a hotel, nor, as far as that went, was Ned. Both of them wore dirty, mud-stained clothes. After the experience of the morning and the ride that followed they looked like a couple of tired and dispirited gypsies rather than Mrs. Edward Delaney and son, late of Grafton, Missouri.

Cliff sensed the reason for her hesitation.

"Tell you what," he said, "there's a Mrs. Moore who keeps a boardinghouse here—a widow woman. I bet you could stay with her."

"Yes," Catherine agreed. "That sounds better."

The cowboys rode up to a small white house sitting among cottonwood trees. It was trim and neat looking; the yard, though bare of grass, was swept clean. Lights shone through the windows. To Catherine, weary and bedraggled, it looked like heaven.

"Do you suppose she'll have room for us?" she asked the boys.

"Sure, Violet will take you if she has to sleep on the floor herself," they assured her.

"We'll just leave you and Ned with her," Cliff said, "and then, first thing in the morning, we'll ride out and tell your husband you're here. Sound all right?"

"Oh, yes—" Catherine said, the words catching in her throat. In the morning Edward would know she was here. The bright promise helped her forget, for the moment, the dark conclusion of her journey.

They stopped their horses, helped Catherine and Ned to alight. Then they led the way to the door and knocked.

A woman came to the door. Catherine was not prepared for the appearance of this angel of mercy the cowboys had promised her. She was a small-boned woman who had become very plump down the years, with the soft flesh of one who likes her food too well. But, here also, was a woman who still saw herself as she had been as a girl, and dressed and acted accordingly. Her hair was red—certainly not the color nature had meant it to be—and it was arranged in an intricate cascade of girlish curls and puffs and bangs. Ear rings dangled from her ears and bracelets jangled on her wrists; her dress was a conglomeration of puffs and ruffles and lace and tucks. Her feet, delicately small for the rest of her body, were encased in high-heeled shoes with beads on the toes.

"Why, hello, boys," she said.

Despite her appearance, she gave a feeling of warmth, a reaching out, a friendliness.

"Hello, Violet," Cliff said, "this here is Mrs. Delaney and her little boy Ned. Reckon they could stay with you?"

"Had a bit of bad luck," Scoop explained. "Lost the wagon and everything they had in a quick rise up on the river."

"Why you poor Lamb," the woman cried, reaching out her two plump little ringed hands toward Catherine. "You poor, dear Lamb. Of *course* you can stay with me. You get right into this house!"

The sun shining in at the window awakened Catherine. She struggled to a half sitting position, thinking she had overslept. She must hurry—she must get on the road. Then, realization came to her and she lay back down, the events of yesterday rushing through her mind.

She was wearing a nightgown, not her own. It was Violet Moore's.

"Now honey," Violet had said the night before, "you just get out of those clothes—you and dear little Ned, too. Clemmie—that's my colored girl—will wash them for you, and by morning you'll have something fresh to get into."

Catherine had not protested. Violet, with her bustling kindness, had disarmed her entirely so that she was once more almost the child that Della would have cared for, ordering her around with brisk and loving energy. She wondered briefly what her mother would have said to this woman, with her assumptions of a youth that was no longer hers, her dyed hair, her fussy clothes. And almost at once she dismissed the thought— it did not matter at all what anyone thought. Violet Moore was kind and beneath her silliness was a real goodness.

"Now for Ned—" Violet Moore thought for a moment. "I'll tell you—I'll just get an undershirt that belonged to my second husband, Mr. Cartwright. He was a small man."

Her second husband, Mr. Cartwright! That meant she must have been married at least three times, for her name was now Moore.

She brought the undershirt.

"Now, Ned," she said, "you can just sleep in this, honey,

and by morning your own little suit will be nice and clean.
Won't that be fine!"

She put so much child-like enthusiasm into her voice that
Ned was convinced, donned the garment without protest.

He even consented to eat his supper in it; Catherine sat
with him, almost too tired to put food into her mouth, wearing
Violet's nightgown covered with one of the woman's wrappers.

"My goodness, honey," Violet Moore had said, bustling
around the kitchen getting the meal together. "You're just real
pretty—and young—now don't tell me you drove all the way
from Missouri by yourself—"

"Uncle Willie was with us when we started," Ned put in,
"but he got killed."

He makes us sound like trash, Catherine thought. Like
brawling, fighting trash. She was too tired, too exhausted both
physically and mentally, to explain. She let the statement stand.
And Violet Moore did not so much as bat an eyelash to hear
it. As far as she was concerned she seemed to imply, it was
nothing out of the ordinary for a man to be killed on the road
down.

She's taking us on face value, Catherine thought. That's
the way Lola did. That's the way Cliff and Scoop did.

When the meal was over, Violet Moore said, "Now, you
go to bed, both of you. And don't you worry about getting up
until you feel good and ready. I'll keep everyone in the house
quiet as a mouse."

Catherine obeyed her, although she did not really feel she
could go to sleep. Her mind was too full of all that had happened. The whole trip had turned to defeat—everything she
had hoped to do had failed. The wagon with its cargo destined
to spell out their future lay at the bottom of the Canadian, lost
beyond any recovering. She had only the clothes on their backs
and, in Della's purse, which she had worn around her waist and

which now rested under her pillow, a little less than twenty dollars—all that remained of the money originally put into the jewel box for emergencies but taken out and used to pay the expenses of the trip after the unspeakable Thad stole Uncle Willie's purse.

But nature must have asserted itself—and Violet Moore must have been as good as her word to keep the others in the house quiet—for Catherine slept the clock around and now it was morning. And although her muscles cried out in protest when she tried to move, she did feel rested. Courage had come back to her, too. She could meet whatever this day brought. She could meet it because, at its close, she would see Edward. For had not Cliff and Scoop volunteered to take him the news of her arrival!

"It's a lot of trouble for you," she told them.

"None at all. First thing in the morning we'll ride out. He should be back by the middle of the afternoon."

"Thank you," she had said, tears of relief and weariness coming to her eyes.

"It's nothing—gosh, it's just nothing at all."

She knew the boys would keep their word. Before too long, Edward would know she was here. And then . . .

Her heart raced at the thought. She jumped out of bed.

There, lying folded neatly over a chair were her clothes, the dress and the underwear carefully washed and ironed. Her shoes had been cleaned, too, and were sitting under it, almost exactly the way she always put them at night. She remembered how Edward used to laugh at her because of this, and she giggled to herself. Ned's things were on another chair, washed and ironed. The Negro woman had evidently brought them in while Catherine and the child were still asleep.

At that moment Ned sat up straight in bed.

"Mama," he asked eagerly. "Will Papa come today?"

"Yes, honey, some time this afternoon. Scoop and Cliff are riding out to tell him we are here."

"He'll be glad to see us."

"Oh, yes, he will, darling."

A thousand times during the long journey down she had dreamed about this meeting, letting the sweetness of it run through her mind. She and Ned would be wearing their good clothes—clean, neat, sweet-smelling. In some way she had never made clear in her mind, Edward would be there waiting to swing them off the wagon, to gather her into his arms, to listen to her story of the trip. Then, when it was finished, he would tell her how wonderful she was, how brave, how right to do this thing which she had done.

It was only a dream, but it had sustained her. There were times when she would scarcely admit to herself that she dreamed this, but always in the back of her mind, in one way or another, it was with her.

Edward would completely justify, entirely vindicate, this trip she had undertaken without his knowledge, without his asking. Not only that, but he would tell her that, by bringing on the necessary things, she had made it possible for them to succeed here. She needed to have this justification—in a measure, she must have it to pay for those other times when she had failed him.

Instead, she had come through to him with nothing. The thought of it was bitterness almost too great to be borne.

"Mama," Ned said, "I'm hungry."

"Hurry and dress," she told him, "and we'll go ask Mrs. Moore if we may have breakfast."

When they went into the kitchen, Violet Moore was bustling around, very bright and efficient.

"Well, hello," she cried. "My, you do look better this morning! No need to ask you how you slept."

"I slept fine," Catherine told her.

"Me, too," Ned said. "And now I'm hungry."

"Of course you are, and you are going to have your breakfast right away! Clemmie had it all ready and waiting."

Clemmie, a vast slow-moving Negro woman did have breakfast ready for them.

"Did you wash my clothes?" Catherine asked.

"Yes ma'am," the woman said.

"Thank you," Catherine said. "Thank you so very much."

"Oh, that was all right," the woman said, with a voice and
smile so much like Della's it caught at Catherine's heart.

"This looks good," Ned told her. "It looks just like Della
used to fix it!"

"Now," Violet Moore asked, once breakfast was over.
"What do you want to do this morning? Go out and look
around the town a little?"

Catherine hesitated. Could she go to town in a calico dress
and a sunbonnet, no matter how clean they were? Except for
the locket, which she wore outside this morning, she looked
exactly as she had on the trip down. She let herself think
fleetingly of the good clothes, buried somewhere in the treacherous Canadian; then she pushed the thought from her.

"Why yes," she said. "I think that's a good idea."

She combed Ned's hair, tied on her sunbonnet, and together they walked out into the street.

The day was clear and sunny. The sky was so brightly blue
it hurt Catherine's eyes to look at it. The air was light and
crystal clear. Cottonwoods rustled in the wind. The whole effect was one of well-being, of vitality, of youth, progress, new-
ness. She found herself walking faster, taking deep satisfying
breaths.

As Cliff and Scoop had said, the town was dominated by

the courthouse and the hotel. The latter was a two-storied rock building, larger than one would expect to find in a town of this size. That was probably the result of Fort Elliot's being near. She could see the cluster of buildings in the near distance, judged it to be the fort.

Impressive as was the hotel, it was overshadowed by the courthouse.

It also had two stories, and was made of rock. But while the hotel was frankly built for comfort, the courthouse stood— square and substantial, dignified and impressive—a veritable temple of justice. More nearly than the fort it looked as if its function was to maintain the law of the land.

The other buildings were nondescript—wooden stores, and of course, the usual number of saloons. Horses were tied to the racks on both sides of the street. Women walked along, some of them wearing sunbonnets, looking very much the way Catherine looked. She saw a few women wearing hats, the sort of women Catherine would have liked to know—gentlewomen who had brought something with them from their own homes, shaping it to meet the needs of this new land. They walked quietly, with assurance.

She came to the window of a little shop. There was a sign, hand lettered, which said, "Mavis Storm, dressmaking." But it was not the sign which attracted Catherine's attention so much as it was the hat in the window. A little hat, with a single pink rose nestling in a swirl of maline—almost identical to the one she had brought from Missouri, the one which now lay beneath the waters of the Canadian.

She stood looking at it for a long time. Once she made a half motion to go inside and examine it more closely. Then she drew back. But she continued to look at it. For the time being everything else was forgotten.

Finally she was brought back to the realization of her surroundings by Ned tugging at her hand.

"Come on, Mama," he said. "Let's walk some more."

She turned, walked on with him.

A little farther down she came to a general store. All kinds of merchandise were piled in front of it and in the windows. She stood looking at the various items thus exhibited. Finally she was aware of another woman regarding her intently. She, too, wore a sunbonnet and a calico dress. She looked tired and there were faint lines in her face, the face of a woman who might have been pretty, had she not looked older than her years.

For one fleeting second Catherine looked straight at this other woman, and then she drew back with a gasp of horror.

It was only the reflection of herself she saw, there in a mirror in the store window.

Herself, a mover woman, wearing a bonnet and dark calico dress, her skin tanned and roughened from weeks on the road —weather-beaten, despite all the precautions she had tried to take.

The sunbonnet—that was what did it! She snatched it off, but that served only to give her a better look at her hair, which seemed faded and stringy now that it was exposed to the light. Moreover, the motion called her attention to her hands, rough and work worn from camp chores.

Catherine turned around so fast she almost jerked Ned off his feet. Quickly, as if a compulsion outside herself moved her, she walked back to the store where she had seen the little hat. She stood a moment looking at it. She felt the purse at her waist. She touched it thoughtfully. Then she squared her shoulders and walked into the shop.

A tall woman with an air of quiet distinction came toward her.

"Can I do something for you?" she asked.

"That hat—" Catherine told her. She was still breathing fast, as much from the shock she had experienced as from her swift rush back to the little shop. "I'd like to try it on."

The woman got the hat out of the window, brought it to Catherine, who put it on.

Catherine sat very still, looking at the reflection in the mirror. This was a magic moment; she had been given back herself. The hat framed her brown hair, making it look only slightly less lustrous than it had been back in Missouri weeks ago, in another age and another world. The shadows under her eyes, brought on by fatigue and weeks of difficulties, seemed to add a look of mystery to her appearance, more intriguing than otherwise. No, that was not quite right. It was not herself she saw, but another woman. For, where once a face with undertones of hesitant uncertainty had looked back at her, now there was strength and purpose. And above all a warmth and vigor and a bright and wonderful delight that she should see herself once more a woman.

"It's your hat," the other woman said quietly. She did not seem to see any incongruity about Catherine's wearing it with a dark calico dress. She did not even find it strange that a woman should sit lost in the sight of her own reflection in the mirror. "It's certainly your hat," she repeated.

Catherine came back reluctantly, as one would return from another, brighter world.

"Yes," she agreed, still not removing the hat, "it's very lovely."

The hat was perfect. Maybe it had been made for her, as the woman suggested. For the Catherine Delaney who had lived in Missouri, once upon a long ago. A woman who had been concerned only with such small matters as whether they should accept an invitation to her mother's for Sunday dinner, and worried because Jessie did not like for Edward to smoke. It was also the hat for the new Catherine Delaney—the one who had driven across all those difficult miles to be at her husband's side. In some subtle way it bridged the gap between these two in a way the other little hat—the one she had brought from Missouri—could never have done.

"If it's a matter of price—" the woman began delicately.

"No," Catherine began. "I mean, that isn't all—"

The woman looked at her sympathetically.

"It would go with almost any kind of dress," she said.

"But I don't have—" Catherine began, and then stopped. She could not tell a strange woman that she had no other dress. Not even a woman who seemed as kind and understanding as this one.

"I even have a dress that would go with it perfectly," the woman continued as if she might have sensed Catherine's thoughts. "Ordinarily I don't carry dresses made up, but an officer's wife ordered it and then had to leave before I finished. She was about your size—I'm sure that with a few minor alterations, it would fit you exactly."

Catherine hesitated.

"Just a moment. I'll get it."

She disappeared behind a partition, was back in a minute, bringing the dress with her.

"Here it is," she said, holding it up.

Catherine looked. It was gray muslin—very smart, very modish, beautifully made. Her hand reached out instinctively to touch it.

"Why don't you try it on?" the woman suggested.

Catherine looked at the dress. She looked back at herself in the mirror. Resolution came to her.

"All right," she said. "I'll just try it."

It wouldn't hurt to try it on, to see herself once more in a becoming dress.

She took off the little hat, laid it on the table. She slipped out of her calico dress. The woman lifted the gray dress, let it slip over Catherine's head. Even before the last fold fell into place, Catherine knew it was right for her, even as the hat had been.

"Try the hat with it."

She put the hat back on, stood looking at herself.

She could have gone anywhere in the outfit. To Kansas City. To Virginia. Anywhere.

"It's lovely," she said.

"Yes, it looks just right on you. Do you live here?"

"Not yet. I am going to. I am Mrs. Edward Delaney. My husband is already here."

"Well, then you will soon find out that Mobeetie is no ordinary frontier town. Women here know good clothes, and wear them. Their husbands expect them to."

*Mobeetie is no ordinary town!* After all, the cowboys had told her this. *The women know good clothes!* That, too, they had told her. *Their husbands expect them to!*

She felt the little purse at her waist.

"You can have the two for fifteen dollars, since I'm left with the dress, and it wouldn't fit everyone. I'd do the alterations free."

Catherine looked at herself in the mirror once more. She looked back at the woman.

"How long would it take?" she asked.

"Not long. There's really very little to do."

Resolution came to her.

"I'll take it," she said.

She felt very confident, as if she had done exactly the right thing.

It was an hour later when Catherine walked out of the shop, with Ned at her side. Her head was high, her cheeks flushed. She wore the gray dress and the hat with the rose on it. Around her neck was the locket. In her gloved hands (gloves also bought at the store) she carried a package. It contained her discarded dress and bonnet and Della's purse, almost empty now.

In her heart was a strange mixture of delight and consternation. Delight that she should know she would be lovely in Edward's eyes; consternation to think of the money she had spent on herself. But the latter emotion she tried to push back from her as she walked down the street with its whispering cottonwoods on both sides.

"Hello, Mrs. Delaney," she heard a voice calling.

She looked and there were Cliff and Scoop reined up almost at her elbow.

"Oh, hello," she said, thinking how pleasant it was to hear her name called in this strange town; thinking how good it was to see the boys again, thinking that by now . . .

"Hello, Cliff. Hello, Scoop," Ned cried, wiggling in happy excitement. "Mama's got a new dress and hat—"

"She sure has. Lucky thing you were with her, or we'd have passed her right up."

"Did you find Edward?" Catherine asked, finding it difficult to say the words. They caught in her throat in her great eagerness to say them.

"Yes ma'am. He was on his way to town already, and we met him."

"Was he all right?"

"Yes ma'am, he's just fine. And say—you better get over to Violet's in a hurry, if you want to be there before he comes."

She scarcely waited for them to finish. She grabbed Ned's hand, started off down the street. She paused a moment, looked back.

"Thank you, boys," she cried over her shoulder. "Thank you so much."

"Oh, that's all right," they called after her. "We were proud to do it."

She was almost running when she came to Violet's house. She saw a horse tied to the hitchrack, scarcely looked at it. And then she heard her name.

"Catherine."

It was Edward's voice. She looked up, saw him coming toward her.

She dropped Ned's hand. All those weary miles she had never forgotten the child. Not once. But now, leaving him to manage as best he could, she flew to meet Edward, her gray skirt making a swishing sound as she ran, the rose bobbing on the little hat, her arms outstretched. He was coming toward her, running as she ran.

"Edward."

"Catherine."

His arms closed around her. He swung her up—her feet were off the ground. There was no reality of earth or sky, only a strange and beautiful state of suspension, and Edward's arms around her, Edward's lips on hers.

For a long and beautiful eternity they were aware only of themselves. They were brought back to the here and now by Ned, who was tugging at Edward's hand. "Papa, Papa, here I am," he was saying.

Edward released Catherine, turned to the child. He lifted him up, hugged him close, kissed him.

"Why son, to be sure you are. My, how you have grown!"

"I'm a big boy," Ned told him proudly. "I helped Mama drive lots of times."

"Of course you helped her."

Edward put the child down, turned to Catherine.

"My God, Catherine," he said, "what's this about the flood?"

"The boys told you?"

"A little. They were explaining how they knew you were here."

"Let's go in," she said. "I'll tell you about it."

They went inside, to the room that had been Catherine's the night before. Ned was holding fast to Edward's hand.

"You knew me, Papa. Mama said you would."

"Of course. I couldn't forget my boy."

"And I knew you."

"You wouldn't forget your papa." He looked around the room, saw a book lying on the table. "Now listen," he said, reaching out to rumple the child's hair, "why don't you take that book and sit on the sofa awhile and look at the pictures. Your mama and I have to do some talking."

Ned obediently crawled up on the sofa, began to scan the pages of the book. Edward turned to Catherine.

"Well," he said, "what happened? At first I thought it was a joke or something, you in Mobeetie, and I didn't even know you had left Missouri. I hadn't heard from you for such a long time, but mail is slow and undependable out here. I figured your letters were just held up. If I had known you were starting out alone, I would have been worried crazy."

"I didn't start alone. Uncle Willie was with me. Did the boys tell you about him?" her voice trailed off.

"Yes, but not much. What happened?"

She told him, crying as she did. Gentle tears, without bitterness.

"Even with him, it was a risk to take," Edward told her, his voice rough with feeling. "Why did you do it, anyway?"

She looked at him, her eyes wide, her lips parted a little. How could she put into words the thing that had brought her toward him, the urgency which had driven her forward when every bit of reason and common sense had proclaimed that she should go back? How could she explain to him all those subtle doubts and fears which had stayed with her by night and by day, making it impossible for her to do other than she did?

Or, how could she make him understand that, with him away, she had lost her sense of completeness, of being the other half of a strong and enduring whole? That she saw the gulf widening between them, slowly and surely, as cakes of ice drift apart in a swollen stream? There was no way to say these things. Not now, there wasn't. Maybe there would never be.

"I wanted to be with you," she said so softly her words were scarcely audible. And then the full meaning of her failure came back to her, something she had almost forgotten in those first bright moments of reunion. Now it struck her again—the sense of guilt that she should have started in the first place without his knowledge or his consent.

"Oh, Edward," she wailed, "I lost everything, everything." The burden of her sorrow and the loss they had sustained spilled over into her voice.

"You are safe—and Ned—that's all that matters."

"But the money—"

"Come here." he said, pulling her down into his lap.

She rested against him, her heart beating fast and strong, even as it had done in those first days of their marriage. She reached up, stroked the back of his head. She traced with her fingers the lines in his face—the parenthesis marks around his mouth and the absurd, questioning uplifted eyebrow. She dropped her head on his shoulder.

"I'm sorry," she whispered.

"Oh, hush," he said thickly. He lifted her face, kissed her several times, his arms tightening around her. "What's money, so long as you are here?" He kissed her again. "If you only knew how much I've missed you."

"I know."

She knew. She had a gauge for measuring—her own bleak desolation without him.

"When the boys told me about the flash flood, I nearly died. I can hardly let myself think about it, even now."

"What are you going to do for seed and a plow and things. How will you farm the claim, now?" she asked.

He moved so suddenly that she almost slid off his lap. He reached to steady her, and she stood up. He stood too. She looked at him, puzzled by the change in him. His jaw was set and hard; the lines in his face were deep. "He looks old," she thought. "Old and troubled." And for a moment she remembered the thought that had come to her, there when the waters were ready to close over her—the thought that she and Edward would never grow old together.

"What's wrong, Edward?" she asked quickly.

"The claim, Catherine," he told her. "I wrote you there was some trouble about it . . ."

"Yes, that's why you couldn't come. What was wrong?"

"It's a long story, but the gist of it is that we may lose it."

"Lose it?" the words burst from her in unbelief. "Why you can't, Edward. You lived on it six months. You made improvements. You did everything they asked you to."

"And so I did. But it was on the wrong section . . ."

"I don't understand. Wasn't it surveyed, and all—"

"Yes," he was finding the words hard to say. "Yes, but here's what happened. The first surveyors up here were private ones; they mostly were trying to get some good land for themselves. Then the state caught on and sent out its own men. When they came, they found things really in a mess. Why the United States Government had to trade sections with the town of Mobeetie, just in order to own the land Fort Elliot was built on."

Cliff and Scoop had laughed about the "squinting boys" and she had scarcely listened, thinking the whole affair had no meaning for her.

"And your claim?" she asked.

"The second survey seemed to show that the land really belonged to a fellow named Gillespie. He's a pretty hard customer —there's no talking reason to him. But the way things looked, there could be a mistake. So I came in to talk to Judge Fisher —I had served on a jury and got to know him—and he agreed to check the records against those down at Austin to see if my claim would hold. So I turned it over to him. He said it would take a couple of months."

"And that's why you couldn't come when you'd said you would?"

"Sure, I didn't dare leave. Gillespie was the kind who'd take any unfair advantage he could. I had to stay here and keep my eyes on things."

"Why didn't you tell me?"

"Because I didn't know how it was going to turn out. There was no need to worry you if I was going to be able to keep the claim after all."

And because I had forfeited my right to share your concern over things that happened to us, Catherine thought. But this she did not say.

"I needed to be here where I could come in and confer

with Judge Fisher," he told her. "My Lord, Catherine—the dugout's there, and a spring. The spring is what turned the trick. Water is the life blood of this land. People will do about anything for a section with a spring on it."

"It's not fair," she burst out. "All the work you put in, and the time . . ."

And the separation, and the loneliness.

They were both quiet a moment, going back over the thing in their minds. There was silence in the room, broken only by the regular breathing of Ned, who had fallen asleep on the sofa.

"I wish you'd look at him," Edward said. "Asleep, already."

"No wonder," Catherine said. "Poor little thing, he's exhausted."

"Anyway," Edward went on, "Judge Fisher sent word for me to come in today, to meet him at his office about two. He has the final decision from Austin. That's why I was on my way in when the boys met me." He took out his watch, checked it. "It's almost that time now," he said. "I'd better be going."

So close—the decision was as near as that.

All the way down she had thought, once she was here with Edward, nothing would matter. That things would go right automatically. And now they had no more than seen each other when he must leave her, when they must face the possibility of a more difficult thing than any she had met on the trip. For here was a threat, not just to possessions which might be replaced, but to the very core of their reason for being here.

"Oh, Edward, do you have to go *now?*"

"Yes, now."

He started to leave, then turned to her. "Why don't you go with me?"

She hesitated only a moment.

"I'll get Violet to keep an eye on Ned," she said.

She picked up the hat she had dropped on the bed when they first came into the room; she put it on her head. She smoothed the folds of the gray dress, she gathered up her gloves. Then she took his arm.

"All right," she said, "I'm ready."

They walked down the street between the rows of whispering cottonwoods, came to the courthouse, standing dignified and solid and substantial. They mounted the steps and entered, found it cool and dim after the sun-washed street. Edward made his way to a door as if he was thoroughly familiar with the place. They walked into an office.

A man sat behind a desk. A distinguished-looking man, middle-aged, looking wise with a wisdom which went far beyond what he had learned in books. Catherine liked him, even before he spoke. He stood up and she felt his eyes fixed on her with well-bred inquiry.

"Oh, hello Edward," he said. The name fell easily from his lips as if he had occasion to use it frequently.

"Hello, Judge Fisher. I want you to meet my wife."

The judge extended his hand to Catherine. "How do you do, Mrs. Delaney," he said.

He spoke with easy courtesy, with courtly graciousness, making no attempt to cover the surprise and approval he felt at seeing her.

"Sit down," he said, and they took chairs.

"Now, I suppose your husband has told you of this claim business," he said, turning to include Catherine in the discussion.

"Yes," she said simply.

Our whole future rests in the words he will say to us, Catherine was thinking. Our whole lives. She found herself looking at him, waiting for those words, hardly breathing—as if he, by his own power could decide this thing in their favor.

Judge Fisher took off his glasses, polished them thoughtfully, put them back on.

"Well, Edward," he said, "I hate to tell you—but your claim was not upheld. The state recheck is in, and it gives the land to Gillespie."

For a moment there was silence in the room. It crashed around them, in a terrible and thundering urgency that beat on Catherine's numbed brain.

The claim is gone, she thought wildly. What will we do now? Go back to Missouri, to Mama's farm? A great revulsion swept over her so that she felt herself shaking with its force. The humiliation of it, the death to Edward's pride. Long ago he had said, "If you want to grow, you have to go West. Go East and you die—inside yourself."

And even if they had to go, where would the money come from? She had lost most of it—had spent the last bit on new clothes for herself. Suddenly she wished she might take the dress and hat and tear them from her, do penance for her foolish vanity. Then she caught the judge's eyes on her, a strange measuring look.

She straightened her shoulders. From somewhere out of her past came the memory of her mother, holding herself with a high disdainful pride even while her own personal world was falling to pieces around her. Remembering, Catherine felt a degree of calmness come to her. And now she was glad that she sat here, not a bedraggled mover in a calico dress and sunbonnet, beaten by life, cowering back from what had been said, but a woman dressed in her best, bearing with pride and dignity whatever might come to her.

For one split second she caught Edward's eyes on her.

*He's glad, too,* she thought. *He's proud of me.* It's good, the way things are.

The judge, looking at her, did not need to sympathize with Edward for having a wife old and broken by hardship. It went deeper than that—he could not blame Edward for allowing her to undertake the difficult journey by herself. Now she looked like a cherished woman, a well-beloved woman, and it was to the credit of both of them that she should do so.

From what seemed like a great distance the judge's voice came to her.

"It's a hard thing to have happen," he was saying. "But that's the law."

He said it as if that settled everything. As if, when the law spoke, they should all be perfectly satisfied with the results. It was a sentiment Catherine could not feel. The law, indeed. She could share the cowboys' disregard for it. It was a bad law that took something you had worked and planned for. This went beyond law. It was a *moral* obligation, like the money for the orphans.

She understood, at long last, Edward's attitude about that. The old Indian had made the thing clear to her. Dirty and ragged and menacing he might have been, but he had shown her that any child in need is the concern of all people. Whatever bitterness she had felt about the matter left her forever after the night of Ned's illness. But this—it was different.

"I don't pretend to think it's easy," the judge went on. "Perhaps not even fair. Gillespie is a hard man. I tried to reason with him, but he's beyond that. He says he has the law on his side."

We'd be better off without law, if that's what it does for us, she thought bitterly.

Judge Fisher looked at her keenly, as if he guessed her thoughts. But it was to Edward that he addressed his words.

"I suppose we must look at it this way. If the law did not uphold a sound legal claim, your place would mean nothing to you, had you been allowed to keep it. If you could reach out and take property—and keep it—then anyone who wanted to come along could take it from *you*. If he was strong and ruthless enough, he could."

"Oh, sure," Edward said, clearing his throat. Catherine could not look at him—she did not want to see what the news of the loss had done to him, to be witness to the death of his dream.

"Sometimes the law may seem to do strange things," the judge went on quietly. "But without it, people would not come here, and without people this region would hold little for you. Actually, it is not just the men with guns at their sides who make a new country. It is also the ones who make and help to keep the law. Still, I am sorry I must be the one to tell you the law has decided against you."

"Of course, I was not unprepared, sir," Edward assured him.

"No, you have not been without warning." He paused a moment. "May I ask if you have any plans?"

"I couldn't make any definite ones," Edward said. "There was the chance the thing might go in my favor. Besides, I wanted to write my wife and ask her before I started anything else. Fortunately, she is here now."

He looked at Catherine, and suddenly it all made sense. Her trip down here. All the hardships, the difficulties, the terrors. Even the loss. They faded into nothing, just to have him look at her and say, "Fortunately, she is here."

"Yes, that is good," Judge Fisher said. "What did you say you had in mind?"

"Well, a man was telling me about a section I can file on

up on the Washita. It's clear," he added hastily. "We checked that thoroughly."

Ah, another claim. But how would they get their start here, without a team, without money for the down payment, without anything?

"Do you have your heart set on homesteading?"

Edward looked at him quickly. "I have to do something," he said. "I have a family, you know."

"You think it has to be homesteading?"

"Not necessarily. I have run a store. I have also farmed. Under the circumstances, homesteading seemed the logical thing. I know that sort of work."

The judge shifted quickly to face him.

"You also know a great deal about law," he said. "Ever since I've been working with you on this claim difficulty I have been impressed with your legal knowledge. I think you told me you once read with a lawyer."

"Yes—he had been a district attorney—"

Bing Sutton, Catherine was thinking. She had objected to Edward's association with him.

"And after I came down here," Edward went on, "I continued reading by myself. It helped to pass those long evenings there in the dugout. Besides—I enjoyed doing it."

"Ever think of becoming a lawyer?" Judge Fisher asked, as if it were the most natural question in the world.

Light glanced across Edward's face; suddenly he was young and full of purpose. Determined, as he had been the first time Catherine ever saw him.

"When I was growing up," Edward told him, "I thought of nothing else. But there wasn't any way of managing it." He hesitated a moment, then went on. "You may think I'm foolish, Judge Fisher, but I'm going to be a lawyer yet. I may be an old man by the time I learn enough law to pass the bar examination, but I'm going to keep on until I do."

"I have authority to give the bar examination. Did you know that?" Judge Fisher said, apparently finding nothing amiss in Edward's ambition.

"No—I did not know—"

"An idea occurs to me," the Judge went on. "For some time now I have felt the need of a clerk and secretary. My work is rather heavy, you know, and I must sometimes ride long distances. You strike me as being the young man for the place. I can't offer you much money at first, but there is something I can offer. You can read law with me. As much as you already know, it should be just a few months before you are able to pass the examination. How does the idea strike you?"

A lawyer! The long dream come true. The first time he had met her he had told her he wanted to be a lawyer. Uncle Willie had said Texas was the place to bring one's dreams.

The judge went on, "After you've passed it—and there's no doubt in my mind but what you will—I could use a smart young lawyer as a partner. Besides," he concluded, making a gallant gesture in Catherine's direction, "now that I've seen Mrs. Delaney, I think we better keep you young people in Mobeetie. We need your kind here."

"Go in with you—here in Mobeetie—" Edward spoke slowly, not quite believing the words even as he said them.

"Yes, at least for a while. Later, maybe we'd move to some other town. There's a new one I've got my eye on, a hundred miles or so to the south. A place called Amarillo. Watch it—some of these days it will be a real town."

Edward looked at Catherine. He looked back at the judge.

"Think it over a few minutes," Judge Fisher said. He got up from his desk, some papers in his hands. "I have to take these to the next office. When you've decided, come in there and tell me."

He went out of the room.

Edward turned to her swiftly.

"Well, what do you think?"

How could she tell him what she was thinking? That now, it didn't matter a bit that she had lost the wagon and its contents. Those things were meant for homesteaders. As it was, she and Edward stood, free and unencumbered, with the last tie to the old life gone, the last demand it might have made on them. Just as she had shed so many things down the long hard way to him, so many personal weaknesses, so many fears and prejudices, so she had also lost the thing that might hold him to a way of life he didn't really want. Or did he?

"You are sure you don't want to homestead? If you are holding back on my account . . ."

She knew he wasn't, but still she had to make the offer. Once before she had kept him from his dream, but not again. Never again.

"Homesteading was a way to come West," he told her. "It served its purpose. Are you willing for me to be a lawyer? Things may not be easy, not just at first."

She went to him swiftly, leaned against him, feeling once more a sense of completeness. He put his arms around her, and suddenly the pieces of their life began to fall into place, making a sharp and beautiful picture, like a whole new pattern emerging at the turn of a kaleidoscope. That was the way a landscape used to do on her journey down here when she had topped a hill and saw before her the whole road she was to travel, spread out mile on endless mile.

Now she could see the road they were to travel, and knew it would be good. The country would be all he said, and he would have a hand in making it so, in time becoming one of its legends. "Ask Judge Delaney," people would say. "He'll know, if any man does." And she, too, would be a part of the legend. "Mrs. Delaney—she drove down to him. Just her and her little boy."

They would be telling the story long after she and Edward were only memories in the land.

She put her arms around his neck. She kissed him twice very quickly. Once for luck, and once because she thought that never in all her life before had she been quite this happy.

"Go in there and tell him yes, darling," she said. "I'll wait here for you."

*Continued from front flap*

her husband. And when circumstances prevented Edward from coming for them as he had promised, the rift in their marriage seemed to widen. Edward needed her, she knew. And she needed to prove herself in his eyes, to measure up to the demands of the life he wanted to make for her. So, with only her small son and her wise but dubiously reliable Uncle Willie as companions, she set out to go to him. At midpoint of the dangerous trip she was suddenly, tragically robbed of Uncle Willie's guidance. But not even then would she turn back. . . .

It would be unfair to deny the reader the suspense and satisfaction of making this "far journey" with Catherine herself, of sharing her adventures, which include a startling encounter with a mysterious Indian, a poignant trailside birthday party, and a terrifying pursuit by an evil stranger!

Catherine's journey is, in a sense, the journey every woman makes toward her love. And as she crossed the vast plains of a growing America, Catherine herself grew to a mature understanding of those simple, enduring values that still beckon each of us onward today. In *The Far Journey,* the reader will find them, as Catherine does, in the daily round as well as in the once-in-a-lifetime moment that reveals them in all their glory.

*Jacket and endpapers by Paul Laune*
*Lithographed in U.S.A.*